KINGDOM OF GLAS

REBIRTH

by K. Vider

CHAPTER ONE

Kaiser held the pillow tightly against his head, hoping to block out the birds taunting him with song, and the bright rays of sun beaming through his window. His efforts, unfortunately, didn't block anything out.

But it didn't matter. It would only be a matter of time before one of his sisters came bursting in. They did so every morning, waking him right as the birds did. Usually, it would be his youngest sister, Lilly, but today, when he finally peeked from the pillow, he found his oldest sister, Alice. Her hand rested stubbornly on her hip, and she had a look of sternness on her face, warning Kaiser he better get himself out of bed or face her wrath.

With a groan, he tried to retreat under his pillow, but a set of little feet rushing through the house ruined any chance he had of returning to slumber.

"Wake up!" Lilly shouted before leaping into the air and falling onto Kaiser's bed. The breath rushed out of him in a *whoosh*.

Lilly began jumping about as Alice took a seat on the edge of the bed. Kaiser was surrounded by admirable foes. He gave up, pulling the pillow from his head and tossing it at Lilly.

"You have to help Guile with the fields today," Alice said to Kaiser before smiling at Lilly as the young girl jumped up and down on the bed. "I fixed breakfast; you should eat before you start."

Alice rounded up Lilly and led her to the door so Kaiser could get ready. He pulled himself out of bed, ruffling his black hair.

He looked different than his sisters. Alice was a year younger than Kaiser at seventeen, her hair as brown as the bark on a tree. Both sisters shared that trait, while Kaiser's was raven black.

He was the only sibling with a different mother. Alice and Lilly had the same mother, but Kaiser had never met his, had only heard stories of her. She had left when he was still a baby.

The three had lost their father five years ago to sickness. Alice and Lilly's mother had died just a few years before him of the same, leaving the two older children to care for Lilly alone.

They lived in a small village just east of the kingdom of Sullvain. The kingdom was too far for Kaiser to find work and make the trip each day, so he was left assisting a family friend with his crops.

"Can I help today?" Lilly asked as she followed Kaiser down the hall, her hands wrapped around his leg as he walked.

Kaiser ruffled her hair affectionately. "You're a bit tiny for the job, sis. Maybe when you get taller."

The two reached the kitchen just as Alice set the plates on the table, steam still rolling off the freshly cooked meal. Their little house was old and broken, with a leaky roof Kaiser had never managed to fix, but it was enough for them. The three were content with their lives, never asking for more. As far as Kaiser and Alice cared, this was as good as it would get, and they could live with that.

Kaiser took a seat at the table across from Alice, and the two helped Lilly prepare her plate.

"I hear Ragnovok has been sighted marching north into Sullvain. Could see war soon," Kaiser mentioned while chewing.

"Can we please not talk about the war at the dinner table?" Alice said, sending a glare Kaiser's way. Talk of war scared Lilly, and for good reason.

Sullvain had seen two wars in less than ten years; the royal family seemed to enjoy picking fights. Rumors of a draft recently swept through the village, but no one was sure if it was true. The affairs inside the castle were of no concern to Kaiser and his little family. After all, he had never even been to the castle in his life.

Kaiser lifted his fork, playfully stealing a bite of eggs from Lilly's plate. The small girl giggled, taking food back from his plate. The two laughed, almost swapping their whole meals before Alice cleared her throat, ending the game.

"If you're finished, then you shouldn't keep Guile waiting."

"I know. He's probably been out there since before sunrise." Kaiser stood, rubbing Lilly's head before he parted for the door.

"We'll bring you some refreshments later," Alice said, taking the plates.

"Tell him we said hi!" Lilly giggled, walking Kaiser out the door.

Guile was an old man who also lived in the village. He had known

Kaiser's father and was one of the only people who could tell him of his mother.

Kaiser found Guile out in the fields. He was a large, fellow, with freckles littering his old face, but his age didn't hinder his farm work. Kaiser quickly jumped in, making up for sleeping in.

"How are the girls?" Guile asked, tossing Kaiser a rake.

Kaiser easily caught it. "Good. They said hi."

Kaiser and Guile got to work, raking and pulling crops from the ground. During their work, Kaiser often asked Guile questions regarding his mother, Alesana.

Apparently, Guile had only known her for a short time. After Kaiser's birth, she left, leaving Kaiser's father alone with his children. Guile had tried to keep to himself, so he'd never questioned her disappearance, and out of common courtesy, none of the other villagers had questioned it either. As far as Kaiser could gather, she had deserted them without a word. One day, his father woke up, and she was just gone.

Today, however, he asked about Guile's time in the war. Years before Kaiser was born, Sullvain waged a war against Mirelos, a kingdom to the east. Requesting such stories always brightened Guile, allowing him to relive his adventures across the Realm. He was old now, but Kaiser gave him an excuse to remember more exciting times.

"Have you ever seen a dragon?" Kaiser asked hopefully.

Guile shook his head, his grey hair swaying with the motion. "No, the Dreava killed the last dragon long before I was born.

They used to roam the South and lived in caves along the coast, but the Dreava killed them all and built their kingdom out of the bones. No one has seen a dragon for at least a hundred years."

Such a thing wasn't what Kaiser had hoped to hear. Kaiser was no adventurer. He lived such tales only through Guile, but how he longed to see such things. He loved to imagine the dragons and their brilliant scales and fearsome claws. They were the old gods no one in the Realm worshiped anymore.

Long before the true god was declared the one and only, all six kingdoms worshiped different gods. Kaiser had trouble keeping track of them all, but he recalled a few. Kessa, the Goddess of youth, and Malkar, the God of blood, were the only two gods ever said to have taken physical form, but no one in the Realm believed in such gods anymore, only the True God.

Kaiser stopped raking, resting his chin on the tip of the rake's handle, staring off into the distance. He wondered what such travels would show him if he could someday leave this small village and see what lay across the Realm, as Guile had in his youth.

"Dreaming of dragons won't help me clean up this field," Guile said with a smile.

Before Kaiser could return to his work, he noticed something in the distance, a gathering near the village entrance. What was going on there? Kaiser couldn't recall hearing about a scheduled gathering or an important event.

It wasn't long before Guile also saw and put down his rake. "A break would not hurt..." Guile walked past, going to investigate the crowd.

Kaiser followed suit and dropped his rake, quickly tagging along behind Guile. The two approached the scene, and Kaiser quickly noted the two men on horseback. They had armor, and their shields had the Sullvain banner on them.

"The kingdom is at war," one of the knights declared, "and Ragnovok forces march toward our capital as we speak! King Sull demands every able man take up the sword for the kingdom and report to the capital for training and preparation!"

The words dropped like a dark curtain over the crowd, bringing with them a sense of despair. Some people cried. Most of the men looked resigned. Women grabbed hold of their sons and husbands, not wanting to see them go and potentially never come home. The village had never been asked to produce soldiers.

"Sir, I'd ask to go in this one's place." Guile stood in front of the knight.

Kaiser shifted uneasily behind him as the old man offered himself up in Kaiser's place. He wanted to speak up, but his words were caught in his throat. He had never fought, he didn't know the first thing about war.

The knight briefly glanced at Guile, cocking an eyebrow. "A noble gesture, but the way your leg limps... you would be of no use to the king. No, we need young and able. He's to report to Sullvain before the end of the week, as are all of those who are able. Those who fail to report will face charges of desertion."

With that, the two rode off, leaving the village with a dark cloud over it.

"So the draft was true..." Kaiser couldn't bring himself to look up from the ground, the realization of what was happening finally creeping into him.

Guile's heavy hand landed on Kaiser's shoulder. "Go home and spend the day with your sisters. I'll take you to Sullvain before the week's end."

The tight lines on his face spoke clearly of his worry, even if he was acting confident.

Later in the night, Guile replayed the day in his head. He recalled the look on Kaiser's face as the lad realized what was happening. The boy was scared, and for good reason. War was not something he had ever witnessed, it would tear Kaiser apart. The powerlessness Guile felt was worse than war itself.

He retreated to his home, huddled by the fire, and thought of all the war stories he had told Kaiser and how he had kept out the worst part of it, the blood and death. Kaiser was no swordsman. He was barely a man at only twenty. Kaiser had never ventured far from the farm life, and Guile knew the young man would die out on the field, alone and scared.

Trying to push the thought from his mind, he removed a long object from a trunk he kept near the fireplace. He pulled away the cloth covering, revealing a sword. As he unsheathed the blade, his eyes admired it as if it had just come from the smith's fires yesterday. It was a fine sword, one he had used years back when he was a soldier.

He took a whetstone and slid it down the blade's edge, trying to sharpen and bring back some of its fight. Guile hadn't fought for the kingdom in years—since before he knew his life in the small village—but he wasn't surprised at how desperate the king had become, drafting young farmhands into the war as if such boys would make a difference. King Sull had never been an honorable man.

They would be fodder for the war.

He sighed, watching the shine of the blade as he sharpened it, preparing it for Kaiser.

"We can run away, leave Sullvain, and go to Valacore or Waltz!" Alice cried out, her legs pacing back and forth across the kitchen floor. "You don't have to go!"

Kaiser had waited until Lilly was in bed to explain what had happened. Alice hadn't taken the news well, her eyes instantly filling with tears and her small body shaking.

Kaiser stood from his chair, trying to comfort his sister. "We can't run... None of the kingdoms would welcome a deserter, and we would live out our days constantly in fear."

Kaiser wrapped his arms around her, allowing her to bury her tear-soaked face into his chest. She tried to stop, her chest fighting for air from the struggle of crying. Kaiser worried about how his sisters would fare without him. He had faith in Alice. He knew she was strong, but he also knew she was capable of only so much.

"I'll come back. I promise," Kaiser said, his hand stroking Alice's hair as she wiped her face.

Finally, she looked up at him, her eyes reddened by her tears. After a moment, she nodded and placed her head against his chest.

The two sat together for most of the night. Out on the porch, they watched the sky and talked about better times. Kaiser had taken her mind off the uncertain future, and finally, she relaxed some. He sighed to himself and watched the stars. He was scared, he knew that much, but he felt numb to it. He had to swallow his fear and be strong for Alice and Lilly.

Kaiser sat on the porch with Alice's head on his lap. She lifted a hand, her index finger pointing up at the red moon. Every so many days, the moon would be joined by its red brother. For as long as history had been documented, the two moons had shared the sky on some nights, while other nights, the red moon disappeared out of sight.

The moons reminded Kaiser of Kessa and Malkar, the God and Goddess. Kessa was said to have remained in the Realm, hiding among the mortals like the white moon, while Malkar left them but would always return from time to time to keep Kessa in check —or so Kaiser had read from a book he had from his youth.

The moons meant nothing of the sort to Alice, who had pointed out the red moon to make a promise.

"Promise me that so long as the red moon returns, you'll think of us. You'll return to us," she said, looking up at him so earnestly.

"I promise," he said seriously.

He looked up at the red moon, and the two watched it in the sky until Alice drifted off, her face finally returning to the peaceful face Kaiser wanted to remember.

CHAPTER TWO

The sound and smell of the ocean was a comfort to Alyssa as she stood out on the terrace, her long black hair swirling about in the sea breeze. She rarely found time to escape the confines of the castle halls, and it seemed, sometimes, she would never see the sky again.

Her pale skin and rosy cheeks were given a golden shine in the sun, its time in the sky coming to an end. Alyssa longed for many things, but nothing more than what she contemplated now. How she wished she could leap from the castle walls and into the ocean. Her legs would give way to fins, and like a mermaid, she would free herself of this prison.

Unfortunately, no amount of wishing granted her the will to jump.

Alyssa watched as guards shuttled past, each one avoiding eye contact with her. She was like a ghost inside the halls. No one spoke or even glanced at her for fear of what the king might do to them. Alyssa was the second youngest of the king's children, and though she had three other siblings, it was her alone who was told to never leave the castle. Her brother, on the other hand, went horseback riding, and her sisters voyaged to distant villages for the most important royal balls.

Alyssa was all but shackled to the stone walls around her, never to leave the kingdom of Valacore.

She laid her arms over the stone ledge and rested her chin on them, sighing as she watched the sunset far away. The brilliant purples and pink held a melancholy tint.

"A fourth royal child? Why have I not heard of her?"

Two men stood below the walls, each wearing full armor. They watched Princess Alyssa from afar.

"She is very important to the king, and he would see no one outside these walls know of her," Foster Dalfair said, turning his sights from the girl to his adopted son.

Grant Dalfair was tall and healthy, his golden hair bright and full, compared to his father's gray head of hair.

After pulling his eyes away from Alyssa atop the wall, Grant followed Foster as they made their way to the barracks. "Surely you didn't ask me to the castle to gossip of the king's secrets?" Grant got straight to the point, his patience as short as ever.

The king speaks of allowing his daughter to exit the castle on occasion," Foster replied. "He believes it'll help calm her wild imagination. I've recommended you as her royal guard."

Foster almost toppled over as Grant bear-hugged him, his old bones popping under his son's grip. Such a title was an amazing honor, and he knew Grant longed to rise in rank finally.

He stepped away, and the smile on his face was warming to Foster.

"Well, boy, don't just stand there; go introduce yourself to your ward." Foster shook his head as Grant left and returned to more pressing matters inside the castle.

The stairs took Grant up to the castle walls, his long legs eating up the distance in his excitement. He was afraid Alyssa would have left by now, but there she stood, still watching the sun setting over the ocean. He had seen her among the castle before, while visiting his father, though he had never questioned her status. He has taken her for a royal, just not as high as the royal family.

The castle of Valacore sat tucked between two mountains, the sea to the east, two peaks on the north and south, and the Resting Plains opened to the west. The kingdom had a large port market, and the smell of seawater flooded the air inside the castle grounds.

"Your Grace," Grant said as he approached, his body shifting to one knee. He was an honor-bound man, learning such things from Foster. He looked up to see Alyssa's smile, her body giving a small bow itself.

"You may rise, Sir...?"

"Grant Dalfair." He stood, his eyes examining the girl he would often see in the days to come. She was young, barley half his height. Grant was lost admiring her long black hair as it ran down the front of her shoulders.

"You are related to Sir Foster?" Her head tilted ever so slightly to the right.

Grant dipped his head in a nod. "I am. He adopted me when I was but a child. He probably doesn't speak of me freely in the Castle; he believes in making a name for yourself."

Alyssa stepped closer, her blue eyes smiling with mischief. "You are to be my shield? So, I may go into the kingdom?"

When he nodded, she squealed like a child, a grin on her face. For some reason, Grant's face flashed, no doubt stained red; no amount of honor could have halted his blush.

Finally, she calmed herself. Although her body adjusted and her hands fixed her dress, her lips still curved into a bright smile at the news.

"I look forward to seeing the city with you... can we go tomorrow?" Alyssa shifted as if to leap at him.

Grant stepped back, his body moving to catch her if she tried. "That's entirely up to your father. Have you never left the castle?"

Grant worried he was treading in places he best not, but he was curious about the girl.

"No, my father loves me, I know this... but he would see me locked away, safe over free and in danger." Alyssa raised her hand, rubbing at her left shoulder as if something under her sleeve bothered her.

Her mood had noticeably changed with the new topic. The excited, joyful girl he had just spoken to wandered into a girl with more serious thoughts, a place he knew better than to ask about. He did the best he could and tried to cheer her up.

"I'll speak with your father about allowing us to go into the city tomorrow evening. That would please you?"

Before he could ever finish, the girl attacked him, her grip wrapping tight around his neck. She nodded her head against his shoulder and removed herself, slipping back some.

"Thank you, Grant."

"I believe it the best course of action. Grant is a capable knight and has proven his prowess against bandits, protecting your very roads." Foster sat across a large table from the King of Valacore, the two aged men discussing the troublesome times. The light from the fireplace illuminating the king's quarters.

"You do not have to sell me on the decision, Sir Foster. I know how trustworthy Grant is. He will be appointed as my daughter's royal guard."

He owed much to Foster. Without the old knight, Valacore would surely have been taken by enemies in the past. Foster had defending Valacore for ages.

"I would ask something of you in return, however," he continued.

The king looked at the map set before them. The table where they sat was carved into the shape of the Realm, from Valacore in the north to Ragnovok in the south. King Valacore had lined the pieces on the board to show Ragnovok and their forces marching north to Sullvain.

"Ragnovok will fall upon Sullvain within weeks." The king

inched the southern pieces north and pondered.

Foster absently tapped his finger on the table. "How does this involve you and your kingdom? Has Sullvain requested your assistance?"

"Yes... They fear the coming forces may be more than they can handle."

It was no secret. Valacore held the mightiest army in the Realm, its forces outnumbering most of the kingdoms combined, but they hadn't been at war for many years, and King Valacore would keep it that way if possible.

"Sullvain provoked Ragnovok. Every year, they try to take more and more of the South as if no one notices." Foster paused. "If you are requesting my judgment, I recommend helping as little as possible. Sullvain will try to use our support to push their territory. Leave Sullvain to their own devices. They provoked the beast; allow them to learn their lesson. Ragnovok is no enemy of ours."

Foster didn't think highly of Sullvain and their methods. Although they worshiped the Given God as Valacore, Sullvain leaned more toward the old ways, with stricter beliefs.

The king gave a wan smile. "It is not so simple, my old friend. I ask that you join my counsel to assist my advisors on the best course. I want to help Sullvain, but just enough that my kingdom is not sucked into their foolish war."

"I will assist your advisors. Tell them to send anything of note to my chamber," Foster said.

Foster's words lifted the weight from the king's shoulder, and he nodded, gesturing for one of his subjects to do as Foster had asked. After all was finished, the two raised their glasses, taking a moment to relax.

"Thank you, old friend. You do not know how much it means to have you help with this matter."

Foster inclined his head respectfully. "It is an honor."

"Did you see him? He's a real knight!" Alyssa ranted on about Grant as her maidens scrubbed her gently, her black hair soaking wet and slicked back from her pale face so the girls could bathe her.

She was young, and in a year or two, she would be married, or so she hoped. She had been locked away in the castle her whole life, so she worried that when she came of age, she wouldn't be married, but kept away in the castle forever. She was a royal, and he was a knight. Not only that, but he was far older than her, in his mid-twenties.

"A princess can marry an older man, can she not? I mean, Grant is brave, and a knight," Alyssa asked her maidens as one of them lifted her arm and scrubbed her side. Black markings swirled around her arm, starting at her shoulder. The markings ran along her skin like a tattoo, trailing down her arm to her hand. She had been born with these markings, and she often wondered if that was the reason she was stranded in the castle.

"Yes, my princess," Evette replied, "but Grant is no lord, and you aren't yet of age. Don't rush into the arms of the first man your heart would skip for."

Evette did have a point. Alyssa was only sixteen, and her two sisters were almost twenty without marriage yet. Her father was a strict and honorable man who refused to marry his daughters to anyone unworthy.

She adjusted herself in the small stone tub. The water was becoming cold, and she was too excited to sit around in the bath all day.

In less than a day, Princess Alyssa would venture out to the streets for the first time. All the books in the library could tell her of the streets of Valacore, but none could show her. The golden stones and the steep walkways led down from the castle and through the kingdom. The main street stretched from the castle gates, twisting and turning through the many districts and, finally, to the kingdom walls. She wondered what the stores would be like, all the people from across the sea and south of Valacore, the warriors and the maidens.

Her heart pounded in excitement, and she couldn't sit still for another second. She jumped from the tub, water splashing about. A maiden barely got a robe around her before she reached the window.

A smile stretching across her face, she looked out over the main street at the small dots below, dots she would soon see up close.

CHAPTER THREE

When the sun rose, Kaiser was already awake. He hadn't really slept much.

For as long as he could remember, his sisters had been waking him up bright and early every morning, their laughter and silly games always a pain to him, but there he was, standing in the hallway watching Lilly sleep, wishing for more of that laughter and silly games.

He wanted to watch her for a moment in her peacefulness, another part wanting to wake her so that he could hear her voice and experience her shining smile. Lilly lay sleeping, but Kaiser could hear Alice further down the hall.

Kaiser took one more look at his sister and left the doorway, venturing to find Alice. He strolled through the old house, avoiding the spots he had learned caused the boards to whine.

Alice was alone in the main room, her hands fighting with the red ribbon she was trying to tie her hair with. She had worn the fabric since she was a child. It had been a gift from her mother before she died.

"I didn't know you were awake," Alice said.

"I couldn't sleep..." Kaiser gently took the tie and finished her hair.

She turned, smiling at him. He could tell she was barely holding back the tears. The two had spoken less than a minute, and already, she was crying for him. Soon, she'd beg him to stay. He missed the peaceful look she had while she slept.

"Please don't." He looked away, lifting his hand to ruffle his bed hair while attempting to avoid eye contact.

"What if I never see you again? All we have is each other," Alice said, her tone pleading, her voice trembling.

Seconds later, he felt her arms wrap around his waist and finally looked at her, seeing her bury her face in his stomach as she cried. Kaiser rested a hand on her head, gently lifting her chin so he could see her reddened face.

"Sissy Alice, what's wrong?" Lilly stood in the hall, wiping the sleep out of her eyes. She gazed at Alice, curious as to why her big sister was crying.

Lilly's face soon fell. "Is Bubby Kai leaving today?"

Lilly ran over, joining Alice as she wrapped her small arms around Kaiser's waist. Kaiser tried to wrap his arms around the two of them, but one look at Alice's tear-stained face caused him to break. He laid his head against hers and smiled through the tears that flowed.

"We love you..." Alice whispered.

Leaving them might just be the hardest thing he'd ever have to do.

The three siblings stood outside on the village edge, Lilly hugging Kaiser's legs while Alice had her arms wrapped around him. Guile was behind them, tossing the few things Kaiser would take with him into the wagon.

"Please be careful. Don't try to be a hero out there." Alice did all she could to keep from crying, and for that, Kaiser was thankful. It was hard enough leaving as it was.

He nodded, kissing her on the cheek before he bent over to see Lilly.

"You listen to Sissy Alice, okay? Don't give her any trouble." Kaiser smiled, using both his hands to ruffle Lilly's hair, forcing her to smile. "That's more like it."

He kissed both his sisters on the head and heard Guile mention the wagon was ready.

Once he said his goodbye, he stepped away from them, facing them as he walked back to the carriage. It was the hardest thing he had ever done, watching his sisters standing by their house as he rode off on Guile's wagon. The hurt on Alice's face broke his heart.

They had stuck together through everything, and he was being forced to leave them.

Soon, they were gone, only the small shapes of the village in the distance. Kaiser watched in their direction until he could see nothing.

"You'll see them again, I'm sure of it," Guile said gruffly.

The words of comfort fell on deaf ears. Kaiser was too heartbroken to listen to platitudes.

"Here, this is for you..." Guile pulled something wrapped in cloth from the back of the wagon and handed it to Kaiser.

To his surprise, it was a long sword. Its blade was beaten and nicked but recently sharpened. Kaiser looked over to Guile, wondering what would make him part with something he must have been close to.

"All those stories I told you about, I used that sword during every one of them," Guile said, looking forward rather than at Kaiser.

Kaiser swallowed hard, touched by the gesture. "Thank you." He wrapped the blade and placed it on his lap.

Sullvain was to the west of their small village, meaning they wouldn't have to worry about encountering any Ragnovok troops coming from the south.

Kaiser was silent the whole trip, wondering why he was being punished for a war two kings had started. He had lived his whole life without bothering a soul, now he was being torn away from his family for someone elses's gain.

It wasn't until Sullvain was in sight that he spoke.

"What sort of person is King Sull?" Kaiser asked curiously.

Guile glanced over at him. "King Sull's a strict man who will do anything to win. It's the only reason he still rules after facing three different kingdoms."

"He provokes these wars?" Kaiser asked in a whisper, more toward himself than Guile.

So, he was to fight for a man who would start a war at the drop of a hat? Kaiser would be risking his life for someone so eager to throw others into the battle.

He sighed, watching as the gates to Sullvain opened, allowing the wagon inside.

Once inside, Guile left his horses and led Kaiser into the streets. Kaiser had never been to Sullvain and wasn't impressed. The place was gray and lifeless, despite all the men and women in the streets. Everyone seemed so cold and scared.

Kaiser slowed down some, his eyes taking in the sights.

Before too long, he lost track of Guile. He scanned the crowd but couldn't find the old man's grey head anywhere.

He heard whispers of a prince as people began moving in the same direction.

He walked with the flow of people until he found the event everyone had been whispering about. He stood along the streets, looking up at a large wooden stage in the square of the kingdom. Five men stood up on the stage. What was going on? Whatever it was, it piqued his curiosity.

He shifted to get a better look, finally making it to the front row of the spectators.

A tall, long-haired man spoke. His appearance seemed that of royalty. Kaiser imagined all the stories Guile had told him had young men like this in them. Able and strong, and Kaiser had never seen such nice clothes his entire life. Behind him stood two knights, one in white armor and the other black, both wearing helmets shaped like a bear's head. He could hear people whispering about Prince Devon and pointing to the long-haired royal.

"These men are deserters, found trying to flee north!" Devon pointed to the two men on their knees, surrounded by the black and white knights. "To desert Sullvain is a crime punishable by death. Let this be a lesson."

Devon's cold eyes looked over the crowd, and Kaiser stared right back, only shifting his sight when the two knights moved forward.

"Sir Oran, Sir Servis..."

Devon turned, stepping from the stage as the two knights rose their blades and brought them down on the two deserter's necks.

Kaiser's heart stopped as the heads hit the wood and rolled off the stage, leaving a trail of blood in their wake. He watched with wide eyes. Kaiser who had never seen a public execution before, he felt his stomach church at sight.

Two children rushed forward, kicking at one of the heads as if it was a toy. All of it made Kaiser question if he was taking up his sword for the right side...

"There you are!"

Kaiser jumped as Guile's hand landed on his shoulder. Guile had missed the execution, but not the aftermath, seeing the two knights' blades covered in blood as they followed after Devon, Prince of Sullvain.

"Come on, lad," Guile murmured as he pulled Kaiser away from the scene.

24

Not long after that gory display, Kaiser found himself in a tavern.

The crowd was not as lively as most taverns he had heard stories about. Most of the joy and rowdiness had been sucked away by the war preparations. Guile brought Kaiser here and bought them both drinks.

"I don't drink..." Kaiser said, pushing the mug a few inches away.

"What you mean to say is you never have," Guile correct. He took a large swig from his mug and slammed it down on the bar before he clanked the mugs together to push Kaiser's back in front of him.

"War is hell. I suggest you find a way to drown it out early," Guile said gruffly.

The old man's words made sense in a way, so Kaiser picked up his mug and took a small sip of the ale. The taste was different and intense, with a bitterness to it. Kaiser coughed at the trail of fire down his throat, placing the cup back down. He wasn't ready for another drink. The sight caused Guile to laugh, and after his laughing calmed, he chugged another.

"Listen... I'll watch over your sisters for you," Guile assured him, his eyes serious. "Just worry about coming home in one piece."

The gesture was kind, and Kaiser appreciated it, but what he would give to return home right that moment. Instead, there he was, sitting in a dirty tavern.

Kaiser nodded stiffly. "Thank you, Guile... for everything."

"Enough of this heavy stuff. I haven't drunk Sullvain ale in years. Drink some more with me." Guile got another mug filled for the two, and they knocked their cups together, a solemn toast to Kaiser and his uncertain future.

Come sundown, Guile would leave Kaiser to be trained by the Sullvain men, and neither of them was ready to say goodbye.

Inside the walls of the castle, Devon made his way through the halls, both his knights following him. He was the definition of a royal—strong, respected, attractive. He was Sullvain's only heir, and he deserved the respect he was due.

After making it through the castle, he pushed open the doors to a large dining room, where the rest of his family sat. They all gathered around a giant feast—his father King Sull, his mother the queen, and two younger sisters.

"The deserters have been made into an example," Devon informed his father as he sat down in his designated spot across from his youngest sister.

"Very good. What of the Ragnovok army sighted in the south?"

Devon crossed his arms, sure the news he was about to deliver would stir his father's anger. "A company has been spotted north of the Scar... Led by the Phantom himself."

The king ceased eating at that, placing his fork and knife on the table. His brows drew down into a frown. "The Phantom? I see."

King Sull brought a napkin to his lips, patting them softly. Devon was prepared for the worst, and even the rest of the family visibly readied for the king's anger. His father was aged, but his tired body did nothing to weaken his rage.

"Command the first line of drafted men to march south," he said levelly.

"But, dear, they are untrained boys," the queen started but was silenced when the king's fists slammed into the table, shaking every plate.

"And all boys must become men! Devon, have them march south. Untrained or not, we will gauge Ragnovok's forces before sending any of our knights."

"Yes, Father." Devon left as quickly as he had entered, Oran and Servis following behind him. Devon would do as he was told, to honor his father.

CHAPTER FOUR

Like a wild animal, Alyssa dashed through the crowd, her long hooded robe fluttering behind her. Grant could scarcely keep up with the girl, weaving and dodging through the people. It was clear the girl had never been outside the castle. Because she was smaller, she easily slipped through the tiny cracks, whereas Grant was wider and had trouble making his way without outright knocking people over.

"Your Grace, please slow down!" Grant urged as he struggled to keep up. If this didn't sway him to take these strolls free of his armor, then he didn't know what would.

His hand pulled the collar of his armor away from his neck, and he tried to breathe, finally watching Alyssa slow to a stop near the market stands. She was so full of energy, and despite Grant's youth, he was finding it hard to keep up with her excitement.

"Grant, you are a knight, correct? And knights fight the enemy in distant lands?" she asked coyly, obviously fishing for a story, but Grant had none fitting for a girl of her age. As honorable as Grant was, he had seen his share of blood. The roads near Valacore had been his duty to protect, and his patrols had pitted him against countless bandits. Grant was no stranger to death.

"Yes, I have been to Sullvain and Dreava... Dreava only when I was a child, though." Grant sorted through the market stand, joining Alyssa on her quest through the random objects.

"You have felt snow below your feet? What was it like?"

Grant was taken back by her imagination, taking a simple thing as snow and fantasizing about it.

"Very cold, and not as nice as you may think it," he replied.

Alyssa grinned, looking up from the stand for only a moment to give him a *you're no fun* look.

Grant had worried at first, thinking such a title as Royal Guard would be just as annoying as it was respectable, but to his surprise, Alyssa was a lively and fun girl to accompany. Grant admired her spirit, even if it was that of a caged bird.

"Grant! Can I have this?" she asked him as if she wasn't a royal, his better. She was a princess, born high above Grant, and yet she acted nothing like one.

Grant approached her as she held up a shiny, red stone. Its edges were jagged, and it held no definite shape. Grant took the rock, looking it over. He placed it down, finding something more suitable among the stones on the table before them.

"Ahh, this would look much better on you." Grant lifted a small stone in the shape of a crescent moon. "It matches your eyes."

Alyssa's smile shined, her eyes fixated on the necklace as Grant circled her, his hands reaching around her neck to move her long black hair.

Alyssa turned to look at him, her bright blue eyes lighting up more brilliant than the stone now resting around her neck. "I will think of you every time I put it on."

Alyssa stood on her toes, giving him a small kiss on the cheek. He shifted from her, uneasy from the way her blue eyes looked at him.

"We'd best return to the castle," Grant said. "It'll be dark soon, and Foster requires my presence. We'll come back tomorrow."

Grant placed a few coins on the vendor's table before the two left. With a few skips, the young girl caught up with Grant, her arms grabbing hold of his as she walked next to him.

"Tell me about Foster. I heard he has been across the ocean!"

"To tell you the truth, I don't believe he can swim!"

Alyssa smiled, laughing at Grant's jokes. As the streets thinned out, Grant and Alyssa walked back toward the castle until a robed man approached. Grant's hand rested on his sword's hilt, as it was clear the man was walking toward him and Alyssa.

"Steady your hand, young knight. I am Father Adan of the church here in Valacore." Despite the old priest's words, Grant didn't release the grip on his sword.

"How may I help you, Father Adan?" Grant asked briefly. Alyssa stood behind Grant, hiding what she could of her presence from the priest.

"I came to show my respects to Princess Alyssa."

Grant's grip tightened, and his left arm moved back some to keep Alyssa behind him.

"I don't know what you're talking about, Father. It's best you move on." Grant grabbed hold of Alyssa's hand, pulling her with him.

The priest gave a smile to the girl as they passed Adan, making eye contact with Alyssa as she went by. The man's eyes and smile caused Alyssa to shiver. The two walked quickly toward the castle, only stopping once they had put distance between themselves and Adan.

"How did he know who I was?" Alyssa looked up at Grant, worrying clear in the tight lines of her face.

Grant shook his head. "I don't know, but I know someone who may."

Grant had returned Alyssa safely to the castle and now stood before Foster. The old man was drowning in a stack of papers.

Apparently, Foster had helped one of the advisors with the treaty, trying their best to find a way out of sending troops to aid Sullvain. It was not so much they wished harm on Sullvain, but they didn't want to get involved in a war they had no part in. Sullvain had started the whole affair, and it was only right they conclude the ordeal by themselves. They had caused two wars, both of which they had started, and now it seemed a third.

"You look busy. Should I come back later?" Grant said, meeting Foster eyes, the old man's glare daring him to leave.

"Fine, where should I start?" Grant smiled, taking a seat near the desk. He flipped through the papers, unaware of what they might be until his eyes found the words.

"War? Sullvain prepares for war with Ragnovok? Are we to help them?" Grant looked over, Foster too busy sifting through the chaos to look up as he spoke.

"It would seem so. The king requested my help in the decision."

"And what have you decided?"

Foster sighed, tossing the paperwork down on the desk and leaning his old body back in the wooden chair, his hands rubbing at his tired eyes.

"As much as I would like to leave them to handle the war themselves, the treaty between our kingdoms means we have to send reinforcements."

Grant was shocked by the words. It was clear that Foster agreed with the advisors on letting Sullvain clean up their own mess, but the action of refusing aid could break the treaty between the two kingdoms. Grant crossed his arms, contemplating what this would mean for the future. Even the kingdoms that were on good terms were still on uneasy footing. Refusing aid could lead to something serious.

A small laugh came from Foster. "Calm those cogs in your brain before you break one of them. Even if we were to go to war, you're a royal guard. Keep your focus on protecting Princess Alyssa."

Disappointment shot through Grant. He was a warrior, his sword meant to be swung. If his father was ever called to war, how could he stay behind? Could he?

"Speaking of royal guards, how did your first trip with Princess Alyssa fare?" The old man leaned forward, his hands pouring two cups of ale. Once the beverages had been given out, Grant answered his question with ease.

"She's a lively soul. The girl takes to the markets as if she had traveled across the land to some new kingdom, but that very subject is why I came to see you." Grant shifted some, taking a drink. "A man by the name Adan spoke Alyssa's name. He said he was a Father from the Given Church."

Foster dipped his head in a quick nod. "Ah, Adan, he is indeed from the Church. The Church—or at least some of its higher members—knows of Alyssa. I will tell you some other time why they know, but for now, you should focus on protecting her."

"She was well-behaved, though, despite her wild wonder. I have no doubt my job will be an easy one." Grant sat down his cup, looking over at Foster. He seemed uncertain of such a thing, as if Grant's job was more important than explained. Alyssa was little more than an excited child, she didn't seem hard to watch over.

"Take care of her. It is your job to see no harm comes to her."

The two sat at the desk, surrounded by paperwork, sipping ale and talking of life. It had been too long since they had spent time together. Foster with his work under the king and Grant's patrols of the roads outside the castle had kept them apart. Grant missed the old man, even if he was too proud to say so. He hoped that his new role in protecting Alyssa would allow him more time with his father.

Ragnovok and Sullvain clashed because of their hatred for one another and their beliefs, but Valacore stood apart from them. It welcomed many people from all walks of life, even if its primary belief was of the Given Church.

Foster had once been a man of the Church, conducting travels away from home on behalf of the Church, but Grant could never see the old man garbed in robes and giving praise to the Given God. To Grant's recall, he had never known Foster to praise any god, which made Foster's dealings with the Church such a mystery to him.

As the night went on, the subject came to mind, allowing Grant to ask the drunken Foster what he pleased.

"When I was a child," Grant began, "you would often leave the castle on behalf of the Church... What purpose could you have had to travel such distances for the Church?"

Grant poured each of them another cup of ale, his cheeks red and his speech slightly slurred. He only hoped the old man was loosened up enough to spill such secrets.

Foster waved his hand through the air. "You speak of years ago; I haven't set foot in the Church since before you could wield a sword. The gods knew if I had left you unattended, you would have chopped off your arm in my absence. You couldn't learn a thing without me there to properly teach it!"

Foster had changed the question, all but answering it. Grant noticed the evasion, and out of respect, he pushed it no further.

Grant snorted into his cup. "How could I learn to swing a sword if taught by the women of the pub? I must have had every gal in the tavern watch me at least once or twice while you were away."

"Do I hear a young man complaining of a woman's companionship?" Foster laughed, his cup empty again.

Grant smirked. "No, you hear a young man with better taste in women than that of his elder."

Alyssa sat in the library, her fingers running along with the words as she read them to herself. Valacore's library was the second largest in all the realm, second only to Dreava's, and so Alyssa had learned many things from the books she had free access to.

Even after her time outside in the streets with Grant, she found herself back inside the library walls, looking up things she had seen today. The relics and jewels, she wondered where all the items had come from.

A new interest she had developed: Foster. Grant spoke so fondly of the old knight that Alyssa had wondered if all the feats he had supposedly done were true. She had heard many stories of Foster, but only from books.

Alyssa rummaged through the books she could find on the

Realm's history, finding only small stories of Foster. His role in the two past wars and even a few stories of him working for the Church were all she had seen. Still, she was hungry for more until she found one page that stood out.

She read it, confused at first, so she flipped through some pages under it. Undoubtedly, the book was mistaken, and she wondered why the stack of books brought to her when she asked of Foster would have a book of Stalkers in it. Everyone knew of the Glas and how they had been extinct for hundreds of years—even Alyssa had heard the tale spoken from her Father's lips during bedtime. She also recalled hearing talk of a few remaining and how Stalkers were employed by the Church to hunt the Glas race down.

Why would Foster's name appear in such a book?

"You are up late... I thought you would have been worn out by your trip outside the castle." The king entered the library, looking over the books she was reading. He seemed curious, flipping a few pages. "Demon hunters?"

"I requested books on Sir Foster, and it must have gotten mixed in with them. I read about him fighting as a mercenary for Valacore when we won the war against Mirelos. Is that when you knighted him? So he would be a knight for Valacore?" Alyssa moved out of her seat, so she could see her father better, ready to hear a story as always.

"Sir Foster is a knight, yes, but he belongs to no kingdom. He has been to and fought for many kingdoms. He grew up in Valacore; his family before him also." The king smiled, ruffling Alyssa's hair before closing the book with his other hand. "I'll tell you more of Foster later. You should get some sleep if you wish to go back into town tomorrow."

CHAPTER FIVE

Kaiser's feet and back ached as he marched with the rest of his company.

He had been given two full days of sword training before they shipped the men out onto the field, leaving Kaiser with almost no experience with the blade Guile had given him. He had heard whispers of Ragnovok forces marching north and even more hints of combat breaking out in the next few days.

Honestly, Kaiser was scared; his heart beat like crazy, and they had yet to fight.

He had become friends with two other drafted men, Nick and Phil, both lowborn like Kaiser. For the two days of training, the three trained together. Nick was the more experienced, although he refused to explain where he had gained such skill with a sword.

Together, they marched south. Every day it grew colder, and it rained for two days. The company had advanced for a week or so, and the enemy was supposedly just over the hill.

Finally, the company stopped, allowing the men to rest. Nick and Kaiser leaned near the fire. Phil was off gathering wood while the other men sat idly, but no matter what anyone was doing, they all had fear in their hearts, and it eased Kaiser knowing he wasn't alone.

He often thought of his sisters when he was around the fire.

He remembered their smiles so as not to forget them. Tonight, the red moon was absent, but he knew it was up there in the sky, hiding. Kaiser gave a weak smile at the thought of his sisters looking up at the same sky, watching for the red moon.

"You should worry about the present," Nick said, sharpening his sword across the fire from Kaiser. The rhythmic scraping was almost comforting in a way. "Thinking about your sisters during combat will get you killed."

He was a strict man and often scolded Kaiser and Phil for not taking things seriously. Kaiser knew he was right, but even then, he couldn't stop worrying about them. What if he died? They would be left alone.

"Give him a break, Nick," Phil said, returning to the fire. He tossed down his load of wood and took a seat next to Kaiser. "The guy hasn't seen his sisters in weeks, and he's all they have. Don't you have family somewhere?"

"No, I come from Mirelos. I came here after my parents died." A simple reply, but meaningful.

Mirelos was far to the east, a kingdom surrounded by marsh and littered with sinful pleasures, or so Guile had said. Each of the men there had their reasons for being there, but Kaiser was only worried about his reasons.

The sky was full of stars, and most men had passed out from the march, but Kaiser, Phil, and Nick remained awake, discussing stories and tales from their past.

"So have you two heard of the Phantom?" Phil pulled a twig

from the stack of wood he had brought and begun drawing in the dirt. He drew a stick man with two spears in each hand.

Nick cocked an eyebrow. "The Phantom?"

"The Phantom. The few men who have seen him on the field say he's almost seven feet tall and wields two spears. He has crimson red hair and rides a demonic horse with red eyes. I heard one guy say he's like a ghost and can disappear into thin air."

Nick rolled his eyes, kicking at the dirt to mess up Phil's depiction of the Phantom. "Are you both so childish to believe fairy tales the enemy side has created to scare us?"

The group went silent, Nick's mood killing the fun of telling stories.

"I don't know anything about the Phantom," Kaiser said after a few minutes, "but I have heard a lot of stories from an old friend. He told me about the gods that abandoned the realm and the dragons that lived along the coast in the south." Kaiser paused for a moment, trying to think of what else Guile had told him. "Men who live across the ocean that can change their shape at will, looking like anything they want, and long-lost races that have been gone for so long no one remembers their names. So, I believe it's possible for a man like the Phantom to exist, but like all the stories I've been told, if dragons can be killed, so can the Phantom."

None of them had ever seen anything as magical as a dragon, but at least two believed in such.

"Well, hopefully, you won't come face to face with this Phantom," Nick said mockingly before he stood, tossing the whetstone to Kaiser and heading to his tent. "Sharpen that thing; it's as dull as a stick."

Unfortunately, it was true. The blade looked like it had seen better days. Guile had done all he could to restore it, but it was still in worse shape than the other swords.

Kaiser and Phil remained awake a few more hours, exchanging stories they had heard about the South and all its creatures, before Phil finally called it a night, leaving Kaiser next to the fire alone. His mind drifted from the stories they told back to his sisters, wondering how they were.

After another look at the sky, Kaiser decided to get some rest and headed toward the tents.

Across the camp, Prince Devon and his generals gathered around their table, charting and plotting their plan of assault. They knew Ragnovok forces would soon come over the hills, but they wouldn't go full force just yet. Sullvain would send the drafted men in first; the more experienced men waited a day's march away, so they could better view how many men and how strong a force Ragnovok had sent. Keeping their forces this far north could have crippled some of Ragnovok's men due to a lack of resources and supplies.

"If rumors are true," General Coloden said, "the Ragnovok may feast on the drafted men after they fall."

"Do you always believe rumors, General Coloden?" Devon asked with derision.

They had no real reason to be this close to the front, but the half dozen companies of drafted men would be hard to control if they didn't head the march themselves. Devon and his generals would fall back to the second wave of knights once battle erupted. It was common knowledge that Ragnovok had the more massive army of the two kingdoms, but it was a matter of how many men they would be willing to send north. Even if Ragnovok had dispatched half their army, if Valacore didn't send reinforcements from the north in time, it would be a close war.

"What of Valacore? Any news from them of reinforcements?" A servant poured Devon a glass of wine, and he leaned back, his posture confident and in control.

"Your father sent requests a few weeks past, but no word has returned," General Coloden explained, taking his glass of wine and gesturing toward the tent door. "It is likely they will wait until the last second if they help at all."

"Our drafted men stand no chance," General Mont replied, "but if we're lucky, we can catch Ragnovok off- guard in a sort of false sense of confidence."

It was low odds, but it was the most they could hope for, using the drafted as fodder and a distraction.

"We can only hope," Devon said, sipping on his wine.

While Sullvain and Ragnovok engaged in war, the smaller villages did what they could to assist. Knights often came by, taking needed supplies and rations from the crops. With Kaiser's absence, Guile had turned to tending the fields alone, his old back and legs throbbing from work.

He thought of Kaiser daily. Ragnovok was a ruthless army, and he worried about Kaiser's safety. Deep down, he knew Kaiser probably wouldn't return; he was young and had never held a sword in his life. Guile knew the trials of war, and it broke his heart to think of Kaiser lying among the dead.

"It sure is a hot day!" Alice smiled, a large cup of water outstretched toward Guile. She helped him as Lilly ran through the fields.

"Stay close!" she shouted as Lilly began dashing left and right through the crops.

Guile gladly took the cup, downing most of the water before wiping what was left off his beard. She had been trying to help him every day that Kaiser had been gone. She was a good girl, a year older than Kaiser. The two were smart kids, and Guile had done all he could to look out for them.

"How are the fields coming?" Alice asked once Guile was finished drinking. She took the cup back, pressing it to her chest while she watched Lilly roam the field.

"It's getting harder for me to work the whole field... Makes you appreciate having a young man like Kaiser around." Guile propped his scythe upon his shoulder and wiped the sweat from his forehead, smiling when Lilly rushed past him. Guile looked back to Alice and saw the same heartbreak in her eyes that he felt himself.

"I could help you with the fields," Alice offered earnestly.

Guile quickly shook his head. "The fields are no place for a lady like you. Besides, who would watch Lilly?"

Alice shyly shook her head. She wanted to pull her weight, and while he understood that, he couldn't allow her.

"Do you think he'll be okay? I can't see my brother swinging a sword." Alice sighed, looking down at what remained in the cup, focusing on not crying.

"I've seen him swing a scythe, he ain't so bad at it. A sword isn't much different." Guile shifted, his aching body preparing to get back at it.

Alice noticed Guile subtly signaling he was getting back to work and stepped back, yelling for her sister. She would leave Guile so he could return to work. Another glass of water, later perhaps. Alice left Guile to work and returned to their house.

She missed her brother, and although Lilly played as children do, she also missed him. It was so different without him around the house. He was a smart young man with a childish side, and it helped Alice to get through the day as an older sister playing the mother.

CHAPTER SIX

The midday hat beat down on Grant and Foster as they traded blows, their dull training swords clashing. They spent most every evening sparring, Grant still trying his best to outdo his father in combat. In a matter of minutes, Grant found himself on his ass and Foster's sword at his throat.

"You let your guard down when you side-swing. Your swing is too slow, and it leaves you open," Foster explained as he reached his hand to help Grant up.

"You have been telling me that for years," Grant grumbled.

Foster smiled slightly. "Yes, and you never listen."

Once on his feet, Grant lifted his hand, pushing his blonde hair out of his face, clearing away the sweat. It was a workout trying to keep up with Foster. Despite being in his mid-fifties, the old man could wield a sword like no other. Grant would have loved to have seen him in his youth. The skill he must have had. Grant had heard many tales of Foster and his feats before he settled down in Valacore. The people used to call him the Dark Stalker.

"You never mention your past. Why is that?" Grant asked before lifting his canteen, drowning himself in the cold water. It was a godsend, considering the workout the two had just finished.

Foster merely shrugged. "Nothing of mention. If you want to hear about the time I killed a dragon or when I fought back a hundred men, go to the tavern and listen to the drunks. There's nothing to those old rumors." Foster took a sip of his canteen, watching as Grant drenched himself in cold water.

"I just thought maybe one or two of the stories may be true," Grant said. "Alyssa goes on and on about you, asking question after question. It has got me wondering the same things about you."

Grant tossed his sparring blade back onto the rack along the wall and moved aside as two guards passed them. "I feel like I know so little about you, the one person I've known my whole life."

Those words revealed what Grant was fishing for. He didn't want to know more about the rumors and legends. He wanted to know more about his father and the man he was before he adopted a son and settled.

"Grant, you know the only me worth knowing. I promise you that." The old man smiled, placing his hand on Grant's shoulder.

"But have I told you about the time I rode a wild boar into battle against the snowmen of Ice Mountain?" Foster smiled, mocking him. "Do you not want to hear it? I saved a princess— hells, I saved five of them on that day!"

Grant sighed and began to walk away. "I have to take Princess Alyssa out. Find someone else to mock, old man!"

As he left the barracks, he looked back to see the goofy smile still on Foster's face.

Grant found his oath would be an easy one to uphold. Each day was spent walking with Alyssa, something he had grown fond of.

He had ditched his heavy knight's armor for more casual wear, allowing him to move freely with her and save him from the heat that beat down on Valacore each day. Grant followed her across the main street, leading to the kingdom gates. She was usually very talkative, but she was silent today.

"Is something wrong, Your Grace?" Grant asked cautiously.

She continued walking, not turning to address him. The two walked further until she came to the gates and watched as the large wooden doors opened.

"Can we go outside the gates? Maybe tomorrow?"

"Your father would never allow it," Grant replied, not thinking of how the words might hurt, but she turned to him, a false smile on her young face.

"I know... but dreaming got me this far, did it not?" Disappointed, Alyssa walked back up the street.

Grant wished he could do something. He had seen her act this way only a few times, and it hurt him. He knew his place was to protect her from harm, but he was powerless to protect her heart from it. He watched on as she walked, her fingers playing with the blue crescent stone he had bought her his first day escorting her.

Grant took hold of her arm, pulling her in the opposite direction. Her blue eyes looked up in worry as he lead her away from the main street and down an alley. His eyes darted from one alley to the next, until finally, they came out at an opening.

Grant stopped, releasing her arm, so she could see what he

had brought her to see. Before them was the ocean, closer than Alyssa had ever seen. They stood on the docks of Valacore; the breeze and smell of the salty air embraced them. She stepped forward, her eyes wide and full of wonder.

"You may not be able to step outside of the kingdom, but you can touch the ocean with your own hands," Grant said, crossing his arms. He remained further back, so Alyssa could have the moment alone.

She stepped over to the edge of the pier and looked down, seeing herself in the clear blue reflection. As she fell to her knees, her hand reached out and gently caressed the waves that rolled in.

When she finally rose, she rushed back to Grant, wrapping her arms around his waist and burying her face in his chest. He was surprised, but he automatically lifted his arms to make room for her.

"Thank you, Grant... Can we come back here tomorrow?" Alyssa looked up at him, tears running down her cheeks. Grant was relieved they were tears of joy; he lifted his hand and wiped her cheek clean.

"Of course, Princess. We can come here whenever you like," Grant said, looking out over the sea behind her. She couldn't be free in the way she wanted, but she could look out and touch the ocean, something that had no walls.

After enjoying the sights for a bit longer, Grant and Alyssa started back toward the castle, Alyssa rushing ahead as she was in a much better mood. Her black hair twirled in the air as she leaped from one step to the next, making her way slowly up the main street.

People watched on, some shaking their heads at the girl's playful manner. Although Grant would normally have requested she calm down, he was happy to see her in such an uplifting mood.

His smile quickly faded when she tripped and tumbled down the steps. Grant rushed forward. When he got to her, his hands gently searched for injuries to make sure she was okay.

"Are you hurt?" Grant's voice was full of worry, and although she seemed in pain, she gave a soft smile.

"You are so worried, Sir Grant! It is most adorable!" Alyssa smiled, her hands rubbing her elbows.

"You ripped your shirt sleeve." When Grant lifted his hand to move the dangling cloth, he stared at what he saw underneath. He'd never seen such a thing. Black markings decorated her skin, wrapping and twirling around in a pattern a snake might make. It began around her shoulder, hid under the rest of her clothes, and traveled down her arm until it disappeared at her wrist.

Alyssa quickly pulled her arm back to hide the markings from Grant as if she were ashamed of them.

"Sir Grant..." she whispered, turning away from him, so he couldn't see her right arm.

"I—I'm sorry." He pulled off his jacket and wrapped it around her shoulders so no one could see her arm. Once she was covered, she looked back at Grant, her shame hidden. Grant and Alyssa quickly walked again, leaving the whole ordeal behind them.

"Maybe I can speak to your father about allowing us to go riding outside of the kingdom..." Grant attempted to change the subject, breaking the long silence. Alyssa nodded, shifting closer to him, showing she was no longer worried about what he had seen on her arm.

As the two left the scene, an old man approached the steps where Alyssa had fallen. His old, wrinkled hands picked up a single piece of fabric that had been ripped loose and left on the stone. He lifted it to his face and examined it, almost taking in its scent.

He had seen the whole thing and bore witness to the markings on Alyssa's arm. The old man blinked, and the whole of his eye became black. He gazed off at the two as if in a trance.

He had seen a secret the kingdom had kept for years.

CHAPTER SEVEN

K aiser stirred, feeling a wind rush through his tent. The cold chill woke him from his sleep, and he rose. His first thought was of his missing comrade, Phil. He shifted, standing from his small makeshift bed, and looked to the empty area on the other side of the tent.

The sound of a scream came from outside the tent, and Kaiser's eyes immediately darted to the tent opening, his heart lurching. It was sealed, but he could see boots racing back and forth at the bottom. He inched closer, his eyes watching in horror as red blood flowed into the tent.

His whole body stopped in place as the warm liquid hit his bare feet and slowly ran around his toes. He was confused, unsure what he would find outside the tent until it burst open, and Phil came running in, his sword in hand.

"Kaiser! Ragnovok has attacked!"

Kaiser barely grabbed hold of his sword before Phil yanked him out of the tent and into the pouring rain, barefoot and without armor.

What Kaiser witnessed next caused his stomach to turn. The sounds of death filled his ears as grown men wept and begged for their lives. He felt the blood wet between his toes as he stumbled to catch himself.

His heart stopped, and everything paused for a moment.

Kaiser watched as men he had grown to know fought and died right in front of his eyes.

This was war. This was what all those stories Guile had told honestly looked like. And there was nothing glorious or honorable about it.

"Kaiser!" Phil's voice fought its way through, and finally, Kaiser snapped back to reality, seeing Phil shouting across the field.

Kaiser ran after him, trying his best to keep up with his friend, but the mud under his bare feet made it difficult to gain any decent traction. He kept his sword close to his chest, not brave enough to pick a fight. He was lucky to make it to Phil without conflict. The hundreds of men fighting around him seemed already engaged, killing each other without sparing him any attention.

Phil quickly motioned toward the other side of the camp. Kaiser couldn't hear Phil over the screams around him, but he had seen the word "Nick" form on Phil's lips. He was looking for Nick, a good idea considering he was the only soldier between them who would know what to do.

Kaiser nodded and followed Phil, but he didn't get very far. Without warning, another man's body slammed into him, and he flew back, hitting the ground hard.

Kaiser fought for breath, the impact knocking the air from his lungs. He struggled to lift the dead weight, but the dead man pinned him to the ground.

The sound of death stepped closer, more bodies hitting the mud around him as he looked on, bearing witness to the Phantom.

As depicted in the stories, he towered above the average man, and his red hair stood out among the others. His black and crimson armor revealed his rank, General of Ragnovok. The Phantom had two blades in each hand, both uniquely curved.

Kaiser quickly fell back to the mud and stopped moving, playing dead, while death itself walked by. Each step the Phantom took, he cut down another Sullvain soldier. Kaiser lay motionless until he realized Phil was still standing.

With a new sense of desperation, Kaiser pushed the body again with all his might, finally, *finally*, sliding free save for his feet.

By that time, the Phantom had found his target—Prince Devon. Kaiser knew he should do something, but he was no hero, and he wouldn't throw his life away to slow the inevitable. If the Phantom reached Devon, the prince would surely die, with or without Kaiser's sacrifice.

Finally, Kaiser was back up and running, his bare feet pounding against the mud. He did his best to maneuver around the fighting; each time his way was blocked by the bloodshed, he turned and found another route, rather than fighting his way through.

As he worked his way through it all, he held his hand close to his mouth, fighting back the urge to vomit. The smell of the dead rose from the corpses littering the field. His legs were growing tired, and before too long, he fell, his knees hitting the earth hard. His whole body fell into the mud and slid.

He was finished, unable to go any further.

He wanted to curl into a ball and close his eyes, wait out the battle and wake up in his own bed. His mind instantly wandered to his sisters, and he cried shamelessly. He wanted to see them again; he wanted to hold them in his arms and make them laugh again.

Kaiser wept until his eyes were red, but when he heard his name spoken, he opened them. Phil was lying a few feet away. Kaiser wiped the tears and mud from his face and crawled through the muck. He inched along the ground, pushing the dead aside, so he could continue without standing.

"Kaiser..." Phil muttered, barely audible among the clamor of the battle. "I don't want to die, Kaiser..."

Kaiser crawled up to Phil, looking around to make sure none of the carnage was getting too close. Phil raised his hand, placing it on Kaiser's cheek. Kaiser didn't know what was happening until he realized Phil's hand left a warm imprint of blood on his cheek. With another look over Phil, Kaiser gasped.

Phil's lower half was mangled and torn; his left leg was severed at the knee, and his right was so cut and damaged, the bone was visible.

"Is it bad?" Phil tried to sit up, wanting to see the damage.

"It's fine. You're fine," Kaiser lied, distracting him so he wouldn't see his wounds.

Phil choked, and bits of blood escaped his mouth, but he attempted to smile through it. He was dying, and Kaiser was powerless to save him, the only friend he had known outside of his little village. Phil would die here in the mud like an animal.

"Go find Nick. He'll protect you." Phil lifted his hand and desperately tried to point in the direction where Nick could be found.

"I don't want to leave you!" Kaiser cried, shaking his head back and forth. He crawled closer, wrapping his arms around what was left of Phil's body.

Kaiser lay there, crying against his dying friend's chest until finally, he could no longer hear a heartbeat.

The battle had broken out unexpectedly, causing Devon and his generals to act fast. The combat overtook the camp within minutes, and the generals hurried off to command their companies. Despite their attempts at gaining control, none had any intention of seeing the fight to an end. Devon and his two knights had fought back most of the enemies, clearing any threats close to the tent.

"Servis, clear our flank! Oran, keep them at bay!" Devon fought back one of Ragnovok's men, killing the man with a quick slash. They underestimated the prince.

"They must take me for a spoiled lordling!" he shouted as another wave of enemies approached.

Servis had gone ahead, clearing a path so the prince could safely fall back and slip off the battlefield. Prince Devon and Sir Oran held back the wave, Oran's sword carving through the enemy.

"Prince Devon Sull..." A challenger stepped forward, the Phantom.

Devon stepped back, a jolt of fear running through him. This was an opponent he never expected, one who might just best him if given the chance.

"Where is your cowardly father? Does he send his children to fight all of his wars?" the Phantom said mockingly, his two blades coming together at the hilts to make a glaive. He spun the two-bladed weapon around and went in for the kill.

Prince Devon tried to step back again. Tripping over debris from the tent, he found himself on his back and staring up at death. His eyes closed tightly, and his pants warmed with piss, but no blade ever came.

When Devon opened his eyes, Servis was standing above him, his claymore sword stopping the Phantom's assault.

"Oran, get the prince to safety!" Servis ordered as he pushed forward, moving the Phantom back a few feet, allowing the prince room to stand.

Oran quickly gathered himself, emerging from the tent, pulling Prince Devon by the arm. Oran retreated with the prince, but before he did, he turned to Servis with a worried look.

Once they were gone, Servis and the Phantom squared off, their blades colliding with a near-deafening clang. Servis was one of Sullvain's greatest warriors, and the Phantom was Ragnovok's, making for an interesting fight.

"I came for the prince's head, but you might be more of a challenge." The Phantom beamed, taking another swing, but it was met with a block, sending the blade sliding up Servis' sword.

"Trust me, I have no intention of dying tonight!" Servis waited for another attack and quickly blocked it. Spinning around, he smashed the backside of his sword smashing into the Phantom's side. Although his blades came up to prevent the attack, the sheer force of Servis' claymore sent the Phantom stumbling back, and by the time he recovered his footing, Servis had dashed after Oran and the prince.

"Cowards!" the Phantom snarled, pulling his two blades apart.

Kaiser had lost track of what was going on around him, and he was unsure of how long he had laid there with Phil, but he finally picked himself up. With one last look at his friend's lifeless body, he crawled again.

After a few feet, he stood, forcing his tired legs to run. He had to find Nick. Every measure of him hoped Nick could somehow keep him safe.

After tracking across the battlefield, he saw his salvation. Nick was fighting, his sword cutting down his enemy, then turning to the next.

Kaiser was exhausted; his feet barely able to take the slow steps he made now. He collapsed to his knees when someone to his right smashed into him, sending him to the ground. He was so close to Nick, but when he opened his mouth to speak, his voice was broken, unable to cry out for his friend.

Kaiser's grip gave, and his sword hit the mud next to him. He could do nothing but sit there on his knees, his eyes barely open as he watched Nick dance across the field. Kaiser thought for a moment that maybe Nick was strong enough to save them all, but then he saw it, the Phantom approaching from Nick's rear.

"N—Nick!" Kaiser finally got out, raising his hand to reach out to Nick.

His plea went heard as Nick turned, looking square at Kaiser as the Phantom's blade ran him through. Nick moaned, struggling against the blade now lodged in his shoulder.

"Are you the best Sullvain has to offer?" the Phantom challenged silkily.

With a surge of strength, the Phantom slammed Nick to the ground and stepped around him, circling his prey. One of the Phantom's blades rested in Nick's back, and the other rose into the air, preparing to execute the wounded man.

"No!" Kaiser pushed himself from the mud, his broken body driving full force at the Phantom. When the Phantom turned,

Kaiser's blade sunk deep into his thigh, piercing the thick muscle. Kaiser stumbled back; he was too tired to lift his sword any higher, and so his attack hadn't been enough.

With a growl, the Phantom ripped the sword from his thigh and grabbed Kaiser by the throat. Despite his fresh wound, the Phantom lifted Kaiser's whole body up off the ground as if he weighed nothing, so high the man was forced to look up at Kaiser.

"Children ripped from their mothers... Is that all the fight you have left in you?" the Phantom asked.

Kaiser's hands struggled to fight the fingers wrapped around his neck. He was losing air, and he was too depleted to break free. Kaiser's vision began to dim as his brain was denied oxygen.

Right as Kaiser thought this was how he would die, he felt it.

The Phantom shoved Kaiser's own sword into his chest with such force, it came out Kaiser's back. Kaiser was dropped to the ground and settled there. He couldn't move, and so he could only look up at the Phantom in fear.

For a moment, Kaiser could see the frustration on the man's face, as if he were hoping for something more. As the Phantom turned, leaving Kaiser to die, all he could do was stare up at the sky. He could feel his own heart slowing and taste the blood fighting its way up his throat and down the sides of his mouth, but the pain from his wounds seemed so far away.

Compared to the pain of seeing the red moon resting above him, and realizing his sisters would be alone in the world, physical pain meant nothing.

CHAPTER EIGHT

The throne room was silent when Foster entered. The king and his council assembled in the center of the room. Foster immediately had a bad feeling as he carefully stepped closer, his hands resting behind his back. Once he joined the gathering, he looked to the king.

"You summoned me?" Foster suspected it was for a dire reason.

"We have been receiving reports that a Glas was spotted on the fields of war between Sullvain and Ragnovok. King Sull currently has it imprisoned, but I fear he may not understand how dangerous his capture is," the king said evenly, but his eyes showed a hint of fear, something Foster had rarely seen from the king.

Foster knew of the Glas, knew what they were capable of. With a quick glance at the stiff postures and tight lines, Foster could tell none of the old men in this room knew what to do. The problem was halfway across the realm from them, but still, it was a force to fear.

"What can you tell us of the Glas, Sir Foster?" one of the king's men asked, fidgeting in his seat. The question was a tricky one. Foster knew more than most, but even that wasn't enough.

"Their race has been extinct for hundreds of years, longer ago than even the dragons." Foster shifted his weight, looking across the room at the window as he tried to recall more. "We presumed maybe a few dozen remained, but thankfully, we have only ever sighted three. You have, no doubt, heard of the Raven? He and his brother are two of the three. He has caused problems for the Six Kingdoms for years, and we know very little about him, including where he resides. The third Glas died twenty years ago."

"Maybe we could find the one who slew it? Surely he knows how to stop them?" the king's aide tossed the idea, and although everyone hopefully agreed, Foster shook his head.

"I was the one present when the Glas died... She killed herself. I highly doubt you could convince this new threat to do the same, and I honestly have no idea how to go about removing one outside of that route. Fire has been known to bring them near death but won't finish them. Once the Raven and his brother discover another of their race is in Sullvain, they'll seek him out. We must act quickly."

Again, the room grew gray, and the group frowned. Foster knew how bad his next few words would be, but it was the only choice he had.

"I will go to Sullvain and, if this rumor is true, kill the Glas," Foster said gravely, knowing there was no other choice. Some of the men relaxed at the burden being lifted from their shoulders.

After a long silence, the king nodded, looking Foster in the eyes. The king couldn't afford to disagree. Sullvain was housing a significant threat in its walls, and if Foster couldn't convince them to end its life, the war would be the least of their worries.

"And if it is true, how will you kill it?" the king asked, idly playing with the rings on his fingers.

"I'll put a flaming sword through its chest. We shall see where it goes from there."

The king nodded. "Sullvain will be expecting reinforcements. I will send a few companies to make your arrival seem less suspicious. If you need anything else, I will see it done."

"Thank you, Your Majesty," Foster said, dipping into a bow. He turned on his heels, going to prepare to do the impossible.

"What do you mean, you're going to Sullvain?" Grant's voice could be heard from down the castle halls and only raised in volume. He was against the plan, and Foster understood why. It was a dangerous one.

"What is a Glas, anyway? Why would the king expect you, of all people, to seek it out?" Grant asked before Foster could even answer the set of questions. The two walked around the room, Grant following Foster as he collected his things to leave.

"Calm down. It's a simple task. It isn't like I'm roaming the countryside hunting a beast. It'll be chained down, like an animal," he said, shoving things into his bag. "The Glas are a powerful race of creatures thought to have been wiped out hundreds of years ago. It would appear one has sprung up during the first battle in Sullvain."

Grant crossed his arms. "Take me with you then. I can help in case something happens," he said, his voice lowering.

Foster shook his head, tossing his luggage over his shoulder. "You are Alyssa's royal guard; you have sworn an oath to protect her at all costs. You belong here with her."

Foster sighed, seeing the pain in Grant's eyes. He knew Grant was worried, but even if Foster wanted to take him, he couldn't.

Foster placed his hand on Grant's shoulder. "Take care, my son."

"I understand," Grant said reluctantly, finally giving up. "Just be careful."

Foster gestured for him to follow, and the two walked down the hall together. Foster would have Grant see him off. He had no one else in the world he cared for more than Grant, and he was the only one he wanted to see before he left.

The day was beautiful, and the sun caused the golden city of Valacore to shine, earning its nickname.

"You should bring the princess out today. It's beautiful."

"Yes, I've already promised her such."

Foster could tell Grant hadn't entirely accepted he was leaving yet. The young knight's curt tone showed it more than his expression. The two finally came to the stables, and Foster approached his steed, a beautiful white horse. Grant had grown up admiring the horse, almost as much a member of the family as himself. The two knights who would accompany him waited near the gates.

"Listen, Grant." Foster turned. "I need you to know something before I go. No matter what happens, you are Alyssa's wall. You can trust no one else when it comes to her. Do you understand? Not the royals, not the Church, not the king. You are all that stands between her and anyone who would use her."

Grant frowned. "What do you mean? Is she in danger?"

"Not for the moment. Stay by her side and see that she never is." Foster reached out, taking Grant's hand as he pulled him in and hugged him tightly. His old eyes fought back the tears.

He fully realized this might be the last time he hugged his son.

Later in the day, Grant walked with Alyssa through the streets. She was in a much better mood than before, but now it was Grant who remained silent and down.

After the long silence became too much for her, Alyssa turned, walking backward as she addressed him. "What is wrong, Sir Grant?"

Grant attempted a small smile that looked brittle around the edges. "Nothing, Your Grace, just thinking."

That wasn't a good enough answer. Frowning herself, Alyssa reached up and pushed his lips into a smile. He quickly brushed her hands away. Alyssa's playful pout became a real one, and she turned her back to him, looking off into the crowded streets.

What could pull Grant from this mood? She'd never seen him like this.

She had an idea, something she thought might cheer him up.

"Catch me, Sir Grant!"

Alyssa bolted down the street with such a head start, Grant lost her in the crowd. She rushed past people, smiling and laughing, while she ducked and ran until she found an alleyway. She would go to the pier and wait for him. It was a perfect plan.

She ran down the alley, taking this turn and that until she found herself at a dead end. She stopped and looked around. She didn't remember that wall being there....

She took a few steps back and sighed, finally admitting to herself she had taken a wrong turn somewhere. When she eventually turned around, she let out a loud gasp, startled by the three men behind her, staring at her.

Alyssa pulled all the courage she had and walked past them. She gasped again as one of them grabbed her arm and pulled her back, pushing her into the wall.

She drew herself up indignantly. "I am a royal! You will let me pass or my knight will—"

"Shut your face, girl!" the large, bald man shouted, raising his hand as if he meant to hit her.

Alyssa flinched, but the attack never came. "Please, just let me pass..."

Her courage had been broken, and she was pleading now, backing up until she could go no further. Her heart thundered in her chest, spurred on by her fear.

The three men kept inching closer, whispering and glancing at each other as they approached. She fought the urge to cry, knowing she had to be strong. To show weakness was to give them an opening to exploit.

She regretted ever leaving Grant, seeing how foolish it was to run from him. She tightly closed her eyes as the bald man reached in, his sweaty fingers grabbing her chin. She could smell his foul body odor, and it made her cringe as she tried to push back against the wall.

"We got ourselves a royal girl. Bet she'd fetch plenty of coins!" He laughed, spit flying about. Alyssa fought against his grip on her chin, but he was far stronger.

"Brock!" A voice echoed through the alley, and the three men turned to see who had called the bald man.

Alyssa was released as Brock left her to address the new voice. She stayed back, still against the wall, praying they'd leave her alone or forget about her. Brock glared at her before he waved his two buddies over, and the three left.

Once they were gone, the boy walked over to greet her. "My name is Dye. Are you okay?"

He was young, around sixteen, like her, and he was handsome, despite his dirty clothes and uneven haircut. He was what she had heard the guards call a Rat, someone who lived in the streets without an actual home.

"I am fine, thank you." Alyssa assumed he had somehow talked the men out of whatever disgusting plan they had for her, and she was thankful for it. She stood, dusting herself off, before giving Dye a smile and announcing her name.

"I am Alyssa Valacore... the king's niece," she lied, knowing full well she couldn't tell a soul who she truly was, and it was unlikely anyone would know if such a niece really existed.

To Alyssa's surprise, the boy fell to a knee, his head bowing to her.

"P—please stand, no need for such formalities!" Alyssa's whole face flamed with heat, and her hand rose to hide the blush.

She wondered if this was what the princesses in all those books she had read felt like when being saved. A handsome young man saving their lives, although her prince was replaced by a Rat. But in all honesty, she hardly cared. He was so handsome.

Alyssa talked with Dye for what seemed like forever, listening to his stories about growing up in Valacore and how he often traveled west to the port cities. She envied him for his exciting life, and it brought her great joy to listen to such stories.

When he asked her about her past, she played it cool, impressing herself by how easily she came up with a fake past. How she lived in a small kingdom near the mountains, so out of the way, no one had ever really heard of it, how she came here to stay with the king while her father was off making treaties or some such. The two talked and laughed, and before Alyssa knew it, they had sat down on some nearby steps and talked more.

She enjoyed his company, the only real company she had ever had outside of Grant who, until that day, had been fantastic company, but this boy was free, something she had always longed for.

"Alyssa!"

She turned, hearing Grant's voice from the alley entrance. She quickly stood, her stomach filled with fear when she noticed the worried look on his face and how it was mixed with anger.

Dye stood with her. Not knowing who the man was, he took a stand in front of his new friend, an action he would soon regret, as he found Grant's sword unsheathed and at his neck. Dye instantly froze.

"Sir Grant! Put your sword away. He is my friend!" Alyssa commanded Grant for the first time since they had met.

Grant's blade stayed pressed against the boy's neck, but after a long pause, he pulled away, gesturing for Alyssa to come to him.

"You know how dangerous it is out here... and how dangerous it is to speak to anyone, let alone a stranger," Grant said tightly.

Grant's eyes stared through Dye. His intent to kill was evident by his expression and by the hard lines of his muscles. Although she wanted to stay, she knew how right Grant was and nodded, stepping over to join him.

"We should return to the main streets, Your Grace." He gave Dye one last threatening look and walked out of the alley.

As Alyssa was all but pulled along with him, her head turned to look back at Dye, and she gave him a happy smile, one he returned to her.

Far from Valacore and Sullvain stood a keep cloaked in the shadow of a mountain. Inside the keep stood a pale beauty. Her hair trailed down her back, almost to her knees. The white roses surrounding her resembled her long, white locks.

She found herself inside the garden alone, her delicate fingers coming ever so close to the roses without touching them. She walked through the garden, her beauty putting all the roses to shame. When she heard the doors open and the sound of two men entering her paradise, she turned. They approached her, both taking a knee once she acknowledged them.

"My queen..." The younger of the two men addressed the white-haired beauty, and she smiled, letting them know they could stand.

Her two loyal knights stood and followed her through the garden as she looked over all the roses that had yet to bloom. The two men resembled each other. The older one went by Draston and was a large man with the build of a bear rather than a man. His younger brother was Laderic, the queen's most loyal knight, and that made him the most valuable asset she had. The queen turned to her knights as they delivered news from the outside.

"We have wonderful news, my queen," Laderic exclaimed, his eyes shining in triumph. "We found the mask, hidden inside one of the churches."

This news brought a smile to her pale lips. "Excellent."

"We have also found one of the marked ones..."

The queen's expression shined; the news brought her much pleasure, and she shifted toward him, taking the small piece of fabric he had in his hand.

"Where is she?"

"Valacore. Under the Church's watch, for the moment."

She absently raised her hand to rest a fingertip on her lower lip as she considered her next move. "Draston, you will bring her to me."

Without question, the large man bowed, leaving his brother and the queen so he could do as commanded. Once he was gone, the queen moved even closer, and her pale hand found its way to Laderic's cheek.

"Is it true?" Laderic asked hesitantly.

She nodded. "Yes, it would seem another of your kind has recently been born again. Wrapped in the blood of war, he has experienced his rebirth."

The queen smiled. Laderic was just as loyal to his race, the Glas. Laderic and Draston were the last of their kind, but now, another was born, and Laderic would undoubtedly do all he could to find his new family member.

The queen pulled Laderic closer, her cheek pressed against his, and he closed his eyes. She was so very fond of Laderic and him so very loyal to her.

Her pale lips inched closer to his ears, and she whispered, "We will find your kind in due time, but we must not turn from our current task."

The queen knew how badly he would want to set out for Sullvain, to bring his reborn brother into their ranks, but he was loyal, and he would follow her commands explicitly.

"Yes, my queen, I will retrieve the mask and bring it to you," Laderic said with steadfast conviction.

Satisfied, she stepped back across the garden and tended to her flowers. As Laderic exited, the queen grinned, her pale fingers finally reaching out to touch the only bloomed rose among the group. The beauty in the rose withered away and died at her touch.

As Laderic marched out of the castle doors, he found his brother standing at the foot of the stairs.

"Draston? Why have you not left for Valacore?" Laderic approached his brother and instantly realized he was full of doubt.

Draston took a deep breath. "I know how strongly you feel about the queen, but..."

"But what? We should be thankful she has opened her arms to us. She's helping us."

Draston shook his head, looking back at the dark stone castle the queen resided in. "The marked girl, how does such a thing benefit our cause? How will it help our race?"

Draston had always had his doubts about the queen, since the day she welcomed the two brothers.

"Do as the queen commands, brother... We won't speak of this again." Laderic's fury showed through his tone, but he held back his rage.

CHAPTER NINE

He could see nothing but the dark void.

For a moment, Kaiser was at rest. Although he was cold, he felt as though he was wrapped inside the arms of something much larger than he. His mind was silent until he saw the light ahead, its rays showing him something outside of the darkness. He couldn't see his hands in front of him, but he could feel them lift, and when he finally reached out to the light, his dark, sweet embrace deserted him, and he awoke to reality.

He found himself alone, without the embrace he had left behind. He cringed, holding his hands up to look at them. It felt as though he had flames burning inside his arms, and for a moment, he even imagined he saw the veins under his skin twist and turn as if alive.

Soon, the burning ceased, and he tried to relax. His breathing returned to normal, and he looked around the room, trying to discover where exactly he was.

The last thing he remembered he was lying in the mud, dying on the fields of Sullvain... He yanked his shirt up, taking stock of his chest where the Phantom had run him through.

To his surprise, he found no wound, only smooth skin. Not even a scar. Was it all a dream? If so, where was he now?

Kaiser went to stand, but his legs were tired and limp, that of a newborn's, unable to lift the weight of his body. He fought with all of his will to stand, using the wall to his advantage. He crawled along the wall until he discovered bars blocking his exit.

He was inside a cell.

The damp and dark surroundings were bright now—he was a prisoner in a dungeon somewhere. He rested against the cell bars and tried to peek out, seeing nothing but a small torch further down the hall in the dark.

He could hear the coughs of others in the cells lining the wall opposite him, but he couldn't see past his own cage.

Kaiser's first assumption was that he had been captured by Ragnovok, but how would he have survived such a wound? A better question was, where had his injury gone? His hand found no wounds at all, not a single scratch.

A wooden door suddenly slammed, and then the sounds of boots splashing through the wet dungeon hall met his ears. He tried to step away from the bars, but his legs gave out, and he fell to the floor. Three men stopped at his cell as he pulled himself to the back wall.

Kaiser could barely make out the men, the two in the back mostly hidden by the darkness. The one standing closest to the cell stared in at Kaiser.

"W—where am I?" Kaiser's voice was broken and came out in clumps. He could hardly get the words out. "Why am I in a dungeon?"

The man moved closer, revealing his facial features. His brown hair was tied up in a ponytail, and his expression seemed mixed. He almost seemed afraid.

"You are Kaiser Noire?" the man asked, his right hand snatching a nearby torch so he could better inspect Kaiser.

Kaiser raised his arm, trying to stop the brief pain in his eyes from so much light all at once. He nodded, shifting back more.

"Do you remember what happened during the battle?"

"W—we were losing... Phil." Kaiser had forgotten about Phil, about how he had died that night. The loss hit him all at once. His eyes burned with tears, but he held them back. When he looked up, the man at the bars seemed shocked by Kaiser's reaction.

"You don't seem the part, that's certain."

Kaiser shook his head, not understanding anything. "The part? What do you mean?"

The three men turned and left without a backward glance. Kaiser forced his exhausted legs up and stumbled over to the bars.

"Please! Don't leave!" Kaiser shouted through the dungeon halls. "Why am I here? What happened?"

The hope he had of getting such answers slowly disappeared as the man's figure faded into the darkness of the halls. Kaiser cried out one last time before laying his head against the cold bars, trapped inside an unknown prison. He could hear the snickering of his imprisoned neighbors as his hope dwindled.

Kaiser's mind was full of confusion and fear. He wanted to go home, he wanted out of the cell, he wanted his sisters.

As Kaiser sat alone and scared in the dungeon, his captors gathered in the main part of the castle. Three men stood alongside the king of Sullvain while he played with his black beard.

"So it is true?" the king asked, unsure if the young man known as Kaiser Noire was indeed as dangerous as it seemed.

"We have multiple witnesses who claim this boy is a Glas," one of the old men standing with the king confirmed as Rageal entered the room.

"Sir Rageal!" The king waved the man over, urging him to join the conversation. "You have spoken to the prisoner? Do you believe this boy to be the threat so many from the battle have claimed?"

"Despite all the claims, the boy seems to be just that, a farm boy. He seems scared out of his wits," Rageal said, looking unimpressed with the boy.

The men pondered over what they would do with such a creature until one of the men was brought a letter. He read it and looked to the king.

"We have a witness who knows him." Before the king could respond, the doors cracked open, and a soldier was led in to stand in front of the king and his men.

"State your name," the king said, eager to hear what the witness had seen.

"My name is Nick Walston." Nick looked at the floor the whole time, refusing to meet the king's eye. "I was in the same company as Kaiser Noire. I've known him for many weeks now."

"And?" the king snapped impatiently.

"I watched the Phantom put his sword through Kaiser's chest. I watched him die right in front of me. Then he came back as something else. His eyes glowed and he was some sort of beast." Nick trembled at the memories of it. "He killed whoever he could reach, Sullvain and Ragnovok men alike. He even wounded the Phantom!"

The group began to whisper among themselves as Nick finished his testimony. Nick stepped forward once more, his once brave eyes full of fear.

"I beg you, kill him! I don't know what he is, but those eyes!" Nick had begun raving and so the king gestured for his guards to remove the young man. He pressed for Kaiser's death even after he was dragged out of the room. The four men turned to their king, awaiting his decision.

"It is decided, the boy is a Glas."

"We should have him killed!" one of the old men spoke up, and the other two nodded at the idea.

Rageal smirked. "We should use him. The Glas are legend and feared by most all who know the name. We can use him to our advantage. We spread the false word that Ragnovok brought it with them to defeat us... we show the men that the Kingdom of Sullvain has captured and defeated Ragnovok's mighty Glas. It will raise morale and give us the upper hand."

Rageal's plan was well-received, and the king did enjoy the idea of acting as though he had defeated a Glas. He stroked his beard again, the smile on his old face already confirming what he thought of the idea.

"Do it, spread the word. I want everyone in the realm to know of Sullvain's triumph over the mighty Glas."

The men all took a bow, leaving to do as their king commanded.

Rageal returned to the king's side. "My king, I have word Sir Servis wishes an audience concerning the battle."

The king beamed. "Yes, let us hear what he says of my son's actions on the field. Send him in."

"Yes, my king."

He had retreated like a scared child, his honor left in the mud.

Devon sat in his royal chambers, his hand tightened into a fist. He was angry at himself, at his failures. He had returned to Sullvain with piss-stained pants and broken honor only to discover a Glas had been found on the field. He could have gained more glory then ever if he had stayed long enough to just walk into the castle gates alongside the men who returned with the creature, but he had returned days before.

His royal knights, Servis and Oran, had brought him back, and although he wanted to punish them, if it weren't for Servis, he would have died at the hands of the Phantom. So now he sat alone in his chambers, too ashamed of himself to show his face.

"My dear son." The sound of the queen's voice surprised Devon.

Entering his room without a sound, she stepped over to him, joining him on the edge of the bed. "Why have you not joined your father's side?"

"I should have been the one to bring the Glas back. I could have gained my father's respect and that of the kingdoms. I failed, I cannot look Father in the eyes." He clenched the bedsheets, looking off at the window, anywhere but at his mother.

His mother placed her hand on his knee comfortingly and shook her head. "You are the Prince of Sullvain... If you want stories to be told of how you defeated the Glas and captured it, then all you have to do is say the word. No one would dare say otherwise."

"But Father knows. He knows I had already retreated like a coward!"

"Do you think your father has done all the feats his court sings of?" his mother asked with a smirk. "I have a wonderful idea, something that will make you feel more like the king you are meant to be."

In his daze of confusion, Kaiser was pulled from his cell, utterly clueless as to his fate. Two guards led him in chains. When they turned and took stairs leading deeper into the dungeon, his heart began to pound in fear. He didn't know where he was, but from the way the three men had looked at him, he was starting to realize he was in enemy hands.

The guards pulled him into a small chamber. Forcing him against the walls, they yanked his hands up and secured the binds to the wall. He struggled against the chains, fear finally pushing him to panic.

The two guards disappeared from the small room, and he was left hanging there. His eyes moved from one side of the room to the other, taking note of various tools and objects. On a long, stained table rested spikes and chains, long blades and hooks.

His heart nearly pounded from his chest as it dawned on him what this room was for: torture.

In a blind panic, Kaiser pulled and fought against the iron around his wrists. He struggled against the chains as if pulling them from the stone walls were possible. His flesh opened and bled, but he ignored the pain and put all his strength into getting free. Harder, harder...

Without warning, the steel door pushed open. A young man dressed in noble attire entered. He pulled the frilled sleeves of his shirt up his arm and stepped closer. Kaiser recognized him from his first day in Sullvain. The man paced the room, his eyes darting from all the horrible blades, then back to Kaiser.

"I doubt you know who I am, a simple farmboy like you. My name is Devon Sull, Prince of Sullvain." Devon's lips curled into a smile and he picked up a long, curved blade.

"Please don't. I didn't do anything!" Kaiser pleaded as Devon got closer.

Devon's hand shot out and grabbed Kaiser's throat to keep him still. He couldn't move his neck to look down, but when he felt the blade pierce his chest, he screamed from the pain. Devon pushed the knife into Kaiser's chest and moved it from one side to the other. Kaiser's legs gave out from the searing agony as his breath sawed in and out of him. Blood ran down his chest, and he heard a small chuckle from Devon.

Several different blades later, Kaiser's body was covered in cuts, holes, and his own blood. Everything throbbed, screaming in agony. He sucked in a painful breathe and cried, his body limp against the wall now. He had felt the blades cut into him, heard chunks of himself hitting the floor.

"I couldn't claim victory over you on the battlefield, but I will give you something that will never heal. At the sight of this gift, despite the truth, everyone will see my victory over the unstoppable Glas."

Kaiser's head hung lifeless. He had lost the will to scream what felt like hours ago, pain taking over his boy, but when he heard the sounds of coals being shifted, he struggled to look up. Devon was approaching him with a long iron brand, its tip glowing a bright orange.

No! Kaiser struggled to move, to free himself, but his muscles refused to move an inch. As the brand was applied to his exposed flash, Kaiser let out a shriek, smelling flesh burning, his own flesh. The iron left a jagged shape burnt into the skin over his right rib cage.

"I will not be labeled a coward! I am the future king!" Devon quickly muffled Kaiser's screams, his eyes looking over his pain with a hint of pleasure.

The coming days brought more misery to Kaiser than he had ever thought possible. Day after day, he was tortured. His body beaten and broken, but somehow he continued to live.

His thoughts were always on his sisters, wanting to live through this so he could one day see them again. But deep down, he knew he wouldn't be leaving this kingdom alive.

Why was this happening to him?

He had no memory of the deaths he was accused of, and he had no lust to kill—so why then was he being punished for something so unspeakable?

He had no answers, just thoughts to help him stay alive.

CHAPTER TEN

First blood had been drawn, leaving both Sullvain and Ragnovok to assess the damage. Everyone was contemplating the meaning of a Glas coming into play. Such an event was massive, leaving both sides to rethink their tactics.

Deep inside the Ragnovok encampment, the Phantom sat, his wounds still fresh and raw, yet he thought little of them. Instead, his mind was on the Glas sighting. The Phantom of Ragnovok had never felt such shame. His fingers rose, touching at the cloth covering his bare chest.

The Glas who had awakened on the field had left him with four new scars across his chest and down his arms. He wanted badly to march on and attack Sullvain while they were unprepared, but he could barely stand—let alone fight. He hadn't felt this weak since his youth.

"Seeath Reinhart, Phantom and General of Ragnovok... beaten by a child." A shadowy figure entered the tent. His frame was slim and frail-looking in comparison to the Phantom, but he spoke the Phantom's real name, and his voice was that of a friend's.

Seeath scowled. "I don't have time for your mockery, Magus, and you would be wise to take this seriously. I know what I saw— the rebirth of a Glas."

His companion nodded his head, his eyes prying at the wounds Seeath had sustained during his fight with the Glas. The two men remained silent for a time.

"We need to kill it," Magus finally.

"We must capture him," Seeath countered.

Seeath and Magus looked at each other, both dumbfounded by the other's plan of action.

"The boy was afraid," Seeath said, shaking his head. "He all but wet himself before he was reborn... If we can somehow get him out of Sullvain, we can use him, temper him like a blade."

"A blade that is just as likely to turn and chop our damn heads off!" Magus growled. "If he is what you claim him to be, you know how dangerous he is. You've fought his kind before."

Magus was right. Seeath had fought a Glas before, one who was thought to be the last—the Raven.

Seeath adjusted himself, his wounds sending a sting through his ribs. He brushed off the pain, much like he did Magus' objection. He had always heeded Magus' advice since they were children playing in the streets of Ragnovok, but this was something Seeath knew in his heart he needed to do. He had seen this new Glas kill, and it was wild, untamed. Completely unlike the Raven. If Seeath could get his hands on the Glas who had been reborn that night, he knew he could tame him to be a force benefiting Ragnovok.

Magus shook his head, but before he could object once more, a knight entered the tent. His haste caught both Seeath and Magus' attention.

"Sir Reinhart." The knight took a knee, showing his respect

before speaking. "A scout from the front line has returned. You need to hear his report."

Seeath nodded, standing from his chair and pulling his belt and sword tightly around his waist. He had nothing else to say on the matter, so he followed the knight out and tracked across the camp. The rain from the night before had left the grasslands muddy and the air damp.

Many eyes watched Seeath in awe. Their leader, the Phantom, walking so soon after his battle with a Glas—it was a sight that brought a glimmer of hope to the men.

Seeath reached the group of men gathered near the makeshift barracks, and the men all snapped to attention.

"Let us hear the report." Seeath looked from one man to the next, unsure of which had been the scout.

Finally, a man stepped forward, his head hung low as if afraid to offend the Phantom. "I was north, scouting for survivors of the battle when I spotted a raven delivering news to Sullvain..."

"Fredrick is a godsend with his bow, sir," one of the men interrupted.

"Aye, I shot it down and read the letter." Fredrick lifted his hand, handing the soaked paper to Seeath, who quickly read over it.

When he comprehended what he was reading, he rushed back to his tent in a rage and tossed the letter onto the small table, gesturing for Magus to take a look. At first, Magus seemed uneasy, inching closer and gently pulling the soaked paper apart as to not destroy it before it could be read. Seeath watched on, taking note of Magus' reaction to the news.

"You cannot possibly believe this? What reason would Valacore possibly have for sending eight thousand men to reinforce Sullvain?" Magus was skeptical, and for a good reason—everyone knew the treaty between Valacore and Sullvain was a shaky one.

Seeath shook his head, returning to his chair to rest his wounds once more.

"King Novok will order a retreat once he gets word of this," Magus said as if Seeath didn't know this already.

The Phantom hated the idea of retreat, but if so many men did march from Valacore... Seeath and his men wouldn't be able to stand up against the combined might of Sullvain and Valacore.

Finally, Seeath turned to Magus, a devilish smirk smeared across his face. "Do you still have spies inside Sullvain?"

"I do. Why?" Magus had the mind of a snake—what he lacked in skill with a sword, he doubled with the strings he could pull in all Six Kingdoms.

"Send word to your spy in Sullvain. I would have him do us a favor before our king commands our retreat."

While the kingdoms played at war, Kaiser's sisters tried their best to survive without him. News of his fate hadn't reached their ears, but Guile had many old war buddies in the kingdom, and he had heard about the Glas. He had known for a couple of days, but still, he couldn't bring himself to tell the girls. How could he? They loved their brother, and it would shatter their hearts to hear the news.

Guile worried about the family, but deep inside him, he wondered if the words he had heard were true. Was Kaiser, in fact, a Glas? Did he really belong to a race that had been extinct so long, Guile had only heard a handful of stories?

He stood at his window, his old eyes set across from his own home where he could see Alice fixing a small feast for her sister. His heart ached at the thoughts in his head. He loved Kaiser and his sisters, but the fear he had of the Glas caused his heart to ache almost unbearable. He sat alone in his home for some time before his solitude was interrupted by a faint knock at his door. He was surprised to find Alice on the doorstep.

"Is everything all right?" Guile asked. He saw just as much pain on her face as he had in his heart.

She shook her head, taking a seat near the fireplace. Guile stepped through the house, bringing her a cup of warm tea. Her smile slowly faded as she accepted the tea and took a small sip before looking away.

"People in the village have been talking..." Alice murmured, "About how many died during the first battle."

Guile sighed, worried for a moment if she had discovered the truth of Kaiser's fate of him being chained in the dungeons of Sullvain. He wondered whether he should tell her the truth.

Guile avoided the subject. "How's Lilly?"

"Fine, asleep. She's a handful without Kaiser to help. I know I often complained of his laziness, but she listened to him... He was softer with her, more understanding."

Guile nodded, understanding what she meant. He rarely spent any time in their home, but he knew from his time in the fields with Kaiser that he was a child at heart, a child who was forced to grow up.

"I... I'm sure he's fine," Guile lied, but at least his lie brought out a smile from her, and she nodded, her eyes still watching the fire crackle and brighten.

"I hope you're right." Alice stood, stepping over and wrapping her arms around Guile's large frame. She needed to know Kaiser was all right, and he had given her that false hope. It took some time, but he finally raised his arms, wrapping them around her shoulders and returning her embrace.

"Everything'll be okay, Alice, I promise." The lies came easy now that he knew they soothed her.

Alice pulled away, wiping the tears from her eyes as she stepped over to the door, looking back at him one more time, her smile letting him know she appreciated his words.

After Alice left, Guile returned to his seat. He looked up at the crest over his fireplace. As his eyes filled with tears, he jumped up, grabbed the wooden crest from the wall, and threw it into the flames.

And he didn't stop there. Next, he ripped the relics of war from his walls until all of it was on the floor, and he joined it, falling to his knees. His wrinkled face looked on at the mess, and he continued to cry.

He had grown old, never knowing what it was like to have a family. War was all he had ever known, and now, when he had grown so close to Kaiser and Alice and Lilly, the war had taken them away.

What would a father do to protect his children? The answer came to him easily: run. Guile would run from the kingdom to which he had given his youth. He couldn't save Kaiser, but he could save Alice and Lilly.

Guile watched on as the Sullvain crest burned in the fire. He would prepare his things, and within the week, he would convince Alice to go north with him because it would be only a matter of time before Sullvain would come looking for the sisters of the Glas.

THE RAVEN

The rain poured down along the stained-glass windows, spilling moonlight into the room. On occasion, the lighting would give life to the dark halls, but in reality, only death occupied the church.

A lone priest ran down the hall, his chest heaving, too afraid to look behind him for fear of what might be following. He rushed down the hall and pushed the wooden doors open, finding himself in a completely dark room. He was in the sanctuary; he knew that much.

He blindly stepped down the aisle, his hands stretched out before him to warn him of any objects he might find in the dark. His panicked flight came to a stop when he slipped and fell to the ground. The old man struggled to lift himself. Outside, a flash of lightning illuminated the room, revealing what he had tripped on.

The aisle was littered with the bodies of his fellow priests. Some were nearly ripped in half, while others were missing limbs.

The priest leaned over and vomited, the sight more than he could handle. When the room returned to darkness, he desperately crawled away from the carnage—but what he found next caused his whole body to freeze. He could see it in through the gloom, almost as if it existed inside of the darkness.

A set of purple eyes glowed from the other corner of the room. They floated among the black, dancing their way closer to him.

"Get back, creature! You are on holy ground!" the priest shouted into the night.

The eyes didn't cease. Instead, the owner answered, "Such words didn't save the rest of your order as they pleaded between screams."

The deep, gravelly voice sent chills down the old priest's spine, and he shifted, prepared to crawl back toward the bodies if the eyes didn't stop their approach.

"You know what I want," the horrible voice said.

The eyes disappeared, and the priest spun in place, frantic to find where the creature disappeared. Another flash of lightning revealed the creature standing directly in front of the priest, and in the next instant, a cold hand wrapped around his neck, lifting him from the ground.

"You are the last of your kind!" the priest gasped, struggling to speak as he dangled in midair. "Let the past go!"

"I'm no such thing... have you not heard? The Glas are returning."

A quick throw sent the priest flying against the stone walls, and his bones broke upon impact. He lay on the ground in terrible pain, but the sounds of the creature stepping closer forced him from the floor again.

"My name is Laderic Velstavor, and I am the Raven. Now, where are you keeping the mask?"

The words were followed by the screams of the priest echoing down the church halls.

CHAPTER ELEVEN

G rant studied the memories displayed along the walls. Foster's old study had become somewhat of a getaway for him, and once again, he found himself standing among the now empty room.

He recalled the last time he sat with his father, both trapped under towers of documents and treaties. Grant wished he could go back to that night and see the old man again. All he had now were the paintings Foster had hung in his study. His father was many things, an artist just one among the list. Grant had been sneaking off to the room since the day Foster left, his way of remembering him.

Grant smiled, looking over the assorted paintings. One of them was of the ocean, and he recalled the story of when it was painted. Foster had been traveling down the shallow coast along the Eastern Sea. He'd said the sun was so beautiful that he couldn't pass the chance to paint it. Grant wondered if ever there was a time when the old man didn't look up, see the sun in the sky, and not feel the urge to paint it.

Further down the wall was a rough sketch of what looked like a golden city atop a mountain, green trees surrounding it from below. Despite it being a sketch, the sight of the drawing brought a sense of adventure even to Grant, who had seen his fair share of distant lands. He couldn't recall the name of the city, but he knew it was found somewhere across the Eternal Sea that separated the two continents. Foster had spent some of his youth there.

Finally, Grant came upon the final painting. He pulled it from the wall and took a seat at Foster's desk, looking down at the art in his lap. It was a small blonde-haired child near the age of ten. His small size was made apparent by the sword hanging over his shoulder. The smile on the young boy's face matched the smile on Grant's, but it quickly faded. Grant couldn't remember the day Foster drew this, and that, coupled with the idea of never seeing him again, took all the joy Grant had found in the painting. He sat alone for a bit longer until the door cracked open and someone entered.

"You miss him?" Adan, the priest Grant had met while guarding Alyssa a few weeks prior, had let himself in. "Foster is a resourceful man... I have no doubt you will see him again soon."

The priest's words didn't help and instead gained Adan a stern look from Grant.

"Can I help you?" Grant couldn't make out the holy man's intention, and he had no desire to spend any more time with the priest than needed.

"You have his green eyes."

Grant rolled those green eyes. "He adopted me. "

"Coincidence, I suppose." Adan stepped across the room, his eyes peeking at the paintings Grant had just finished reminiscing about. Grant hated the way Adan looked at them as if judging the skill of the artist rather than seeing the soul that was put into them.

"Why are you here?" Grant was growing impatient, and it showed.

"I came to invite you to a council meeting. Some... events have transpired, and the king has called his advisors to the table." Adan stepped away from the paintings and stepped back over to the door.

"Why are you inviting me?" Grant demanded. "I'm just a knight."

Adan nodded, looking back at Grant for a moment as if to re-confirm something. "A knight who has yet to find his purpose. Maybe you will find it at the meeting."

Riddles, Grant thought, *is all the damned Church is good for.*

He watched as Adan slipped back into the hall, leaving Grant to question whether he would attend this meeting. He looked back down at the painting in his lap, seeing the young boy in the picture. He shook his head and set it down on the desk.

For five nights in a row, the princess had escaped the castle walls. Like a rogue hidden in the shadows, she crept across the castle floors and out onto the stone walls where she could climb, with some skill, down the vines that grew there. She imagined herself as one of the fabled Ratha, a band of warriors that wore all black and moved in the dark of night.

Alyssa had read about them from the many books at her disposal, read about their clan across the ocean and how, for the right amount of coin, they could kill anyone in the world. Alyssa was one of them, if only in her head.

She inched down the vines, making sure not to fall or knock loose any rocks as that would alert the guards. Finally, she peeked down, debating if she was close enough to the ground to leap. With a mental shrug, she did just that, jumping from the vines and hitting the ground hard.

She stumbled, but a pair of strong hands caught her. Heart stuttering, she looked up to find Dye. He had apparently been waiting for her to make her daring escape, just as he had been for the last five nights. Alyssa smiled, happy to see the street rat of all people.

"I hope I didn't keep you waiting!" she said brightly.

The two walked along the streets while most of the city slept. Usually, Alyssa would have been scared of all sorts of evil that lurked in the night, but Dye would protect her. He knew the streets of Valacore better than she ever would, and so they walked, her arm tightly around his.

"Tell me about the world," she said, her arm reaching up above them as if pointing toward the horizon.

"You act like I've seen all of it!" Dye laughed, and just his smile brought the same to Alyssa's face.

"Um... Tell me about the kingdoms! Which ones have you been to?"

Dye lifted his hand, his fingers rubbing his chin as he thought about the question. "I have only been to Mirelos and Sullvain... Both are very gloomy, but each in their own way. Sullvain follows the teachings of the Given God like Valacore, but only in the old manner."

Although Alyssa was listening, she couldn't help but admire the way his little tan nose wrinkled as he concentrated.

"Mirelos follows no teachings. Their king is said to have a hundred wives, and mercenaries from all over the realm gather there for the booze and jobs."

"Is that not the kingdom that was built atop a swamp?" Alyssa asked as if she was unsure, but she knew it was. She had read about all the kingdoms, but she hoped he would give her more detail.

Dye nodded as they walked, making sure to take the back streets to avoid any guards along the main street. "I've never been south of the Scar, but I've heard nothing but savages live that far south."

"But what about the dragons? Did they not live along the south coast?"

Dye shrugged, less excited than Alyssa at the mention of dragons. "If you believe in that kinda stuff, yeah."

Dye had seen plenty of the world, much more than Alyssa, and she could tell that Dye didn't understand how much she envied his freedom.

Alyssa grabbed hold of Dye's arm and turned to him, her eyes full of adventure. "Let's run away! We can go west, across the

Great Bridge!"

Dye took a shocked step back. "But what about your family? You're a royal."

He was right, and she was disappointed in herself for not coming up with a better past for her new identity. She shook her head anyway, still determined to see the world with her newfound friend.

"I know my father loves me, but he would see me wither away in a castle before I ever see the outside as it should truly be seen." She pulled his hands to her chest, holding them tight. "Please, Dye, show me the ocean."

The street rat pulled her hands back toward him some and smiled, that single act washing most of her worry away. "You should consider what you're leaving behind, and if you still feel this way in the days to come, maybe I'll consider."

His words weren't the ones she had hoped to hear, but still, she smiled, nodding her head as the two began walking again.

Back inside the castle, Grant stood among a room of important men. He felt out of place, but still, he had joined the council. The king sat at the head of the table, with his most trusted advisors filed in beside him. Adan sat midway down the table, and Grant stood along the wall in the back. He tried to stay out of the way, as he had no idea what the meeting was even for. He was puzzled as to why a high priest like Adan would be invited to the table.

"We have called this meeting to address a rising threat to the realm, and how Valacore can best handle it," one of the king's advisors said, and then he sat down to give attention to the king.

"We have received word of a Glas in Sullvain of late," began the king. "This, as you all know, is old news. But it would seem that Glas is not the only one. A few nights ago, one of the churches to the west was burned to the ground... The entire order of priests was found among the ash. Most of the bodies had been torn apart."

Immediately, the room filled with whispers and panic. The word "raven" began popping up, something Grant was growing increasingly curious about.

"The only surviving Glas we knew of before the recent events in Sullvain was the Raven. He has been gone for some years, but it would seem the Sullvain Glas has stirred him out of hiding."

"Who is the Raven?" Grant spoke up, his arms crossed as he looked at the king. The whole room looked toward him, almost as if to scorn him.

Of all the people, Adan spoke up in his defense. "The Raven is a Glas, the sole survivor of an ancient race we thought had been wiped from the realm... Well, sole survivor until recently, that is. Sullvain claims they captured one that Ragnovok had been using in their army."

Adan's information opened a whole new threat for Grant's father and his quest to Sullvain.

"What is it he wants? Why cause so much trouble?" Grant

asked, needing to know the answers and how that affected his father. A part of him worried this was what Adan wanted.

The priest met his eyes. "We suspect he wants his kin."

"Then why attack a church that isn't even located in Sullvain territory?" It was clear from the looks that Grant's questioning was beginning to annoy some of the members. He was asking questions they either had no answers to or didn't want to answer.

The king stood from his seat, looking directly at Grant. "Should you not be tending to matters more befitting a royal guard?"

The king's words were heard clearly, and Grant nodded, giving his apologies before exiting and leaving the room of old men to themselves. Halfway down the hall, Grant stopped, looking back at the council room door. He was beginning to see events beyond him, and Grant felt helpless in comparison.

CHAPTER TWELVE

The Kingdom of Sullvain had erupted with talk of Prince Devon and his victory over Ragnovok. Most everyone took in the lies Devon spewed and his mother, Queen Sull, encouraged them. None of the truth came out, and Devon had everyone in the Realm believing he had captured the Glas and that it had been a servant of Ragnovok. While Ragnovok knew the truth, the rest of the Realm believed Sullvain. Devon was a hero, a great warrior like his father, both shrouded in lies.

"My prince, your father has asked for you," Oran said, but Devon looked out of his window over his future kingdom.

"Have you ever seen such a beautiful sight, Sir Oran?" he asked, but Oran didn't reply. Thinking nothing of Oran's silence, he stepped past him and pulled the chamber doors open. "I intend on taking a walk through the kingdom later. Prepare my trip."

The prince, with the grin still on his face, departed for the throne room, leaving Oran and Servis.

Servis sighed once the prince was gone and shifted to pull his helmet off.

"Godsdamned brat... I all but saved his royal ass from the Phantom, and he dances around in the glory. As if he didn't piss his breeches that night," Servis growled, stepping over to Devon's desk and sitting in his chair.

"Lower your voice, brother!" Oran demanded. "Lest you want

the whole castle to hear you bitch about the prince."

Oran shook his head and watched his brother Servis sit down. Oran was the younger of the two and—as he often pointed out—the more responsible of the two. Servis was a god in combat, but he was reckless and had a temper. Especially when it came to the royals.

"Sometimes I wonder why you ever became a royal knight if you despise them so much." Oran turned, making sure the chamber door had been closed, worried Servis had spoken too loud.

"If not for you and your wits," Servis retorted, "I would have moved off to Mirelos or someplace."

"Mirelos is just one huge brothel." Oran stepped back over to his brother and removed his helmet.

"Yes, but so is Sullvain. At least Mirelos doesn't try and hide the fact."

Oran sighed, giving his brother a stern look. The two resembled each other in many ways. They shared the same brown hair, and although Servis' eyes had a more battle-worn look in them, they both had the same brown eyes.

"Just keep those comments to yourself," Oran said, rolling his eyes. "No one needs to hear you talking ill of the royal family."

"Godsdamn the royal family!" Servis spat, his jaw ticking. "Have you seen the so-called Glas Devon claims to have defeated? He sent me to check on it... He's a child, younger than even you. What sort of family tortures a child and brags about it? Is that truly the sort of family you want to loyally serve?"

"Prepare the prince's trip and keep your opinions to yourself," Oran said as he made to leave the chamber. "I prefer my only brother keeps his head."

With that, Oran left Servis alone.

He leaned back and closed his eyes, questioning his brother's misplaced loyalty.

The two had grown up in Sullvain, barely making ends meet. Their father had been a knight and had been cut down during the Coin War between Sullvain and Mirelos. After his death, their mother took her own life, and the two were left alone on the streets of Sullvain. Oran quickly took to training, hopeful he would be like his father and become a real knight.

Servis, on the other hand, damned the royals and only fought for his knighthood so he could keep an eye on his young brother. There was not a day that went by that Servis didn't wish he and his brother could flee Sullvain and start a new life as something other than warriors.

On the other side of the castle, Devon entered his father's chamber. The stout old man was found examining the war-torn blades that decorated the dimly-lit walls.

"You called for me, Father?" Devon's confidence had disappeared, leaving the child among the father. He stood in silence and awaited his father's command.

King Sull pulled one of his blades from the wall and revealed the shining steel. "You have been boasting of your victory over the Glas."

The king's words made Devon swallow hard, a lump in his throat. "I—I... Mother said..."

"Your mother is not the king!" King Sull turned, his old eyes looking on at Devon in disapproval. The queen had spun her web, talking tales of Devon and his capture of the Glas. Even King Sull himself believed them at first, but it wasn't soon after that Servis had revealed the truth to the king.

"You see this sword?" the king asked. "I killed hundreds of Mirelos men with this sword alone. I did not retreat. I did not need my knights to drag me away from danger!"

The more he spoke, the more his voice filled with fire until he finally had to sit down. Devon rushed over, helping his father to his chair but was quickly pushed aside.

"You are my only son... Because of this, I expect much out of you." The king lifted the sword, handing it to Devon. "The man who witnessed the Glas turn in the field, he warns us the Glas may have family in one of our villages east of Sullvain."

The old king tried to regain his posture, taking in a deep breath. His anger had caused him to have a spell.

"I would hope you are capable of fetching a few young girls." King Sull turned to grab his glass of wine, then looked up at Devon, who was still standing silently with the sword in his hands. "Do you need me to walk you to the door, boy?"

Devon shook his head and made a quick rush to the door,

pausing for a moment when he heard his father speak again.

"Take a few men with you in case the girls are indeed Glas like their brother. Do not take Servis or Oran... They have done enough of your heavy lifting."

Devon left the chamber, his bowed posture fading. Instead, it was replaced by rage. Servis was the cause of this. He slammed his fist into the stone wall and cursed Servis, causing a few of the castle maids to run away in fear.

"Servis."

The knight had always thought himself more of a warrior than Devon, and now he was running to the king with the truth of that night. Devon wanted to go find Servis and show the fool his place, but he would have to wait until after this mission. He was to ride east and find the two sisters. He hated the fact his father was sending him to fetch children. Surely, this wouldn't regain him any lost respect from his father, but he would do as he was told.

Devon was the oldest of the Sullvain children and the only son. He had always had tremendous weight on his shoulders, and at times, he could be a bit too proud of his position. The idea that Servis had gone straight to the king angered Devon more than anything could.

Servis had caused Devon to look weak in the eyes of his father, and for that, the knight would pay.

Devon had gathered his men, preparing to ride out, when he noticed one of his father's advisors standing near the stables.

"Rageal?" Devon stopped his horse near the man. He often had information he was willing to part with.

"Going off to find some sisters?" the man asked knowingly.

How Rageal had come across this information, Devon would never know. It came as no surprise that Rageal knew so much.

Devon nodded his head, giving Rageal a look that let him know he didn't have the time for games.

"I have some friends who say they know where the girls are... East, just past the river."

"And what exactly do you expect for this information?" Devon could have just left it at that, but he knew how Rageal and many other members of the court worked—if you didn't repay the information, it was likely the last you would receive.

Rageal smiled. "My lord, I give you these words simply to serve... But if you would be willing to give me access to the dungeon, a glimpse at the Glas would be most educational to a man such as myself."

Devon had to think the request over but finally nodded, looking past Rageal to one of the guards.

"See that Sir Rageal is allowed to come and go from the dungeon as he pleases. But be wary, Rageal... A Glas is nothing to toy with."

Devon strode off, leaving a smirk on Rageal's face.

It didn't take Rageal long before he found himself inside the dungeon. The prisoners he passed moaned and cried out as a new face walked the halls. He had visited the Glas when he first woke but hadn't been allowed to return since the Glas had been moved deeper into the dungeon.

It was a long walk through the filthy place before he came to Kaiser's cell. He found the Glas curled up in a corner, his spirit broken from the torture he had been subjected to. Rageal peeked in the best he could, trying to get a look at the damage that had been done.

Kaiser was already smaller than when Rageal had first met him. He recalled the boy's panic when he first woke up in the cell, and although he was in bad shape then, he was near death now. Kaiser had been starved and beaten. Rageal took note of the brand burned into Kaiser's side. A symbol that resembled a G, King Sull's way of saying the Church had defeated the Glas, just as it had so many years ago.

Rageal had no ties to the Given Church—not that he would ever admit it out loud. Seeing the torment Kaiser had endured, Rageal had no desire to worship such a god.

Kaiser hadn't seen Rageal standing near his cell. He backed away, trying to put distance between himself and whoever was trying to enter the cell.

"I'm not here to harm you," Rageal said, trying to ease the

boy's fear, but no amount of words could take back the panic in Kaiser's eyes. Rageal reached inside the cell and set down a small bag. Inside was half a loaf of bread. He knew Kaiser wouldn't dare come for it while he remained.

"I cannot begin to imagine what you've been through, but know you have allies. Outside of Sullvain, you have piqued the interest of others." Rageal pushed the bag as far as the cell bars would allow and then stepped back.

Kaiser's eyes darted from the bag then back to Rageal. "I—I didn't kill anyone," he croaked finally.

So, it was true. He had no memory of what happened during the battle with Ragnovok. After the Phantom had killed Kaiser, he had returned, fueled by his Glas blood. He had killed hundreds of men before he was finally subdued and returned to Sullvain.

"Why are they doing this to me?" Kaiser shifted, and the sight of his small arm reaching out for the food sickened Rageal. The weight Kaiser had lost in just a week amazed him in a most unpleasant way—the boy's arm was nothing but skin and bone.

"I'm not who they think... I can't be," Kaiser whispered as he took hold of the bag.

"This world is unkind," Rageal whispered back, watching as Kaiser began shoving bread down his throat.

Rageal stood, stepping over to a small well in the darkened corner of the dungeon. He took an old broken bowl and scooped up as much water as it would allow, then he offered the water to Kaiser. The broken young man spilled most of it in his hastened attempt to drink it.

"They can strip you of your pride. They can even burn you." Rageal looked to the brand on Kaiser's skin. "But there is one thing they can never take from you."

Kaiser looked up at Rageal, his eyes pleading to know what it was.

"They can never take that hunger inside, your hunger for vengeance. Keep it hidden, and when you're finally offered the chance... You can show them the same pain they have shown you."

CHAPTER THIRTEEN

"I have not seen Sir Foster of late. Is he well?" Alyssa walked by Grant's side, the two casually taking their trip outside the castle walls. The sky had been dark and cloudy, but Alyssa begged Grant to come out anyway, and so he had.

He hesitated to respond to her question, unsure if he should talk about the Glas discovered in Sullvain. "He's away, though not for long."

Grant wanted to believe his own words. Ever since Foster had left, Grant had been different. A part of him was gone. He had few friends and no family outside of Foster, so the old man's absence had a considerable impact on Grant.

"When he returns, do you think he might be able to talk my father into allowing us to go outside of the kingdom?" the princess asked.

Her curiosity was growing beyond their short visits to the market. She wanted to see more of the kingdom, of the world. She was but a sheltered child before, happy to be outside of her room —but with each trip into the streets, she wanted more and more.

"We should be content with our walks for now."

Alyssa's frustrated sigh met his ears. She adjusted herself, stepping a few feet away from him. "Fine... You should ask my father about it."

She held her head up and spoke with that royal tone Grant so rarely received. She waited for his response, but he didn't take her words lightly and stopped in his tracks.

"Do you have any idea how dangerous it is for you to walk these streets?" Grant asked roughly, turning on her. "You whine about your siblings and all the fun they get to have, but not even they are allowed to mindlessly stroll down the streets of Valacore. They are as much a prisoner of the kingdom as you, only you're spared the pains of being paraded about as a royal child. I won't ask your father because you have no business being outside the kingdom. You are a princess, and it's time you realize that seeing the world isn't something a princess is entitled to."

The two stood in silence. It took a few moments, but when Alyssa's eyes filled with tears, Grant realized how rough he may have been with her.

"Alyssa, I—" Grant raised his hand to stop her, but she was already gone, running back to the castle. He thought to chase her, but instead, he stood in the street.

Grant sighed, already regretting his words. A single droplet of rain hit him on the top of his head and ran down his blonde hair until it landed on his cheek. What a beautiful day for rain, he thought as the rain droplets became a downpour.

The merchants and citizens began rushing back into their homes, but Grant remained standing in the middle of the street. He was starting to wonder if his role as royal guard was meant for him. He had gained it only because of Foster, and with him gone, Grant felt lost.

As he closed his eyes to embrace the rain, a voice broke into his thoughts. "Sir Grant?"

"Yes?" Grant opened his eyes to find a small boy standing before him, a hood over his head to protect him from the rain.

"This here letter is for you. Comes from Sullvain."

Once Grant had taken the letter from him, the boy ran off, leaving Grant alone. He stepped over to the nearest building to protect himself from the rain as he read.

Dear Grant,

I will arrive in Sullvain soon, but I assure you that you are missing nothing. These people are mad with some sort of idea that they can control a Glas. I told you not long ago that the Glas were to be feared, and I did not lie, but this boy they claim to be a Glas, he must be your age or younger. What they may have done to him makes me question who is more the monster. I did not send this message to bother you with such events, though...

I have been thinking of the questions you had recently been asking me and felt it was time you learned a bit about me, as you wanted. In my family home outside of the kingdom walls, you will find a fireplace. Check the bricks around the right side. What you find is a gift I received from a very dear friend. I want you to have it, from father to son. Use it to protect those close to you.

Foster Dalfair

A small glint of happiness fizzled inside him at knowing his father was at least in good health.

He began walking, at first toward Foster's family home, outside of the kingdom walls, but soon, he went off track. His feud with Alyssa caused him to wander in a different direction. Instead, he walked further into town.

Grant had done many things but never had he prayed. He wasn't a religious man, but then why was it that he found his way to the church? As he pushed the doors open and stepped inside, he was soaked, his hair sticking to his face.

Despite all the people inside the church, it was silent, and not an eye looked up to see who had entered. He walked down the center of the nave, looking at all the people in rags, wet from the rain. This was their salvation. Grant wondered if they thanked the Given God, or if they thanked the men who had worked their hands to the bones to build such a building. Grant couldn't bring himself to give credit to a god for things a man had built or gained for himself.

"Can I help you, Sir? Is there something wrong?" One of the priests approached Grant, causing him to turn.

"No, Father, nothing's wrong." Grant had been caught off guard. The priest was clearly just as confused by the presence of a knight inside the church.

"Then faith has brought you here?" the priest asked, and Grant paused, unable to answer. The priest gave Grant a smile and patted his wet shoulder. "Make yourself at home, my son. Our doors are open to all, especially the lost."

As the priest began to walk away, Grant asked, "Is Father Adan around?"

Grant hadn't seen Adan since the meeting he had invited Grant to.

The priest gave him a strange look. "I believe he is at the castle, my son."

Alyssa had returned to her room, tears streaming down her cheeks as she plummeted into her bed. She couldn't believe the things Grant had said to her. Why had he been so mean?

She rolled to her side and wiped the tears from her face, trying to calm herself. She couldn't see the beautiful sky that often calmed her outside of her window today. Instead, she noticed the clouds and rain. After her tears had stopped, and her breathing finally calmed, she sat up on her bed.

Maybe Grant's words had been truthful, and she was beginning to act a bit spoiled. She straightened her dress and took in a deep breath, trying to overcome whatever pain Grant had caused. The more she thought it over, the more she could understand why he didn't want to take her outside the Kingdom.

Alyssa fixed her black hair and straightened her posture, preparing herself to go back out. She needed to speak with Grant about what he had said. She did enjoy their walks, and she didn't know why Foster had left the kingdom, but she was beginning to realize that was why Grant had been so different.

She wouldn't apologize—far from it—but she would let Grant know she understood his concern and that she may have been just a bit spoiled with her request. Once she was ready, she stepped outside her room, looking down the hall toward Foster's chambers. Grant had been spending a lot of time there since Foster had disappeared. Alyssa wasn't sure if the storm outside had caused the halls to seem darkened or if it had already gotten that late, but it seemed the further down the hall she traveled, the brighter the candles along the wall shined.

Alyssa peeked into Foster's chamber, her blue eyes scouting the room, but she didn't find Grant. She pushed the door open and sighed, stepping further into the room. She had only been in the chamber a handful of times, mostly when she was smaller. Alyssa had seen the paintings and drawings on the walls before but was always rushed out of the chamber and never really got the chance to admire them.

She stepped along the wall and couldn't help but smile at the pictures. It warmed her heart to think of Foster sitting in the woods somewhere, drawing the waterfall she was now looking at or standing in the streets of Mirelos to illustrate the massive castle. The sights added to her longing for adventure, but the yearning was replaced by curiosity when she noticed a picture missing from the wall.

Her small figure spun around, looking about the desk until she found it. A little blonde child holding a sword. Alyssa giggled at the sight. Such a young Grant, and even then, he was handsome with that adorable face full of courage. Alyssa wondered if it was such a rare sight to see so much of a father in his son even when the son was adopted.

Alyssa heard a shout from down the hall and dropped the picture. Once she put it back on the desk, she looked back out into the halls.

She could hear words being exchanged and started toward the voices. The further down the hall she got, the more she could make out. One voice belonged to her father, the king, but she couldn't make out the other. Alyssa shifted closer to the door, finding it strange no guards were posted outside her father's chamber.

She pressed her face against the crack in the door. Her father stood near the fireplace, and behind him stood another man. It took her a moment, but she finally realized she had seen the man before, the first day she had gone walking with Grant. She watched the priest place his hand on her father's shoulder. She had never seen her father so upset, so distraught.

"M'lord... I know you have grown to love her as your own, but it's no longer a matter of if, but when. The Raven is on the move, and we all know he will come looking for her."

"Then we will fight him! He is one Glas against an army of Valacore men!" the king shouted, causing Alyssa to jump. The way he was acting was beginning to scare her, and she was confused by their conversation. The Raven? Glas? What were they talking about?

"You haven't seen the Glas and their destructive power," the priest replied, shaking his head gravely. "You knew when you took her in, this day would come. The Raven has already discovered her markings, somehow... We cannot allow him to find her."

Alyssa's heart began to race. The markings, they were speaking about her?

She slowly backed away from the door. She had her back against the wall when she heard the words that stopped her in her tracks.

"He can't be allowed to find her. She must be killed. We tried it Foster's way, but she has become too much of a threat."

Panic took over, and Alyssa ran down the hall, not stopping for anything as she made a dash for the castle walls. It was already dark out, and her escape was just like all the others. She slipped past the guards and out onto the wall. From there, she lifted herself up like every other time she had snuck out of the castle, but this time, she was running for her life.

Would her father really have her killed because of her markings? She liked to think he loved her more than that, but the way the priest had spoken and how her father was handling it... She wondered if he had a choice.

Alyssa stopped with one leg over the ledge. She looked back to the castle, and all she could think about was Grant. A side of her knew he could protect her, but she questioned if he could protect her from the king and the will of the priests...

Pain like no other shot through her as she started down the wall, leaving her home behind.

CHAPTER FOURTEEN

The days had all merged together, leaving Kaiser unable to recall how long he had been a prisoner. He had all but given up when Rageal began sneaking into the dungeon with food and water. Kaiser often wondered who were the allies Rageal spoke of, but he didn't dare ask.

For days, he had been left alone. None of the royals had come to his cell, and the large masked man who had branded and often tortured him had slowly disappeared, leaving only Rageal and his visits.

But just as Kaiser began to hope, it all faded.

One afternoon, Kaiser woke to a group of guards entering his cell. Before he even knew what had happened, they'd shackled him and dragged him out of his cell.

"Where are you taking me?" Kaiser asked, his voice rough, hardly sounding like him anymore.

No response. They turned right and went up the stairs, in a direction Kaiser had never been. He watched as the stone walls transformed into beautiful red stone. He was finally out of the dungeon, but why?

The guards led Kaiser down the halls, past room after room until finally, they came to the throne room. A crowd of people gathered in the great hall, all eyes watching as he was brought in and roughly chained down to the floor.

He was to be on display.

Even while the thought sickened him, Kaiser made no attempts at running. Even if he wanted to, his legs were too worn and beaten to make it very far. So he was mocked and viewed by the royals as they dined.

The smell of the foods reached Kaiser, causing a nauseating pain in his pitifully empty stomach. What he wouldn't have given for a bite or even scraps. He kept his head down, flinching when a group of royal children tossed their finished bones at him with sadistic laughs. His mouth watered at the sight of even the smallest chunk of uneaten meat on the bones, but he didn't move.

Instead, he closed his eyes. He had felt so much pain the last few weeks. Compared to that, he could live through this easily.

As the day went on, he found he was mostly left alone, with nothing but stares and looks of disgust. Was he indeed a monster? Kaiser had no memory of what he was accused of, no memory of killing anyone.

As Kaiser pondered what he was, the crowd turned from him, putting their focus on the throne room doors as two figures entered. Kaiser knew one of them, Devon Sull, Prince of Sullvain. He had visited him in the dungeon more than once. Mostly, Devon simply sat in the corner and watched as the masked man burned and cut at Kaiser's flesh. The second man was a stranger to Kaiser, though his name was quickly announced.

K. Vider

"Presenting Foster Dalfair, royal advisor to King Valacore," a guard said loudly and clearly to the room.

The crowd began to whisper and hush at his name. The name must have been known even in Sullvain.

"King Sull," Foster said as he approached the king.

The king opened his arms as if to invite Foster closer. "Sir Foster, it brings me great joy to see you visiting us here in Sullvain."

King Sull and Foster exchanged pleasantries, then Foster's attention turned to Kaiser.

"Is this the Glas that has everyone around the realm telling tales?" Foster stepped over, taking a knee near Kaiser, who kept his head down. The old knight seemed uneasy.

After a few minutes looking over Kaiser, the old knight stood and looked back to King Sull. "You are sure this child is a Glas?"

The crowd gasped as Foster questioned the king's claim.

"Of course, it is! I watched it kill our men!" Devon snapped.

The crowd went silent as Foster stepped across the throne room and approached Prince Devon.

"I have fought a Glas before, Prince Devon. If this boy is indeed a Glas, then he is far too weak to be boasting about having been defeated. Kill him now and spare the realm any chance of him becoming what the history books tell us a true Glas is."

Enraged by the insults, Devon clenched his fists at his sides as he turned to his father for help. King Sull gave Foster a slight glare, but no firm punishment came for the old knight. Instead, King Sull smiled.

"We will be rid of him soon, Sir Foster," the king said easily, "but first, we would like you to join us during our ceremony to boost morale. My son has brought some very special guests."

Soon after, the small crowd went back to their festivities, acting as though Foster had never insulted the prince. Between the drinking and eating, three guards came in to take the Kaiser away, and Kaiser was actually glad to be back in that cell.

Foster watched as the guards took the Glas away, curious as to what the king had planned for this evening. He politely excused himself from the conversation and made his way after the guards. Keeping back far enough not to be noticed, he followed the two guards further down the hall until King Sull appeared out of nowhere and slammed his hands on the wall, keeping Foster from going any further.

"Sir Foster... You seem to be lost, the party is this way."

Foster looked past the king, trying to see the Glas as he was taken around the corner at the end of the hall. "Where are you taking him?"

"You will see when everyone else does. Come, let us talk."

King Sull lead Foster into one of the many rooms in the castle, showing him to a seat. As most of the castle, the room was full of trophies to remind the old king of his better days. Foster took note of some of the massive game that had been mounted on the wall.

"Ragnovok creeps ever closer to our door, Sir Foster." Sull lifted a glass after pouring drinks.

Foster and King Sull had little in common, but they both shared age. Both men had graying hair, and although they were near the same age, it was clear Foster still had some fight left in him, while the king was already limping toward death.

"The King of Valacore received your request for aid, and yes, we will be sending some."

"Some?" King Sull forced a tight smile, one that was full of thinly-veiled hostility. "Ragnovok will not be turned away by 'some' men... We need Valacore's military might. Does the king have no intention of holding up his end of our treaty?"

Foster took the glass that had been poured for him, taking a little sniff of it before setting it back down. "The king wants to see Ragnovok turned away, yes... But spilling blood over something as small as who owns what side of a bridge is not something King Valacore wants to attend to every time he receives a letter from Sullvain."

Foster's words struck a chord apparently.

The king stood, smashing his glass against the wall. "You come into my kingdom as if an ally, but it is clear Valacore has no intention of supporting us!"

Foster could see the conversation was taking a nasty turn.

"We are supporting you... As I have mentioned, we have men marching to Sullvain as we speak, and King Valacore himself has sent me to help with the disposal of the Glas. We simply don't wish to prolong this war more than need be."

Foster must have said something right because the king calmed some. A harsh look remained on his face, but it disappeared when his son entered.

"Father, the people await you in the square. The ceremony is ready."

The news brought a smile to Sull's face as he looked across the room to Foster. "Come, let us put this matter away and enjoy our evening delights."

The people of Sullvain had flocked to the square, gathering around the very place the two deserters had recently been executed. They roared and shouted as if awaiting an event of some sort.

It was a quick walk from the castle to the square, and once Foster arrived with the king, the crowd roared even louder. Foster looked out over the people, joining King Sull at a small seating area above the square so the royal family would have a perfect view. Inside the viewing box, Foster found the whole royal family —Queen Sull, their two daughters, and even Devon and his two knights in full armor.

"What is this?" Foster asked, a hint of worry mixed in with his curiosity. He suddenly had a bad feeling about all of this.

"Just take a seat, Sir Foster," King Sull said, dropping into his own impressive jewel-encrusted seat.

Despite the king's request, Foster remained standing, stepping over to the edge to look down at the scene.

Below them, the Glas had been locked in a stock.

Unable to move his arms, Kaiser kept his head low, staring at the ground. He was exhausted and ready to give up. He could hear the crowd chanting, cursing him. On occasion, a stone hit him. Kaiser didn't move; he just stared down at the little droplets of blood the last stone had caused, each new drop landing one after another until it was a small puddle, forming directly under where his head was hanging down. The crowd kept on, calling him monster and demon, but finally, the cursing stopped, and the crowd's attention turned to something else.

Kaiser pulled his head up, and tears filled in his eyes at what he saw. His sisters stood across the square from him. They shouldn't be here. He didn't want them to see him like this, didn't want them to be in danger.

A new sort of desperation fueled him as his arms yanked at his restraints, but he was too weak—even in a healthier state, he wouldn't have been able to break free.

"N—no..." His voice emerged for the first time in weeks, crackled and broken. He went from whispers to shouts. "N—no! They didn't do anything!"

A group of knights pushed his sisters, forcing them to move onto the small stage at the center of the square.

The knights tied the sisters to poles. Lilly cried as Alice tried to calm her, whispering words of comfort.

Kaiser kept pulling at the stocks, every bit of him crying out for his sisters. *Take me,* he thought frantically. *Take me but leave my sisters alone!*

Kaiser watched on, unable to stop the knights as they stacked branches and wood around the feet of his sisters.

"Burn the monsters!" the crowd screamed, cheering the knights on.

Why? How could these people be so sick and murderous?

Kaiser cried and screamed, not giving a damn that the whole castle was watching. His screams grew and grew, and by the time the fire was lit, he couldn't breathe, his screams so loud.

The flames danced around the two sisters, and their cries soon overpowered even Kaiser's as they were burned alive. Black smoke rose from the square, and the cheering silenced, all attention now turned to Kaiser.

His screams and cries were that of a madman's as the small puddle of blood slowly shifted, running toward the stage like water downhill. The tiny pool was alive, moving and turning in the direction Kaiser so desperately wanted to go.

King Sull stood from his seat as the locks on the stocks began to crack and snap loose. "Secure him! Now!"

Kaiser's screams turned into deep growls, and streams of blood replaced his tears. He somehow snapped the locks on his restraints. When two knights rushed to stop him, he tossed them aside like dolls. Kaiser's feet stumbled forward toward his sisters' now lifeless bodies, still engulfed in flames.

His heart in tatters, he stepped closer, the blood trailing behind him in the dirt as if it had a life of its own.

"Lilly."

Kaiser stopped, eyes still brimming with tears of blood as he looked up at the burning stakes.

"Alice."

Kaiser lifted his hand, reaching out for what was left of his sisters before he collapsed to the ground, and darkness consumed him.

CHAPTER FIFTEEN

Freedom. Something Alyssa had never fully experienced in her life. She had taken off in the dead of night like some sort of criminal running from the law. She had felt such guilt and sadness weighing on her as she left, but now that she was out in the fields, the wind blowing in her hair, she couldn't bring herself to think of what was far behind her. As Alyssa ran about, jumping into puddles and running across fallen logs, Dye followed close behind, a single horse trotting beside him.

She had run to him, begged him to take her away.

They had traveled for days. Dye said he would take her west, to the Great Bridge, and from there, they would venture into Farera, the land across the ocean. Dye had told her of his time near the ports to the west, all the different types of travelers he had met, like the wild men who didn't speak the language of man. He swore he had even seen a petrified dragon egg.

"Would you like to see a dragon? I would." Alyssa leaped into another puddle, sending a splash of water into the air, wetting the bottom of her dress. She paused for a moment, shocked by the splash but then began laughing.

Dye rushed over, taking the sleeve of his ragged shirt and patting her hair. He was nothing but a street rat in Valacore, but out here, with her, he was her hero. She smiled, shaking her head as he dried the curls on each side of her bangs.

"Wouldn't you be afraid?" Dye asked. "Dragons eat people, you know."

"Dragons could communicate with us, silly. The civilized ones do not eat humans." The two began walking again, Dye nodding his head as if he knew such things. "I read a book once that told the story of King Arnor Dreava," Alyssa continued. "He used to speak with the dragons. He built large stone buildings all along the southern coast for them, and in exchange, they left the humans alone."

"Of course, dragons can't build stuff themselves." Dye grinned. "So where did the dragons go then?"

"After Arnor died, one of his sons was killed by a dragon. The oldest son then started hunting them." The idea of all the beautiful dragons being killed saddened her.

"I've heard of dragons being spotted near Farera... Maybe they flew across the ocean, trying to get away from those crazy Dreavaians?" Dye said, nudging Alyssa's shoulder.

"Maybe."

The two traveled all day and finally slowed around dusk. Dye spoke of an old hut he knew nearby, a place they could get some rest. Alyssa followed close behind, her eyes darting about at the beautiful trees and mountains. She had only ever seen such sights in books and paintings. She stood silent for a moment, looking over the lush green trees covering the mountain range along the path.

Once they arrived, he pointed down the dirt path going past

the hut.

"Down the path here is a little village, probably a good idea to get changed out of that dress, maybe get us some food." Dye handed her a small bag and placed it in her hands. "Don't take too long, we need to get rest and keep going."

Alyssa nodded and rushed toward the village. Once there, she slowed to a walk. She watched the people come and go along the streets. It was a small village, with only a couple larger buildings.

She had never seen such a place, only read about them in books, but she had never heard the name of this tiny little town. She had grown up seeing Valacore, and she was so accustomed to its glory that seeing such an area outside of the kingdom surprised her. Alyssa stopped in the middle of the village, looking around for any shops. She pushed the wooden door open and was greeted by an older gentleman.

"How may I help you?" he asked as he put some clothing on a broken shelf.

The shopkeep was very polite, and Alyssa thought it was nice being spoken to like an average person. She stepped over to some of the clothes and ruffled through them.

"I am looking for something more fitting for travel." She paused, worried she should change her speech. Dye had been raised in the streets, causing him to talk casually, while Alyssa's accent reflected her upbringing and could easily give her away as a royal.

"Heading to Valacore, are you?" the shopkeep inquired.

"No, we are—" Alyssa stopped, correcting herself. "We're headed to the Great Bridge, just came from Valacore."

She smiled inside, proud of how lowborn she could make herself sound. When she finally found an outfit, she turned to the shopkeep, who had a puzzled look on his face.

"Are you sure you're coming from Valacore?"

"I am, why?" Alyssa placed the clothes on the counter.

"It's just, the Great Bridge is west of Valacore, and if you're coming from Valacore, then you would be heading south to get here." The man took the gold Alyssa sat on the counter as she pondered what he had been saying.

She gave the man a smile and took her new clothes. On the way back, she wondered if what the man had said was true. Why would he lie to her? But more so, why would Dye be taking her in the wrong direction?

She shook it off and made her way back to the hut. She trusted Dye—she had spent so much time with him that she knew he would never lie to her. Surely, he knew what he was doing... right?

"Did you get some new rags?" Dye asked as Alyssa stepped through the broken hut door. He had put a small bed together.

"Yep!" She rushed in, jumping full speed onto the old bed, sending dust flying into the air. The sun was beginning to go down, and Dye seemed tired. Alyssa, on the other hand, was so excited she couldn't stop thinking about traveling.

Dye crawled into the bed to lie down while Alyssa sat up, looking out of the window. It wasn't long before Dye passed out, and she laid herself down. She watched him sleep, and she wondered if she would ever get tired of traveling with him.

The king and the Church had been frantic with the disappearance of Princess Alyssa.

The king had ordered search parties to comb the roads outside the kingdom. The people of Valacore would never know of her absence as her entire existence had been a secret. The king was doing all he could to find her, but his focus was on the man who failed to watch her, Grant Dalfair. He had been given the role of her royal guard just months ago, and already, he had failed. No one knew if she had been kidnapped or if she had, for some reason, run away—yet either way, Grant was to blame and there would be consequences for his negligence.

Grant was brought before the king and his council. He knew he had failed, and he would take his punishment without excuse—but his heart was heavy with worry for Alyssa. She was young and naïve and now out in the world alone.

The old men of the council whispered to each other in the darkness of the room, and the king looked down at Grant, ready to pass judgment.

"We gather here to lay judgment upon Grant Dalfair for breaking his oath and failing to protect his ward, my daughter, Princess Alyssa Valacore." The king stood, and his men stood with him. "We have decided, because of your guardian, Foster Dalfair, and his loyalty to the throne, you will be spared of any imprisonment."

Grant looked down in shame. He was being spared because of the reputation of his father only.

"We sentence you to ten lashes." The king raised his hand, and two knights approached Grant, ripping his shirt down the back to expose his bare skin. The cool air caused bumps to break out across his skin.

Grant didn't fight back. He wouldn't fight back, whatever the punishment. He would accept it like a man.

"You will also be stripped of your knighthood and exiled from Valacore," the king declared.

Grant's stomach sank at that, but he had failed in his duty, and he deserved punishment.

Two guards grabbed each of Grant's arms, keeping him in place. The *crack* of the whip was near deafening in the silence. As the first lash ripped across his flesh, his body tightened and jerked at the lick of pain, but he didn't struggle. Merely gritted his teeth and bore it.

"One!" the masked man behind him shouted before rearing the whip back and bringing it back down on Grant's back. He felt the second lash cut across his skin. "Two!"

Grant was to be exiled from Valacore. He had failed his kingdom, but most of all, he had failed Foster, and that was worse than anything. He took the remaining lashes without hesitation.

By the fourth lash, blood ran down his back in a warm trickle.

By the fifth lash, the blistering pain was so great, his legs threatened to give out from under him. Only the guards keep him on his feet.

By the sixth lash, he cried out at last, unable to keep silent any longer.

By the tenth and final lash, he was close to passing out and couldn't support his own weight.

When all was said and done, he was delivered to the doors of the castle and left in the rain. Come sunrise, if he was found inside Valacore, he would be executed.

For a long time, Grant lay there in the rain, unable to move. The water, while agony on his back, was cool and helped ease some of the pain.

After some time, he struggled to his feet, his back on fire, bloodstains seeping through the rags he had been given. He stumbled through the streets until he found himself at the front gates.

He had no idea what to do now. His whole life had been to serve the Valacore family. It was all he knew, but now he was unwelcome there. Grant stood in the rain for a moment. Eyes closed, he tilted his head back and let the rain wash over him. He had gone to the church before, lost and unsure, but now he was more lost than ever. His life had spiraled out of control, and he wondered if he had hit bottom yet.

Grant left the walls of Valacore and come to a stop at his father's old house. The place had seen better days, all its shelves and tables covered in dust. He wanted one last chance to look over it, to take in its memories. While taking in the familiar sight, he remembered the letter he had gotten from Foster.

Grant pulled the now-crumpled paper out and stepped over to the fireplace and began feeling around for the brick Foster had mentioned in his letter. Finally, one of the bricks gave, and Grant pulled it out. When he reached his hand in, he found something wrapped in cloth. Frowning, he pulled out something long and thin.

He carried it over and placed it on the dusty table, unwrapping it to reveal a beautiful sword. Grant lifted the blade in awe. Its edges were made of some sort of red material that resembled glass, transparent to an extent.

Grant swung the sword twice, impressed with its weight and craftsmanship. He held it up closer and examined it. Etched into the blade near the hilt was the word *Valor* and on the other side of the blade was the letter A.

"Valor, huh?" Grant ran his finger along the red edge and looked upon it with confidence. At that moment, he decided he would use this blade to find Alyssa and bring her back safely.

He returned the sword to its sheath, but before he could wrap it back inside the cloth, the front door creaked open. In the next second, Grant drew the blade and whirled around, prepared to defend himself.

Standing at the door was the priest he had run into on that rainy day.

"Father?" Grant lowered his blade.

"Come with me now, my son. Father Adan wishes to speak with you at the church."

Grant was unsure if returning inside the walls of the kingdom was the best idea considering his banishment.

"It is about your father and the dangers he has gone to face," the priest continued grimly.

Foster?

CHAPTER SIXTEEN

The execution of the two girls had Sullvain up in arms. Some were inspired to push Ragnovok back, while others condemned the burning of innocent girls.

"I thought I would find you here." Oran peeked through the doors at the top of the bell tower in the middle of Sullvain. It was Servis' hiding place when he needed time away from the castle. Oran dared not speak more than needed about the events, but he was far more loyal to the Sull family.

"The prince doesn't seem to have noticed your absence."

"Fuck the prince." Servis didn't bother turning around. He stayed seated on the tower's edge, looking out over the kingdom. He had been missing from the castle since he departed from the burning.

"I bet they are so proud of themselves..." Servis muttered disdainfully. "Burning children."

"Servis, they were Glas!"

"If you truly believe that, then you're no better than them!" Servis jumped up from his spot, stepping back into the bell tower room. As he walked around the bell, he finally caught sight of Oran standing at the door.

"Brother," Oran whispered. He knew how Servis felt, but still, he couldn't bring himself to hate the family as his brother did.

Once Oran had gotten close enough, Servis grabbed his

brother by the shoulders and shook him a bit. "They were children, Oran! Little girls and those sick bastards burnt them for some sort of sport!"

Tears streamed down his cheeks, and he finally caved, his face hitting Oran's shoulder as he wept. Oran couldn't think to do anything other than wrap his arms around his brother.

"Servis..." He paused, not knowing what to say. Oran had watched it happen, had witnessed the grins and laughs while the sisters burned, but he knew he couldn't move from his place. He held his duties as a knight above all else, but seeing his brother break down made him wonder for a moment. Had their father's loyalty been misplaced? Oran couldn't imagine it.

Hours went by, and the brothers had sat down to talk, sitting across the room from each other. Servis had calmed down, but still, he hadn't spoken.

"Do you remember when Father took us to the bridge over the Scar?" Oran picked a small pebble up from the floor and began playing with it as he spoke of better days. "He said if you dropped a pebble into the Scar and it made it to the bottom without hitting the sides you could make a wish... We spent hours trying, but every time we hit the cliff sides."

Oran looked at the pebble in his hand, a smile creeping over his face without his consent. "Then, right before Father took us home, you dropped a pebble in, and I remember holding my breath until, finally, it disappeared into the depths. I always wondered what you wished for?"

Oran tossed the pebble toward Servis, and it landed at his side. A few moments passed before Servis shifted, picking the pebble up. He remained silent, rubbing his thumb over the small stone.

"That was the day before Father marched toward Mirelos... My wish was that he wouldn't go, that he would stay with us, with mother."

The two brothers stopped, and Servis tossed the pebble down the shaft under the bell.

Inside the castle, the royals all slept; their day had been full of eating and drinking to celebrate the burning of their enemies. Meanwhile, Rageal was wide awake in his chamber. He had many scrolls laid out, and he went through each, stamping and signing what needed to be done. He was one of the king's most respected advisors, and although that kept him from suspicion, one mention of his trips to the dungeon would call his loyalty into question.

Rageal's time with Kaiser had helped the boy survive this long. What little food Rageal could get to him had helped put some meat back on his bones. With the burning of the sisters, Rageal knew King Sull was losing interest in keeping the Glas around. He would have to act fast if he wanted to help the boy.

He shifted to the window of his chamber and looked out over the forest to the south of Sullvain. Ragnovok forces were just a dozen miles away, but come morning, the Valacore men Foster had promised would arrive, and Ragnovok would no doubt be pushed back. Rageal's window of time was closing.

"Master Rageal..." The voice crept in from the halls, and Rageal turned to find Foster. He had never met the man, but he had heard many tales. Foster was known in the South as the Dark Stalker.

"Sir Foster, how may I be of service to you?" Rageal gestured for the old knight to come in, grabbing two glasses from one of his shelves.

Foster entered, looking about the room and even more carefully over the scrolls. "I noticed your absence from the event yesterday... I thought all of Sullvain would be keen on seeing such a show."

Rageal showed a less than honest smile and shook his head as he poured the two a glass. "I cannot say I am all that interested in the burning of small girls. I believe I had witnessed you coming back from the burning a bit early, no?"

The two exchanged pleasant jabs at each other. Rageal worried why Foster would have come.

"As you have no doubt heard, I was sent to make sure the Glas is destroyed." Foster took the glass of wine from Rageal. "I have spoken to a few of the palace servants since the Glas arrived."

"Why so? If you don't mind my asking." Rageal took a seat at his desk.

"If Ragnovok truly used the Glas in combat—which I highly doubt—they will, of course, want it back... I'm simply making sure no one inside the castle could help them do so."

"And has your investigation come to any sort of conclusion?"

Foster set his glass down without taking a single sip. The old man began walking around the room, placing his hand on the small candle at Rageal's window.

"It would seem you have visited the dungeon more than a few times, Master Rageal." Foster stopped his pacing and turned, looking Rageal in the eyes. "Surely a man in such high respect of a king could not possibly be a Ragnovok spy."

The room fell silent, and Rageal felt a small bead of sweat drip down his forehead. He wouldn't let Foster scare him.

"Would it surprise you if it turned out true?" Rageal asked carefully. "Don't act like you don't see it, the lack of sanity in this castle... The king has slipped, and Devon is walking the same path. They burned two children!" Rageal lifted his glass up, finishing the entire glass of wine between words. "I have heard tales of your deeds, Sir Foster... I know you aren't a bad man, but trust me when I say you're wasting your time trying to help King Sull."

He could tell some of the words had made it to Foster as the old knight looked away.

"I look out for the entire realm's well-being," Foster replied after a moment, "not Sullvain alone. You are a smart man, Rageal, and I respect that—but if you are indeed a spy, I cannot let you stop the death of that Glas. Come morning, I'll be informing the king of what I've discovered. If you have anything to hide, I sug-gest you ride while the night cloaks you... leave the Glas to meet his fate."

The warning was straight and well delivered, and Rageal believed every word. He watched as Foster stepped back to the door and exited. It would seem the window of opportunity Rageal had before was even smaller now, and tonight would be the night he made his move.

He rushed over to the window and lit the candle. His eyes looked off into the forest, and a small flame shined through from the depths of the trees, letting Rageal know his signal had been seen.

Kaiser hadn't moved since he woke back in the dungeon. He couldn't think of anything other than his sisters, but each memory was crushed by the terrible sounds of their screams. Each time, he pulled his hands up to cover his ears, but the screams were coming from inside, so his efforts were in vain.

Over the past few weeks, he had heard one of the men a few cells down repeating a small rhythm over and over until even Kaiser knew its lyrics. It seemed the small batch of words was the only thing that could keep the screams at bay.

Rocking back and forth, he mumbled, "And when the dragon woke, he asked them to be fed; but when no one would feed him, he fed on them instead."

Kaiser went on and on, lifting his hand to wipe the tears away. He had lost everything, and he had no idea why. He had heard the word Glas but had no clue what it meant. Kaiser was lost now, gone... He had made a promise to Alice, and now it would never be held.

The sounds of the dungeon door opening interrupted his grieving. He could hear small whispers from down the hall and then, finally, the sounds of a body falling to the floor. A small torch made its way through the dungeon until it reached Kaiser's cell.

"Can you walk?" Kaiser recognized the voice. It was Rageal. He didn't reply; instead, he looked down.

"Damn it, boy... now isn't the time to be a broken fool."

Rageal fiddled with the keys until he finally found the right one and swung open Kaiser's door. Rageal quickly picked him up and dragged him out of the cell, sitting him next to the small well. Kaiser looked up and watched as Rageal pushed some of the bricks out of the wall and revealed a hidden path. He turned, grabbing Kaiser by the shoulders.

When he didn't bother to stand, Rageal growled, "You want to die then, is that it? You want the bastards who killed your sisters to take your life, too? Get your ass off the ground and live, survive!"

Rageal slapped Kaiser across the face but still, he didn't move. What was the point? There was nothing in the world worth escaping for, not anymore. King Sull had seen to that, the royals had taken the only two people he loved.

Rageal lifted him up and began carrying him as best he could.

The path led into a cave that later joined up with water streaming out of the castle. Rageal followed the stream for a while until he came to a small set of stairs leading down into darkness.

"Listen, boy... I know you feel as though all is lost." He sat Kaiser against the wall and pulled a small dagger out, placing it in his hands. "I told you the first day I met you what it was they could never take away from you... the hunger."

Rageal pointed down the stairway and lifted Kaiser's head so he could see his eyes. "Go, survive... and when the time is right, return here and judge the bastards for what they have done to you."

The words sparked something in Kaiser as he finally looked up, his hand grasping the hilt of the dagger. He couldn't fathom killing the king, the prince, or anyone at all, but something in his stomach tugged at him. Rageal's words had fed something that wanted to believe those things could done.

"Go... follow the stairs to the bottom and out into the forest, my allies are waiting for you." Rageal stood and backed away.

Kaiser struggled to his feet and weakly started down the stairs before Rageal returned back to the dungeon.

Kaiser was tired and weak, his body drained as he stumbled and fell down half the stairs. Although he fell, he never let go of the dagger, as it was all he had left to defend himself.

When he finally reached the bottom of the stairs, the path led out beside a small river. He could see the forest from there, and he began limping toward it. His struggle was made worse when he tripped, falling over something. He tossed and turned in the mud until he finally got on his knees and looked down. All around him were the bloodied remains of Ragnovok men.

Kaiser's stomach turned, and he vomited what little was in his stomach. He hadn't seen such gore since the battle months ago.

"Look what we have here. Even after overhearing Foster and Rageal's little exchange, I didn't think he would really try and let you go."

Kaiser wiped the mud from his face, trying to make out the figure belonging to the voice. It was Prince Devon and his knight, Servis.

"See, seemed coming out was a good idea!" Devon drew his sword, stepping over the bodies as he made his way toward Kaiser. "We found some friends waiting on you, Ragnovok scouts. You see, I could have delivered Rageal's traitorous head to my father before he released you, but now that you have escaped, I'll regain father's confidence by delivering a dead Glas!"

Kaiser backed away, holding the dagger up as his last line of defense. When Devon reached him, he used his sword to smack Kaiser's dagger to the side and then lifted the blade up.

"Devon, Prince of Sullvain, slayer of the last Glas!"

Devon grinned, his blade quickly coming down. Kaiser shut his eyes tight, but instead of a blade, only mud splashed into his face. Devon had fallen, and behind him, Servis stood.

"Servis! What are you doing!" Devon struggled to stand, but Servis kicked him to the ground while another kick sent Devon's blade into the river.

"Earn it," Servis whispered under his breath, hatred in his voice as he backed away from the two.

Eyes flashing, the prince turned and quickly jumped at Kaiser, pinning him in the mud. Both were unarmed, but even if Kaiser was in full health, the prince was a slightly larger man, so he had the upper advantage regardless.

Kaiser's arms struggled to keep Devon's hands from completely grasping his throat. His vision began to blur as the prince strangled the life from Kaiser. His hands slapped and pushed at his enemy until, finally, they fell to the sides, and his struggle ended.

Devon slowly let up, sitting up on top of his victim. "Ha HA! I did it!"

As Devon turned, no doubt looking for Servis, Kaiser desperately reached for the dagger, inches away. So close... If only he could get it, maybe he'd have a shot...

Kaiser's dirty hand finally closed around the handle. Without an ounce of hesitation, he raised the dagger from the mud and rammed it deep into the side of Devon's neck, twisting for good measure. As the pressure left his throat, Kaiser gasped for air, his muddy hand finally releasing the blade.

After a moment, Devon fell on top of Kaiser, leaving a stream of blood slowly pouring into the mud. He tried to push the dead prince off him, but he no longer had the strength. He gave up, letting his body go limp as he passed out.

CHAPTER SEVENTEEN

Grant had been taken to the church near the castle, an idea he wasn't particularly fond of. If any of the King's men spotted him, the priest who had fetched him would surely be in as much trouble as Grant.

He stood near the small stable window, looking out at the strangers passing by. Just the night before, he had thought he'd never see the inside of Valacore's walls again, but there he was, hiding away inside a church stable. The priest had left him there with promises of fetching Father Adan.

Grant pulled his hood on tighter as he considered leaving the stable. He cursed the gods, kicking the wooden wall before he stepped toward the door, unable to wait any longer. Just as Grant swung the stable door open, the priest arrived. He gave Grant a confident look, and Grant followed him.

The day was winding down, and it had become safe to travel along the streets. The two men made their way straight to the church without taking any turns. Just as before, the church was full of people praying. Grant stopped at the door, something preventing him from entering. He had no idea what made him do so, but he removed his hood, his blonde hair falling.

He was afraid of being found out, but something told him he could trust these people. They were the homeless, the hungry, the rejected, and at the same time, they were loving and caring beyond what they could physically give.

The priest had stopped near the front of the church, looking back at Grant as he took in the sight. Grant stepped over to one of the small children—their mother had been praying, and they sat scratching at the ground in boredom. The child was so thin, a stick compared to most Valacore children.

Grant took a knee, a friendly smile on his face. "What is your name?"

Grant received a strange look from the child, catching him off guard but not scaring him.

"Jona... Are you a knight?" The boy smiled back then pointed to the sword at Grant's side, Valor.

"No, I'm not." Grant looked at his father's gift, and the sight caused painful thoughts. "Say, are you hungry?"

Grant rummaged through his small pack and pulled a loaf of bread out. The child's eyes widened, and he stared intently, eagerly waiting for Grant to half the food.

"You have to share with the other kids, okay?" Grant handed the loaf over, and the child rapidly nodded his head before running off to the children across the church.

No one had noticed the act but the priest, and all he could do was smile. The smile soon vanished, however, and he called for Grant.

"We must hurry."

The priest's words caught Grant's attention, and he nodded, giving one last look at the children in the corner as they dived the bread. Once they had reached the back rooms of the church, the priest shifted to a large wall painting, struggling briefly to raise it from the wall hook, and set it to the side. A slight gust of wind from the tunnel blew his hair before he gestured for Grant to follow him.

"Where are we going? What is this place?" Grant followed him through the opening. He guessed these tunnels led into the mountains of Valacore.

They finally came out of the tunnel into a large room brightened by hundreds of candles littering the walls. Men in robes sat on their knees, softly humming. Grant slowed to a walk. He wondered who these people might be and if they truly worshiped the Given God. When he realized the priest hadn't stopped, Grant jogged to keep up.

"Grant Dalfair, I am glad you came." Father Adan was surrounded by a table of books and as many candles as the other hall.

Grant looked around the room, more entranced by the old books and relics scattered about than by Adan. He wondered why the church would have a hidden chamber.

When he remembered why he was here, he looked to Adan. "The priest who brought me here said you had information regarding my father?"

"Straight to the point, as always." Adan shook his head, amused. He leaned over the old table, pushing a book toward Grant.

Grant looked it over, confused by how this book tied into what he had asked. He lifted the book, dusting it off as he pulled the old cover open. Hand-drawn images of men with some sort of blades and spikes coming from their bodies littered the pages.

"What is this?" Grant flipped the pages. They were all the same.

"It is all the Church has on the Glas... Which is not much, unfortunately." Adan watched on.

The book held Grant's attention. He set the book down, pointing at a specific page. It was a single man facing an enemy army. The man had a red blade and jet-black hair.

"Is this a Glas? Can a single Glas really stand up to an army?" Grant wasn't scared by the idea, but somewhat amazed.

"Yes, it is the reason they no longer exist." Adan nodded, offering Grant a seat. "Hundreds of years ago, the Glas ruled a kingdom, some think it rested where the Scar is now. They were a savage warrior race, wielding unbreakable blades made of red metal we know nothing about, even to this day."

Adan looked around the room at the books. "The Church had found a way to stop them, somehow trapping them inside their kingdom and sealing the kingdom into a different realm altogether, though we can't be sure how much of the story is true. We have no idea how they did so, but it saved us all. The Glas had begun venturing from their lands, conquering other kingdoms."

"If they were all killed, then who is the man that attacked the church to the west? The Raven?" Grant had so many questions, and now it seemed he found someone able to answer them.

Adan's head dipped into a nod. "He is indeed a Glas, the last of his kind. Until recently. Why he is still alive, or how they keep appearing, is of little concern... We need your help, the king needs you."

Adan's tone was that of a serious man as he looked Grant dead in the eyes. "The Raven is after Princess Alyssa. The king knew, but with Alyssa being such a secret, he had to make your punishment as real as possible."

Grant's heart dropped, just the idea of her being harmed by them sending him into a rage.

"Why?"

"Her markings, along her arms, I'm sure you've seen them. The Church placed some sort of spell upon the Glas kingdom, making it impossible to find... We are not clear on exactly what they need to break the spell and find the kingdom, but we have reason to believe it involves her markings."

Adan opened another book, showing it to Grant. "Some texts speak of a sword and mask involved in the spell. We also believe a child born with the markings is needed, but we have very little information on such. We do know the Raven hunted for the child when she was born, and we brought her here, to be raised safely inside the castle. At Foster's request, of course."

"Why would you want me to help you?" Grant looked down, avoiding the old priest's searching gaze. "I failed."

"Yes, but not by your own fault. The king, the Church, even your father, we all withheld information that could have prevented this. Find her and return her to the Given Church, and the king will lift your exile. Help us save this world from the Glas."

Adan looked on as Grant thought the task over. He was being given a second chance to protect Alyssa. He didn't care about the Glas, the relics, a secret war, only finding Alyssa.

He gently closed the book and looked up. "What do you need from me?"

The tavern hall smelled overwhelmingly of ale. The crowd roared with stories of war, sex, and money. Grant had never entered such a place before. He was no stranger to ale but had only had it in the company of his fellow soldiers and not to the point of abusing it.

Yet here he was, venturing into such a place for the sake of the world.

Grant pushed his way past the men and women, trying to be as unnoticeable as possible. Adan had sent him here to find a tracker known as Gabriel Tread. He had no idea what the man looked like, but Adan was sure he would be here and that Grant would need him if he were to track Alyssa and find her before the Glas.

When asked, the bartender knew precisely where Gabriel was and pointed Grant in the direction. Once he fought his way through the crowd again, he stopped in front of a table. He was not pleased with the sight.

"Are you Gabriel Tread?" Grant asked, trying not to grimace.

The man with his feet up on the table shrugged, too busy with his face buried in a bar maiden's breast to be concerned with some youngling.

"'Pends on who might be askin' for me?" Gabriel's statement was muffled by the bare skin his cheeks were smashed between. Only after he lifted his head did he notice Grant. "Oh, look, girls, a fancy knight!"

Gab smiled, lifting his cup up and chugging the rest of his drink.

Grant let out a deep sigh, worried this man would be of little use to him. Before Grant could say another word, he was shoved to the side and bumped into a few drunks. When he finally caught himself, he noticed a large man standing in his place, now facing Gabriel.

"Ya cheated, you sack of shit! Ain't no way a man can throw knives like that! I want my coin back!" The angry drunk grabbed hold of the table, flipping it so he could reach Gabriel. The two women who had been hanging onto Gabriel screamed and ran off.

A frown grew on Gabriel's face. "Come on, chap... you're scaring the girlies off."

He lifted his cup to the man, a peace offering. A quick slap sent the cup across the room, and the man shook his head before pulling a dagger out. Just as fast as the dagger was revealed, the large man found a long sword to his throat.

Grant stood to the side, Valor unsheathed and against the skin of the man's neck. Valor's beautiful red edge glimmered, and every soul in the tavern looked toward it.

"I have had a very long day... and this man, drunk as he might be, is coming with me." Grant reached his hand out, and the man gave over the dagger.

Once he had the man's weapon, Grant lowered his sword, putting the beautiful blade away. "Run along."

The man gave Gabriel a nasty glare before he pushed his way back out of the tavern.

"Adan sent me to find you. I am Grant Dalfair, and I believe we have a long trip ahead of us."

The whole hall was quiet, except Gabriel, who was struggling to stand up. He grabbed hold of an empty mug, trying to drink the air before he sat it down.

He looked Grant up and down, smirking. "I think Imma like you, kid."

CHAPTER EIGHTEEN

His time had come, and he was ready. Rageal had spent most of his life living in Sullvain, but he had always been loyal to Ragnovok. Finally, he could step out from behind the hoax.

His sentence would be death, that he knew for sure.

He had aided Ragnovok in obtaining Kaiser and, in doing so, had gotten Prince Devon killed.

Rageal sat in the dungeon. His left leg had been broken, and his face was swollen from the beating he had already received. Despite the pain, he couldn't help but crack a smile. Finally, that little shit had gotten what he deserved. Rageal laughed at the thought but quickly stopped due to the pain in his jaw. He had no regrets, even if he died.

"Why did you let him go?" A voice came from the shadows, but Rageal wasn't spooked. He had noticed the man's presence for some time.

"The boy did not deserve death... and Sullvain deserves everything that it has coming," Rageal said, recognizing the voice. "Did you not go with the prince that night, Sir Servis?"

Servis stepped from the shadows. He looked ill. Rageal had an idea of what was troubling the young knight. He had served the king for many years, and he had seen Servis among most of them. The two rarely ever shared words, but anyone with a sharp eye could tell Servis was troubled by the family.

The young man leaned into the bars of Rageal's cell and looked at the ground. "I... I let that boy kill Prince Devon. I could have stopped him."

"You knew the prince better than most, you knew which of the two deserved a fighting chance."

"That's just it, I don't regret letting him kill Devon. I just worry for my brother's safety... If they were to find out, they would kill us both just for being brothers." Servis shook his head, pushing himself away from the bars and halfway back into the shadows. "I—I'm sorry. I just needed someone to know, someone who would understand."

Servis gave Rageal one more look and rushed out of the dungeon. On his way out, he passed a hooded man.

"Well, well, I seem to be very popular these days," Rageal joked lightly.

Once the hooded man had reached the cell, he removed his hood.

"Foster Dalfair, what can a traitor like myself do for you?"

Rageal knew it had been Foster who turned him over, but what he couldn't wrap his head around was why Foster had given him the chance to release Kaiser.

Rageal shifted, trying to get a better look at the old knight standing near the cell. "Well...?"

"I understand why you did it." Foster's old eyes looked down at him and his bruises, a hint of sympathy in his voice. "I don't blame you for releasing the Glas. No creature, man or otherwise, deserves what the Sull family has done to that boy."

"Kaiser... His name is Kaiser Noire," Rageal said tightly. "The Sull family best remember that because one day, he will be more powerful than this pathetic family could ever fathom, and they will find him standing at their doorstep, looking for justice."

Rageal relished the thought of them getting what they deserved.

"Your men in Ragnovok cannot tame him. He should have been put out of his misery, so he doesn't become what I know he's capable of becoming." Foster shook his head, stepping back from the dungeon cell. "You think he can be controlled, but he cannot. You'll turn him into a weapon, and he'll destroy everything, your-selves included."

The old knight pulled a small bottle from his cloak and tossed it to Rageal. "I will ask the king for mercy on your behalf."

Rageal snorted. "Don't bother. I would rather die loyal to Rag-novok than kiss the feet of a murderous king."

Royals swarmed the throne room, each demanding justice for the prince.

"War! March unto Ragnovok!" someone cried.

The crowd cheered, but the king didn't respond, his old head hanging down. He had lost his only son, and that fact was evident on his face.

Foster stepped into the center of the room, trying to calm the crowd. "Marching on Ragnovok would solve nothing. I speak for Valacore, and if the Kingdom of Sullvain attacks Ragnovok, we will not send support. We will not send our troops any further south than they need to be."

The crowd quieted, worried that, without Valacore, they couldn't survive south of the Scar. That quiet didn't last long. Soon, the crowd erupted again, demanding some sort of justice, be it war or otherwise.

Foster stepped closer to the throne, his long sword removed from its sheath. "On behalf of Valacore, I will travel south and kill the Glas for Sullvain."

The throne room went silent, and not a soul spoke. The king's head finally rose from its slump, and he looked at Foster, curiosity in his eyes.

"I will need a few men, ones I can trust." Foster looked over his shoulder at Oran and Servis. "The prince's knights would like vengeance, no?"

Oran nodded, but Servis merely looked at his feet, attempting to hide his shame.

"You, Foster Dalfair, the Dark Stalker, would do such a thing?" The king stood, the thought of justice for his son bringing new life to him.

Foster gave the king a nod. "I shall, but I will need more men."

"You may take Oran, Servis, and however many men you need... I want that Glas' head on a pike outside of my walls!"

The king's shouting caused the room to shudder. Foster was

the only one who didn't flinch.

He would go south and find the Glas. He would kill the boy known as Kaiser, but despite his words, he wouldn't do it for Sullvain. He did it for every kingdom's sake.

Come sunrise, Foster would ride south with his party. He had already sent word back to Valacore to inform them of his goal.

Sitting at the desk with nothing but time before he left, he began to regret leaving Grant behind. Foster, of all people, knew Grant was one of the best swordsmen in the realm, even if he let his guard down while sparring. Foster was no longer in his prime, and although he had hunted the likes of Glas before, he worried he was no longer able...

A knock at Foster's door snapped him out of his thoughts, and he looked up to find Oran.

"I hope I'm not bothering you, Sir Foster."

"Not at all, come in." Foster gestured toward the chair across the desk. "What can I help you with?"

The young man seemed timid, finding his way to the chair as quickly as possible.

"It's about the Glas," Oran admitted, his eyes looking over the books littering Foster's desk. "Is it true what some of the royals say? That, in your youth, you hunted Glas and other creatures for the Church?"

Foster shifted in his seat, uneasy talking about the past. "It is true. I once hunted what few Glas remained, and other Stalkers before me have for hundreds of years after the defeat of their kingdom."

"I—I can tell you are a good man, Sir Foster. When they killed those girls... I could tell it bothered you." Oran looked down. "Such things bother my brother also. I could tell he felt bad for the Glas, Kaiser."

"Sir Servis is your brother?" Foster was a bit surprised. Yes, the two shared some looks, but Servis was a tall young man, much taller than an average man, and Oran was just shy of being the average.

Oran nodded, finally cracking a smile. "Have you ever regretted killing them? The Glas?" he stuttered.

"When I was young, about my son's age." He looked down at the desk. "The Church gave me orders to kill a Glas that had just been reborn. I knew this person, the Glas they had sent me to kill... I didn't want to kill them." Foster's voice lowered. He hadn't spoken of his role in the church in years, not even his son knew of it.

"I loved her, though I was too weak to admit it then."

"Did you kill her?" Oran gasped at the thought of Foster killing his lover.

"I did." Just speaking the words broke Foster. "I left the Church after that... I could no longer take pride in what they had me do. But, Sir Oran, don't take my words the wrong way... Kaiser Noire is a Glas, and no matter how much you may pity him, allowing him to live is a danger to everyone."

The door to Foster's room busted open, and Servis rushed in, shock written across his face. Foster and Oran both stood from their chairs.

"What's wrong?"

"It's Rageal!"

Minutes later, Foster stood in Rageal's cell, his arms crossed. It had happened while the guards were changing shifts. The prisoner had taken the bottle of wine Foster had given him and broken it. He had taken his own life, something he had warned Foster he was willing to do.

Rageal was laid out on the cell floor in a puddle of his own blood, the broken shards of glass still lodged in his throat.

He took notice of Servis, standing across from him. Foster could tell Servis had some sort of connection to Rageal, but whatever it was, it could be of no harm now.

He stepped over, taking a knee next to the lifeless body. His hand brushed down Rageal's face, closing the dead man's eyes. Once he had stood up, he stepped past Servis.

"Whatever you came to speak to him about earlier... you best leave those words here. Nothing can come of being connected to this man." Foster gave the young man a fair warning before rejoining Oran to prepare for their leave in the morning. Foster stopped at the stairs and looked back at Servis. He still stood staring at the dead man. He was facing himself, his loyalties. If the boy wasn't careful, he would meet the same fate.

CHAPTER NINETEEN

Small beams of light hit Kaiser's face, waking him from his sleep. He was too tired to move or sit up, so he lay there staring up at the canvas that covered the wagon he found himself in. He could feel the bumps from the path they rode on, although he had no idea where he was or who had him now.

He sighed, glad he could rest here without worry of harm, even if it were on its way. It was in this peaceful moment that he heard talking from outside the wagon.

He forced himself onto his side, trying his best to peek out of one of the small holes in the wagon cover. Kaiser's stomach lurched when he saw who it was. The Phantom, Seeath Reinhart, was riding along the side of the wagon.

The last time Kaiser had seen this man, he had put a blade into Kaiser's chest.

He quickly regained himself, trying to peek at the man next to Seeath. He was tall and slender with a streak of silver in his hair, not a warrior at all. He seemed to know the Phantom quite well.

"You'll be lucky if the king does not try to kill the Glas the moment you reveal him. The Raven has caused many problems already, and then you bring a newborn Glas to Ragnovok's doorstep?"

Seeath gave the man a sharp look. "Calm yourself, Magus. If the Raven comes looking for the Glas, I can handle it. Besides, having our hands on this Glas could make us a larger factor than ever. Imagine our strength if we truly had a Glas under our command. If we had such strength before, we wouldn't be retreating from Sullvain today..."

So, Kaiser would be in danger once more. He wondered if he would ever be able to rest. He rolled back over, and closed his eyes. The realization finally hit him, the day his sisters had died. Kaiser clenched his fist, tears forming and streaming down the sides of his face.

Until then, he hadn't gotten the chance to grieve, to fully take in that he would never see his sisters again. The two of them were gone, and he would never hold them again. He remembered the sounds of them running through the old house, and it pained him to think of that house empty now, empty and cold...

The tears left a clean streak down his dirt-covered face, and he reached his hand up to wipe them. His chest heaved as he tried to remain calm but he couldn't, not with the kind of grief that threatened to tear him apart.

The throne room of Ragnovok was draped in dark curtains, and only a single throne sat in the middle of the room. The king and his two children awaited Seeath's arrival. Both standing at the king's side.

When he finally entered, the young prince and princess rushed over. The princess wrapped her arms around his waist, and the prince gave him a respectful bow.

"We are happy to have you back, Sir Reinhart, no matter the outcome of the war." The young prince gently pulled the princess from Seeath, allowing him to address the king.

Seeath didn't get such a friendly greeting from King Novok as his old body struggled to stand from the throne. He had a look of disappointment on his face.

"So Valacore forces turned the tide of battle, then? As we stood at Sullvain's doorstep no less."

"Yes, my lord. Foster Dalfair, an advisor from Valacore, came with a company of men and half an army following a few days behind." Seeath stood, looking to the king for a moment, unsure how the next few minutes would play out.

"I see," the king said simply, giving nothing away in his tone or expression.

"We have not returned empty-handed, however. We have returned with the Glas, the very one Sullvain lied about finding among our ranks." Seeath held his breath as King Novok looked about the throne room as if he had expected to see the Glas.

"The Glas is still wounded from being tortured at the hands of King Sull, but I believe with the right training and motivation, we could use him as a Ragnovok weapon." His idea was out; now he hoped the king felt the same.

The two children watched on, just as curious as to what their father would say. For several long moments, the king was quiet.

"The Glas nearly destroyed the realm and even the last remaining one has been a blight to us since his rebirth, and here you stand, hoping to tame one? You forget who gave you those scars across your chest." The king looked from Seeath to Magus. "How do you feel about this? Do you agree with Reinhart's plan?"

Magus glanced at Seeath. Seeath knew he hadn't agreed at all, but the two were childhood friends, and Magus wouldn't leave him in the cold.

"I don't feel as strongly about such a plan, but I trust Seeath knows what he's doing."

The king thought it over, his skinny fingers rubbing his chin. He was getting slow in his old age, relying on Magus and Seeath to keep things in check. He took a seat back on his throne and looked to his only son, Prince Julius Novok.

"You will rule someday, I leave this to be your decision." King Novok gestured toward his son, and all eyes fell on him.

He was still young, a few years younger than the Glas boy, Kaiser. Maybe it was this fact that made him feel for the boy, or perhaps his respect for Seeath, but Julius nodded, looking to his father, then Seeath and Magus.

"We will keep the Glas," Julius said confidently.

The king nodded. "So be it," he said simply, seeming to trust his son's decision. The king stood, ending the small meeting.

Outside the throne room, Seeath found Magus waiting. He knew he was in for an ear full.

"I do hope you know what you're doing. This creature could be the ruin of us." Magus crossed his arms. "I want you to know this, Seeath, if he shows the smallest hint of being a threat to our kingdom, I'll kill him."

Seeath understood and would kill the Glas himself if need be. Ragnovok's safety came before all else.

The sound of birds woke Kaiser like it had so many times in the past. He pulled himself up and expected to find cells or something of the sort, but instead, he found himself perfectly fine.

Frowning in confusion, he reached out, softly running his hand over the silky blankets he found himself on top of. Kaiser shifted to the edge, using all his strength to stand.

He wasn't sure what to make of his new surroundings. He was in a room, larger than any he had set foot in. Kaiser took in the size; certain it was larger than both the rooms in his house combined. The bed was made out of fabrics only a royal could afford, and across from it sat a fireplace with two tall windows on each side.

Once he noticed the window, Kaiser limped over, looking out at the kingdom below him. Wherever he was must have been in the South. Snowfall rested atop the mountains but disappeared before getting any lower. He could see a small town just down the hill, so the keep or castle he was in must have been on high ground overlooking its kingdom.

Once he was finished surveying the view, he stepped over to the door and found it unlocked. He hesitated, knowing this could be some sort of sick trick, and he didn't have it in him to be tricked anymore. His experience with royals so far hadn't given him a reason to trust any of them even a bit.

He decided to take the risk and carefully pushed the wooden door open. The halls were long, branching off straight and left. Kaiser could see guards standing down the hall in front of him, but they seem to pay him no mind, so he took the left hall.

He took note of all the framed pictures along the way, mostly royals who all looked alike. Each of them had light gray hair, even the younger ones. Once he reached the end of the hall, he took a sharp turn to find two more guards. He expected them to grab him, but instead, they just stood in place, giving him only one room to enter.

Kaiser cautiously entered, and the smell of fresh food almost knocked him over. Mouth watering, he rushed over. No one else was in the room... After only a moment of hesitation, he started grabbing food. He took a handful of peas in his left hand and a piece of a chicken leg in his right, and he shoveled it into his mouth. It was as delicious as it smelled. Maybe even more so, considering how little he'd had in his stomach lately.

If this were a trick and he would soon die, at least he would die with a full belly.

As Kaiser stuffed himself, he heard the door creep open and spun around. It was Seeath. Kaiser stopped in his tracks, afraid of how the man would react.

"Please, continue." Seeath motioned to the food, stepping

around Kaiser to take a seat at the table. Once Seeath was seated, Kaiser took his own seat at the other end of the table, eating the food a bit slower now. "Do you know where you are? What has happened?"

Kaiser shook his head at the first question, but how could he possibly forget the events of the last few months.

Seeath smiled, his teeth showing, making Kaiser uneasy. "You're in Ragnovok. I know what you've been through. The Sull family deserves everything coming to them. I assume you knew of Rageal, the man who helped you escape. He was a spy for our kingdom." Seeath hesitated a moment before continuing. "I'm aware we met on the battlefield as enemies... but you no doubt realize who the real enemy is—the Sull family."

Seeath stood, stepping across the room in Kaiser's direction. He froze, dropping the food onto the plate as he swallowed his food hard.

"I have spoken in your defense. If you vow your loyalty to Ragnovok and its family, I promise you will never be a prisoner of any family again."

Kaiser was too afraid to look up at the man. "And if I don't?"

"You'll return to the life you experienced for the last year, in chains," Seeath said emotionlessly.

Put like that, Kaiser had little choice. He couldn't go back to being chained.

He'd rather die than live like that again. The never-ending pain. The gnawing hunger. The disconnect from reality. The bone-deep cold.

Kaiser swallowed again and finally met Seeath's eyes. "Okay."

Kaiser soon found his ultimatum wasn't so bad. He was lying in a small tub, his body limp and mostly submerged, with only his chin above water. Steam rose from the water's surface. He was in heaven, even if just for a moment. As he enjoyed the warmth on his sore muscles, he thought about everything. About his home, his sisters, Guile.

He wondered what had come of Guile when the Sullvain men arrived. Kaiser liked to think he fought, but then he was saddened at the idea of the gentle giant dying.

Kaiser lifted his hands from the water and splashed his face, cleaning the dried mud from his face, cheeks and behind his ears. He had lived in dirt and filth for the last month or so, and now, finally, he was clean. His hair had grown out almost past his shoulders, which made cleaning it a challenge.

After he cleaned himself up, two women entered the room. He shifted to cover himself, his cheeks heating. They scuttled in quickly and surrounded him.

"W—wha—" he stuttered.

Before he could question what was happening, they grabbed at his hair, lifting it above his head by the handful. The sounds of scissors snipping his long black hair gave way to strains of it falling into the water.

Seeath must have sent them to clean him up. Kaiser had been told he would meet the king soon, but not until he was cleaned up and presentable. This would be the second time he had ever met a king, but the first time he was not a prisoner, although he somehow still felt like one. Ragnovok may have been taking care of him thus far, but he had no choice in the matter. It was a choice between serving King Novok or remaining in a cell.

Kaiser sighed, closing his eyes while the maids trimmed his hair. He would relax and get rest. Seeath had mentioned swordplay training starting within the week.

"A weapon?" he whispered to himself, wondering why anyone would think him capable of being such.

CHAPTER TWENTY

It had taken Grant all morning to get his new companion out of bed. Gabriel had been more of a burden than help thus far, and as the two rode out of Valacore, Grant could still smell the ale on him.

"Are you going to be able to ride like that?"

"Like what?" Gabriel rubbed his eyes with one hand while the other blocked the sun from his face.

Grant rolled his eyes. It was clear Gabriel was hungover.

Gabriel stopped his horse no more than a mile out of Valacore. The path branched from there, one road going west while the other headed south. Grant stayed mounted atop his horse while Gabriel stumbled off, using the road post to hold himself up.

"Which way?" Grant looked west, trying to peer far beyond his sight. "Alyssa always talked about traveling west, to the Great Bridge... We should go that way."

Grant had already made up his mind, but when he looked back to Gabriel, the half-drunken man was on his knees, his hands scooping up handfuls of dirt and lifting the soil to his nose. His nostrils flared, and he closed his eyes. Grant didn't dare disturb him—the man was in some sort of trance.

After a few minutes, Gabriel dropped the soil back to the ground and stood, dusting his knees.

"South," the ruffian announced. "She went south. And she has a horse and one other person with her."

Gabriel tried to collect himself for the bumpy walk back to his horse while Grant sat staring at the man in disbelief.

"How could you possibly know such a thing? She left days ago." Grant was still unsure if the man was serious or not.

Gabriel, on the other hand, had already begun the slow ride south. "Like you, little knight, the Church hired me for a reason. Let's go find this girl of yours."

Grant *really* hoped the man was sober enough to know what he was talking about.

The two men continued south. A day had already passed, and only on occasion did Gabriel get off of his horse to "speak to the land," as he put it—and only once did the man vomit from all the drinking he had done the night before.

Grant was galled that he had to tolerate the drunk, but with his tracking skills, he couldn't afford to leave him behind. The sun was lowering over them, and soon, they would have to stop for rest.

A small village sat ahead, only a handful of houses littered in among the fields and crops.

"Let's stop here," Gabriel said. "We can ask 'round 'bout the girl."

Grant shook his head. "No. We keep riding. We can't lose any time."

Grant was half past the village when he realized Gabriel was no longer behind him. When he turned, he found Gabriel slowing to a stop at the town.

"What are you doing? Did you not hear me?"

"Oh, I heard you all right, and I think you're a bit foolish. You can ride all night long, but all you'll get is a dead horse and sore feet." Gabriel leaped from his steed and led it over to a tree near the village edge. "'Sides, I already saw two places she's been camped. She's probably sleepin' like a babe right now... We might as well get some rest at the same time."

Grant disapproved of the plan, but there was little he could do. Gabriel already prepared a small firepit near the tree line and had wandered off in search of firewood, leaving Grant alone.

He sat silently, the fire in front of him reflecting in his eyes. His whole body trembled, wanting to ride on, but he knew Gabriel was right—they needed rest. He was just worried about what would happen if they didn't get to Alyssa in time.

He pulled Valor from its sheath and set it on his lap so he could look over it. The beautiful red blade was a reminder of his new oath. He would use this blade, not to defend a royal family, but to defend those close to him. And Alyssa was just such a person. He had failed Foster, but this sword was his chance, his redemption.

"That blade... Where did you get it?" Gabriel emerged from the shadows, tossing a few twigs onto the fire before taking a seat across from Grant.

Grant put Valor away, sliding it under the small blankets he had prepared for himself.

"Not a talkative one, eh?" Gabriel said. "Well, we all have our secrets, I suppose... You can tell me when you're ready. Thought you might like to know, though, I dropped by the village and asked around about our girl. Shopkeep says a pretty little thing did come through there. Said she was by herself but talked 'bout a traveling companion."

"That must be her... So, we are on the right track." Grant was relieved for the first time since they had begun riding. Hope blossomed in his chest.

"One last thing, though. He said she thought she was heading west... Whoever has our girl has her thinking she's heading somewhere she isn't."

Gabriel's words caused Grant to look across the flames. "We ride as soon as the sun rises... We can't lose their trail."

Gabriel smirked. "Don't you worry ya pretty blonde head, pup. I could trail 'em to the islands of Farera and back."

Right, Grant thought skeptically. *Good to know.*

Further south, midway between Valacore and Mirelos, Dye and Alyssa sat among some trees. Their fire was low, and the sounds of owls and other night animals echoed between the treetops. They had traveled further than Alyssa could have ever imagined, and she was just now realizing how big the world truly was.

She sat near the small fire, wrapped in her blanket, but she could feel the bite of the wind even through its warmth. Her eyes looked up, watching Dye as he fumbled through a bag he had pulled from their horse. He was acting so different than before, no longer the young adventurer she had met in the alleyways back home.

Home, she thought—how she wished she could see her family. She missed the days before all this. Alyssa wasn't stupid, and she could tell Dye no longer had the same spark he had shown her when they escaped Valacore.

"How far away are we? From the Great Bridge?"

"Why do you keep asking?" Dye nearly barked at her, still frustrating himself with whatever it was he was trying to get from the bag. "We'll get there when we get there."

Alyssa sunk back into her blanket, pulling it up to cover her chin. She felt more alone now, on the road with Dye, than she had ever felt back inside the kingdom. At least then she'd had Grant. How she missed her knight. Alyssa's eyes darted up when Dye finally stood, holding the dagger he had struggled with.

"W—where are you going?" Alyssa asked, her heart skipping a beat.

"To get some firewood before we sleep. Stay put."

"Are you sure? S—should I go with you?" Her words fell on deaf ears as Dye disappeared beyond the trees.

As the minutes ticked by, Alyssa grew more and more afraid, the animals of the forest taunting her with their calls. The sounds of twigs snapping from every direction caused her to inch closer to the flames. She could only see as far as the fire allowed, leaving all manner of creatures to lurk just beyond the shadows.

"Dye? Is that you?" No reply came from the darkness, but footsteps marched closer. "Dye...?"

Alyssa shifted, trying to predict where the footsteps were coming from. Finally, figures appeared from beyond. She had hoped that if not Dye, Grant would appear to save her.

To her dismay, three strangers strolled out of the darkness, all of them eyeing her like a prize.

CHAPTER TWENTY-ONE

For three days, Foster and his crew of Sullvain soldiers marched south. Ragnovok was less than a week's ride south, but for some reason, the old knight had taken his team east after crossing the Scar. Oran had noticed this change of direction, but said nothing—he trusted Foster and kept marching. Servis, on the other hand, was becoming suspicious. He wondered if Foster could be trusted, but Servis never trusted anyone except his brother.

"He's leading us east, toward Dreava..." Servis grumbled. "Yet we know the Glas was taken to Ragnovok!"

Servis somehow managed to keep his voice to a whisper, yet both he and his brother watched Foster closely as they marched. The Valacore knight had been quiet since the group began traveling, saying almost nothing the whole trip. Only Oran had spoken to Foster—he trusted him, but Servis didn't.

Oran finally caved, giving his brother a smile. "I'll talk to him, see why we're heading to Dreava."

Oran gave his brother a pat on the back and began walking ahead. Servis crossed his arms, watching.

Oran jogged up to Foster's side. "Sir Foster, do you have a moment?"

"Of course, what is it?"

Oran shivered. He and his brother had never traveled far from

Sullvain, and they were unaccustomed to the cold of the South.

Wordlessly, Foster pulled one of his fur coats from his shoulders and reached it out to Oran.

"I wanted to speak to you about our destination." Oran didn't take the fur coat at first, but then he acquiesced and wrapped it around his shoulders. "We know the Phantom, Seeath Reinhart, has taken the Glas."

Foster inclined his head. "Yes, we do."

"Then why are we not heading to Ragnovok?" The two kept walking, the company of roughly twenty men marching behind them. Foster looked back at them, Oran doing the same.

"Do you think our twenty men will be able to go into Ragnovok full force? No, we would quickly be killed by the Phantom without a doubt." Foster gestured forward, toward what Oran could only explain as a wall of white in the distance. "I know people in Dreava who will help us. With any luck, we can find a way to kill the Glas without ever stepping foot within Ragnovok."

Oran nodded, still trusting Foster and his plan. It wasn't long until Oran stopped, catching a small white snowflake in his hand. He had never seen snow before, only heard of it. During the winter months it got cold in Sullvain, but never snowed. It was exciting to him, somewhat.

Foster had walked on ahead before noticing Oran had stopped. He turned to look at Oran, giving him an old smile as he looked up as snow began fluttering about the area.

The whole crew of Sullvain men stopped to marvel at its

beauty, some opening their mouths to catch flakes like children. Through the snow and carefree crowd, Servis stood, his arms crossed and eyes forward.

Another few hours of marching east, and the men were no longer amused by the cold. They shivered and sneezed, some even bundled together to keep warm. Foster was the only one of them truly warm within the snow. The fur coat given to Oran had helped some, but the further east they went, the colder it became.

"Do you know of Dreava? The history?" Foster asked, looking over at Oran and giving a small laugh when he noticed Oran's red nose and cheeks.

Oran shook his head, teeth chattering under the cold.

"Dragons used to fly these skies. You could hardly walk ten paces without seeing one, but then a young Dreavaian prince was killed by one... Soon after, all the dragons were hunted and killed."

Foster lifted his hand, catching some of the snow and watching it melt in his hand. "They say it has snowed every day in Dreava since the last dragon took his final breath."

Foster wondered how many times Grant had begged to hear that story as a child. He was always fond of the more majestic bedtime stories, but then that boy who had been full of wonder grew up to be a soldier with a smart and realistic head on his shoulders. Foster missed that curious child. He missed Grant.

"Hold!" Foster lifted his hand, causing the men behind him to cease their marching. There was something up ahead...

Far ahead of them, a group of three men came riding out from the tree line. Each of the men had fur on, a clear indication they were from Dreava. Once close enough, the three men stopped, looking over Foster and his men with caution until their leader, a young man with long brown hair, caught sight of Foster.

"Foster Dalfair? Is that really you?" The young man leaped from his horse and pushed through the snow that now reached the men's lower calves.

It took Foster a moment to return the gesture, finally realizing who it was they had run into. "Harrion Dreava, Prince of Dreava."

Foster met the prince halfway and was caught in an unexpected hug from the young man before he even blinked. Harrion was a tall man, his arms long and strong like a prized prince should be. It didn't surprise Foster to find the prince out in the woods. The young man had always been up for hunting, even against the rest of the Dreava family's wishes.

He finally released Foster from the bear hug and gave him a pat on the shoulders. "It has been years! What brings the Dark Stalker to Dreava?"

Foster could have gone without answering, and Harrion would have still been able to guess—the company of Sullvain men and flags told plenty.

"Is this about the Glas and Ragnovok?"

Foster gave his young friend a nod, returning the pat on the shoulder. "You know I wouldn't have come if it wasn't important..."

He could tell Harrion was unsure, but a sigh of relief came when the prince's worried face turned to a smile.

"This is no place to talk," Harrion said. "Your men look half frozen. Let us get to Dreava and talk in the warmth."

Dreava was a calm kingdom, its residents typically keeping to themselves, which meant the tavern had maybe a dozen men already in it when Foster and his men arrived. Foster knew finding a room for them all would be a task, but he would address that later. For now, he needed to speak with Prince Harrion. The two had sat down together, and a barmaid brought both a mug of ale.

"How is your father?" Foster had heard rumors of the king being sickly, but he wanted to hear it from Harrion before he spoke of it.

"He's fine. A bit sick but nothing serious." Harrion grabbed hold of his mug, taking a large drink. "How's your son, Grant? I haven't seen him since we were kids."

Foster nodded, taking hold of his own mug. "He's a royal guard in Valacore, as best a man as any father could have hoped."

Foster looked up from his mug to find Harrion smiling. He looked like Grant. Harrion had the same build, and despite being a sturdy young man, they both shared that boyish grin.

"I remember when you taught us to ride horses. Grant caught on so much faster than me." Harrion held his mug up high. "To good memories!"

"To good memories."

Foster watched as Harrion leaned back in his chair, getting comfortable. He knew this was as good a time as any.

"I would like an audience with your father, if possible," Foster said. "I know he's ill right now, but the Glas threat is far greater than you could imagine... Ragnovok has already taken the Glas inside their castle. I fear this won't end well for any of the kingdoms."

"I shudder at the thought of what could frighten the famous Death Stalker. I'll do what I can to get you an audience," the prince promised, "but you must realize Ragnovok and Dreava have been at peace for decades... Helping Sullvain kill the Glas would be an act of war. Not to mention the court would have to agree..."

Foster nodded. "Of course. I remember well that nothing happens in Dreava without the court's approval."

Harrion tapped his mug on the table twice, and the barmaid rushed back over. "They have been worried lately, about my father and even more so about my half-brother and his role in the court. I know how close you are to my father, and myself... so I will do what I can, but I won't allow Sullvain to drag Dreava into a war with Ragnovok."

"I would never ask such if I expected war," Foster assured him seriously, meaning it. "I wish to settle this as quietly as possible."

Harrion nodded in agreement, taking one of the new mugs. "Now that the serious talk is out of the way, let's see if all that fancy Valacore living has dampened your drinking abilities!"

Foster merely grinned.

The walls were dark, and only candles gave sight to Foster on his way through the castle doors. He tried his best to carry the drunken Harrion into the large hall leading to the throne room. The castle was as Foster remembered, clad in black bricks and decorated with dragon bones. He wondered if the kindhearted Harrion ever grew weary of the sight and its reminder of death.

Once Foster had gotten the prince to the end of the hall, he stopped and looked up the stairs. At the top of the stairs, he saw a beautiful young lady, a few years younger than Harrion. She had hair as brown as Harrion's, though shorter, stopping at her shoulders. The cold winter sky kept her skin pale and her eyes shined like blue ice, a trait the Dreava family was known for.

"Sir Foster, has it been so long you do not recognize me?" Her voice was sweet, with a regal undertone.

Something in Foster's old head clicked, and he smiled, looking back up at the girl. "How could I ever forget such a beautiful face?"

He hadn't seen Dawn Dreava in years, not since she was a small child. The once small, rotten-mannered child had become an elegant beauty. He could even hear it in her voice.

Dawn gave Foster a kind smile and then looked to Foster's luggage, her older brother.

Foster shrugged as best he could. "I warned him not to try and out drink me."

The small giggle Foster's comment got from Dawn assured him she was still just as kindhearted as Harrion.

Dawn's maid quickly rushed over, taking the limp Harrion from Foster's shoulder and helping him further into the castle. Once the two were alone, Dawn took a few steps down the stairs until she was able to speak without being overheard.

"Thank you for helping him back to the castle. I think he sometimes forgets he is the prince. The way he goes off hunting and drinking." She shook her head in disapproval.

"Think nothing of it, Princess. He would have done the same for me." Foster brushed his shoulder off, rubbing the soreness out of it before he noticed a change in Dawn.

"Are you here about the Glas?" she asked bluntly.

She got straight to the point. Foster respected that.

"Yes, I was hoping your father would be able to assist me, even in the slightest."

Judging from her frown, Dawn didn't like the idea. Her icy-blue eyes cut right through any sort of lies Foster could have come up with. It was clear she was no longer a child.

"Father is in no condition to speak with anyone... I will arrange an audience with the court. That is all I can do for you, Sir

Foster." Dawn's maid had returned to her side just in time for the short meeting to end. "I heard you have men with you. Will your company be staying within Dreava?"

"Yes, Princess. I had hoped to find warm accommodations for them. They aren't accustomed to the cold."

Dawn turned her head, looking at her maid. "See that Sir Foster and his men are given rooms and free meals at the tavern. They are our guests and should be treated as such."

Dawn and Foster locked eyes, and he could now see she was colder than her brother. He would have to be careful not to push his stay in Dreava.

CHAPTER TWENTY-TWO

"Again."

How many times had he hit the ground already? Two dozen, three dozen? More?

Kaiser pulled himself up to a sitting position. Seeath stood a few feet away, his practice sword resting on his shoulder. Kaiser had been training with Seeath all day and had yet to hit him.

After a few deep breaths, Kaiser finally stood, dusting the dirt off.

"Come at me again." Seeath swung his blade about, preparing to counter Kaiser.

The feat wasn't hard as Kaiser rushed in, slashing at Seeath. A quick deflect and kick sent Kaiser stumbling off balance once more, slamming into the ground hard. The impact took his breath away.

"I—I can't!" Kaiser pleaded, not wanting to keep getting knocked to the ground.

Seeath rubbed his chin, scrutinizing Kaiser. "Hmmm."

In the middle of trying to breathe, Kaiser noticed a small girl at the doorway. The two had been sparring in the castle courtyard, so Kaiser had seen servants and guards running about before, but this was the first time he had noticed the girl. She must have been a few years younger than Kaiser. Her gray hair stood out. It looked like the men in the portraits Kaiser had seen the day before.

"Princess Fiona Novok," Seeath answered the question Kaiser was thinking to himself. "She's a shy girl, rarely speaks to anyone other than her brother, Julius."

Seeath reached down, grabbing Kaiser's hand and pulling him up. "Did the Sullvain men teach you how to wield a sword?"

Kaiser struggled to lean down and get his practice sword. "They gave us swords and dummies to swing at.... Nothing more."

Seeath nodded, stepping over to the small rack that held the practice weapons. He snatched a polearm from the shelf and tossed it to Kaiser. "Hold that as you would a rack or scythe."

Kaiser did as commanded, gripping the pole with his left hand below and his right higher toward the blade. What was that going to accomplish?

"You're left-handed? Did you not think to use your left hand when swinging your blade?"

Seeath's question was more of a scolding, and Kaiser's eyes instantly fell to look at his feet, feeling shame for some absurd reason. "I—I haven't swung a sword before."

"And at this rate, you never will." Seeath took the pole from Kaiser, tossing it back to the rack. "Not efficiently anyway."

Seeath gathered the swords, returning them to their places. The training was over for now, and while Kaiser had wanted it to end, he wasn't glad. He was disappointed in himself.

Seeath shook his head, tossing Kaiser a rag to clean the sweat off with. "Stop your whining. If you ever want to defend yourself, you'll need to grow up. Take a walk around town, get familiar with your new surroundings."

Once Seeath returned to the castle, he made his way to his room. Upon arrival, he found he wasn't alone. Magus had let himself in.

"Have I ever told you how much I hate you coming into my chamber unannounced?" he said dryly.

Magus gave him a small smile, playing with one of the swords displayed among Seeath's walls.

"You have." Magus ran his finger to the tip of the blade and then quickly turned. "How is your little weapon coming along? I believe I overheard some of the guards laughing about how many times you knocked him down in the first hour of training."

Seeath wasn't in the mood for Magus' comments right now. Kaiser's training was starting off worse than he had hoped. He glared, keeping what he wanted to say to himself.

After Magus received no reply about the progress, he lifted his chin. "I see. So, it seems not all Glas are born to fight."

Magus mirrored Seeath once he moved across the room. The further into the room Seeath went, the quicker Magus stepped across the room, mindlessly playing with the swords along the wall. Seeath's chamber was covered in blades, some he had crafted for himself, while others he had taken from slain foes.

"Kaiser may need more work than I had expected, but in time, he'll learn," Seeath said gruffly, hoping he wasn't lying.

Magus tilted his head slightly. "The healer said he had never seen wounds like his heal so quickly... It would seem your weapon can at least take a beating."

"Yes, all but the brand... That doesn't seem to have healed."

Seeath had noticed the brand along Kaiser's right ribcage while they were transporting him from Sullvain to Ragnovok. It seemed a Glas couldn't heal from fire so easily. It was good to know, at least.

"I mean to give him access to the library... Maybe the idea of learning about his race will spark an urge to become something greater." Seeath looked over his shoulder at Magus.

"Yes, encourage him... Maybe he will become a monster like his ancestors." Magus' words were spiteful, and Seeath was relieved to see the man take his leave from the chamber.

Despite their friendship, Seeath and Magus often disagreed on many things. It had been that way ever since childhood. Magus had grown up a noble, his family always close to the Novok family —but Seeath had been little more than a smith's son, lucky enough to befriend a royal. Seeath always thought highly of Magus and his advice, but that didn't stop the two from arguing often, both fussing and fighting until one gave up.

Standing at the edge of his bed, looking at the blade Magus had been playing with before, Seeath wondered if maybe this disagreement held more than just a fuss.

Eyes fell upon him from all directions, and whispers circled from one crowd to the next. Kaiser wondered if leaving the castle was such a good idea. He could hear some words clear as day.

Glas.

Monster.

He had come to know these words very well while in Sullvain's dungeon. It seemed even in Ragnovok, he would be known as such. Growing weary of all the attention, Kaiser ducked into a small alley, finding himself near the edge of town.

His heart swelled at the sight of the open plains in front of him. They reminded him of home, even though these planes were more barren and grayer than the ones he remembered. Kaiser took a few steps into the field, his eyes tightly shut as his hands reached out and felt the tall blades of grass brush against him.

Freedom—for the first time in almost a year.

Despite his closed eyes, tears streamed down his cheeks, and he smiled a broken, weak smile.

"The fearsome Glas, come to save Ragnovok!"

Kaiser was startled by the voice, quickly turning to find three men. He had seen them earlier in the day, watching his training with Seeath.

"He doesn't look like much of a threat," one said mockingly.

The three men approached Kaiser, one pointing straight at him. "Look! He's even crying!"

The men laughed, the rounder one even dropped over, holding his gut as he cackled.

Kaiser wrapped his arms around his middle, taking a step back. He wanted to be away, back in the castle.

"Go ahead then, run away. Go be some other kingdom's problem. Ragnovok doesn't need some child."

"No." Kaiser's defiance nearly went unheard as he spoke just above a whisper, but the leader of the three men had heard him. Kaiser didn't want to be here, but he wouldn't be pushed again.

"What was that boy? Do you have something to say?" He stepped forward, a quick pace toward Kaiser.

"I said—NO!"

In the next instant, the man's palm smashed into Kaiser's nose, sending him stumbling back. Off balance, he fell to the ground. Kaiser's eyes watered from the pain throbbing in his nose.

"Cry some more!" The man pulled his foot back and kicked Kaiser in the side.

On his back now, Kaiser couldn't decide if his hands should cover his face or sides.

"You! What is your name?" The three men stopped, turning back toward Ragnovok to address the new voice and its question.

Kaiser looked up to see Prince Julius Novok standing nearby, two guards with him. The boys fell silent, the leader taking a step away from Kaiser.

"Well? I asked you a question," Julius demanded, cocking an eyebrow.

"We were... trying to stop the Glas," the one who had kicked him stammered.

"Y—yeah, he was trying to escape."

Julius shook his head and waved his hand, gesturing for the men to leave. The three rushed by, each giving a quick and respectful bow. As the leader of the men passed, Julius gave a small warning.

"If I see you three anywhere near the Glas again, I will have you executed."

His words fell around them with all the weight of an executioner's blade.

Once it was only Julius and Kaiser in the field, the young prince approached. Kaiser was lying on his side, one hand covering his head while the other covered his side.

"Are you all right?" Julius reached his hand out, and Kaiser peeked up from under his cover, trying to decide if he should trust the prince or not.

Finally, he reached up, allowing Julius to pull him up to his feet. Kaiser's nose was a dark black color and had a trail of crimson blood running from one nostril. Compared to all he had been through, a busted nose wasn't such a bad thing.

He brought his arm up and wiped the blood from his face, then looked at Julius. Kaiser thought it eerie, the royal tone the young prince put out. It reminded him of the royals of Sullvain, but this young royal was different somehow.

"Kaiser, was it? My name is Julius Novok, Prince of Ragnovok." Julius smiled, laughing at himself. "You probably already guessed that, though. Sir Reinhart was looking for you. He wished to show you something. I often come walking so I thought I would look for you."

When Kaiser didn't reply, Julius crossed his arms. "Come, let us return to the castle."

Kaiser's walk with the prince was a quiet one. Kaiser didn't speak a single word, the scars from his last royal encounter far too fresh. Julius didn't seem to be offended by the fact, which eased Kaiser's worry. After the walk back, Julius led Kaiser to Seeath's chamber.

"I see you found him," Seeath said as they entered. "Faster than the guards no less."

Seeath's compliment brought a smile to Julius's face. He obviously thought highly of Sir Reinhart.

Seeath placed his armor to the side, slicking back his red hair before he joined the two out in the hall.

"What happened?" Seeath looked over Kaiser's nose, almost like a father figure.

"Some of the soldiers attacked him near the edge of town. I took care of it," Julius said, and Seeath nodded, gesturing down the castle halls.

The two followed behind him until he reached a set of stairs leading down. The stairs took the three to another hall with a single door.

Seeath pushed the large wooden doors open. "You've heard many things about your race, I'm sure."

Through the door was a massive library filled to the ceiling with books. Each wall was lined with shelves and several more were spaced out in rows.

Kaiser was in awe, stepping into the bright room ahead of the others. He had never seen so many books in his life. This was amazing.

"If you take your training seriously and show progress, I'll allow you access to our library."

A small, old man came from within the room, two books in his hands. Once he arrived, he offered one of the books to Kaiser. The cover was made of red leather and was titled *Lore of the Glas*. Many of the pages seemed to be missing.

"This is Walton," Seeath said, gesturing to the old man. "He will assist you with finding whatever books we have on the subject of your people."

Kaiser flipped the cover open and began scanning the pages. It was the first time in many years that he felt wonder.

"You do know how to read, correct?"

"Yes... Guile taught me. He said if I were to ever be more than a farmer, I would need to learn." Kaiser quickly rushed over to the nearby chair and sat down, his eyes never leaving the page.

"So you'll continue your training?" Seeath asked, not hiding his amusement. "I can expect progress?"

Kaiser nodded his head, not looking away from the only clue as to what he was. The idea of learning more about the Glas ignited a fire in him.

CHAPTER TWENTY-THREE

The cold water rushing under her feet sent chills down her back. Where was she...? How she had gotten there...?

The waters swirled and splashed like the colors of a painting, and even the snow falling around her seemed like small white smears of paint.

Dawn reached her hand out to touch the flakes, but as if reacting to her desire, they whirled around her, engulfing her until her whole body was cold, and she could see nothing but white.

When the snow finally dissipated, she found herself in complete darkness, alone save for one pale figure standing in front of her.

He was nude, his skin as white as the falling snow, his hair as black as night. Dawn opened her mouth to speak, but she found no words would escape her throat. While she struggled to speak, she noticed a trail of crimson running from his eyes.

The first string of blood poured down his face, dripping to his chest. It made its way further, but as it approached his feet, more began pouring from his eyes until a large puddle had formed and his white body was near painted red.

Her feet desperately tried to flee backward, but each step took her nowhere.

The white figure lifted his hand as if in pain, reaching out for her. The large puddle of blood began slithering forward. She could hear the white figure crying, his sorrow as clear as anything she had ever felt.

As the blood reached her feet, it rose and took the shape of the white figure. A red glass version of its creator. Its glass hand rose like the white figure behind it, but its outreached hand touched Dawn's cheek, and its coldness shocked her. Her whole body trembled.

As its hand moved down her neck, she suddenly realized she, too, was naked. The hand continued, tracing down her collarbone. Dawn could feel her chest heaving and her face warm with a blush.

As the crimson glass hand grazed her naked hips, she gasped and sat upright—safely in her chamber bed, her body still hot and trembling.

"I had another dream..."

Dawn Dreava walked the halls of her father's castle with an older man, Elder Hollen. He was the only one among the Elders she trusted, and one of the only people in the kingdom who knew of her visions and dreams. She had told Hollen nearly every dream she had, how real and dangerous they seemed.

"Tell me then," Elder Hollen mused, "was the one-eyed lion in this one as well?"

"No..." She swallowed, remembering back. "I was in the darkness with someone else—he seemed so sad and confused. He seemed to have been reaching out, but could not reach whatever he was longing for, and so his blood began to move beyond his reach, taking a glass form and—"

Dawn blushed, not daring to speak of how the glass figure had touched her.

Elder Hollen stopped at a large doorway. "A glass form, you say? Hmm..." Elder Hollen closed his eyes, his old hand rubbing at the tip of his chin. "I will find all the books we have on such magic and have them brought to your chamber. In secret, of course. Before that, I must tend to your guest, Sir Foster."

Elder Hollen peeked into the doorway they stood in, getting a glimpse of the old knight waiting inside. "Is it true? Is this Sir Foster really the one known as the Dark Stalker?"

"He is," Dawn replied. "I remember Father telling me stories of Sir Foster, about how he hunted cursed souls... I always thought the idea was silly, given how gentle and caring he was to Harrion and me, not to mention his own son, Grant."

Despite being rather strict with Foster when he arrived, Dawn thought highly of the man.

"Well, I will do what I can to aid him for you, Princess." Elder Hollen's words eased Dawn, and she gave him a quick hug before he marched into the room with Foster.

Foster stood in the middle of the large chamber, his eyes examining the different flags hanging over the seats. Each area and its chairs belonged to a faction of the court. A fox, a torch, and a dragon. Each represented a different ground among the court Elders. If the three houses couldn't agree on a subject, then the king would be asked to coincide with one of the grounds, and that would determine the end verdict.

This was how most matters were decided in Dreava, from declaring war to judging someone of a crime. Foster had come seeking an audience with the king, but instead, he found himself speaking to the court—and not even the full court, but a single Elder.

"Sir Foster, Princess Dawn has told me much about you. I do hope you and your men find Dreava a pleasant stay." Elder Hollen reached his hand out, offering a respectful handshake. "I am Elder Hollen of the Dragon Court."

"Thank you, Elder Hollen. My men are pleased to be in the warmth. I hate to be so blunt, but I am curious, where are the other Elders?" Foster gestured to the empty seats surrounding the two men on all sides.

Elder Hollen sighed, folding his hands within his robe. "As you know, the king is sick. The other Elders thought it a waste of time to gather only to refuse you."

"So I'm being denied an audience with the court and the king?" Foster shook his head, turning to leave. If it was a waste of everyone's time, then there was no need for him to be there.

"Please, Sir Foster. If you were being denied, the princess would not have asked me to meet you. She trusts you, which is more than most in this kingdom would gain from her."

Foster stopped just short of the door and waited as Elder Hollen moved closer, his words mere whispers now.

"The king, he sleeps... He was simply sick a few weeks back, but now he will not wake. Harrion and the court thought it best to keep this fact a secret, but Dawn has asked that I inform you why the court has denied you... She believes you come in good faith and wants to hear you out." Elder Hollen reached out a small parcel.

Foster took it and found a map drawn onto it. A map of the South, of Dreava and Ragnovok. A path led through the forest and came out inside Ragnovok territory, just a few miles from the kingdom itself.

"Be wary of the forest. Deserters of the war abandoned Ragnovok and dwell within it. If you need supplies, Princess Dawn has a servant. Send word to him, and he will contact Dawn directly for you."

Foster nodded, slipping the map under his belt. He had but a few more steps to take, and he would be able to rid the realm of the Glas hiding inside Ragnovok.

"Tell the princess I am very thankful."

Though Foster had the feeling he would see her once more before he left Dreava.

Far below the castle windows, children ran about in the snow, kicking and throwing it at each other. Such playful times were of the past to Vale, bastard son of King Dreava. He leered down at them, admiring and despising them all at once.

At one time, his father had treated him as such, as a true son. Vale was just another royal child, but he found the older he grew, the more he had to compete with his older brother, Harrion. The ever handsome and ever capable Harrion Dreava, prized son of the kingdom and rightful heir to the Dreava throne.

Vale's hand shook from the mere thought of his brother and all the praise that had been continuously poured upon him. With a burst of rage, Vale slammed his fist against the glass, cracking it.

Cursing, Vale rubbed his hand, sickened by his outburst now that it was over. From behind him, he heard the quiet moans of his father from the bed.

In his slumber the past month, King Dreava had whined and cried, but no one knew if it was nightmares or pain he was experiencing.

Vale hoped for the latter.

He hadn't always hated his father—for the longest time, his father was all he had. Vale never knew his mother, a chambermaid sent off after his birth. King Dreava hadn't been able to stand the idea of sending his child off with her, even a bastard.

Vale moved to the bed, looking over his father's frail form. He brushed his father's cheek. "Oh, my dear, dear Father... If only I could put you out of your misery, out of my own misery."

He had often dreamed of becoming king. He and Harrion would play as such, Harrion the gallant knight and Vale his rightful king. Back then, it was play. But now? Now Vale truly wanted that throne, and Harrion would have it first.

Vale reached behind his father, plucking the pillow from under his limp neck. He held it tightly to his chest, tears forming in his eyes. Vale leaned over his father and gave him a soft kiss on the forehead before he set the pillow against the king's face.

"Dear Father, false hope is all you ever gave me." He gripped the pillow harder and pressed down. His mind was set, his actions already in motion—until suddenly, the chamber door cracked open and Vale jerked back as if he'd been burned, pulling the pillow back to his chest.

"Brother? I didn't know you were here." Harrion entered, his voice just a small hush as if he would wake the sleeping king if he spoke too loudly.

"I came to check on Father..." Vale beat the pillow some and tucked it under the king's head. Harrion seemed to have no suspicions, so Vale played along.

"I hate seeing him like this." Harrion stood at the foot of the bed, his face pinched. "I spoke to some merchants from across the sea, they say they have herbs that can awaken him, but they can only come as far as Sullvain."

Vale looked across the bed at his brother in confusion. "You cannot possibly mean to send someone to fetch a patch of herbs. If anyone were to hear of Father's sickness...."

"I know, this is why I will ride myself before the week is out. I have already sent word to the merchants. They don't know who's purchasing the herbs."

"Any word from the court?" Vale asked, changing the subject. "About my request?"

He had recently requested a position among one of the three grounds of the court. If he couldn't be king, he would rise some other way—but his request had gone unanswered.

"I have spoken to some of the Elders, but not all believe you should have a seat among them. Vale... I know how you must feel." Harrion gave him a sympathetic look, and Vale wanted to slap it off his face.

"Prince Harrion?" A young maid had entered the room, looking down. "Your sister is looking for you."

Harrion nodded, stepping over to his brother and giving him a firm hug. Harrion was a bear in comparison to Vale, so Vale stood little chance of escaping the embrace. After Harrion left, Vale's fist clenched so hard, his fingernails cut into his flesh.

"How could you possibly understand...?"

CHAPTER TWENTY-FOUR

S uccess, he thought, trotting along the dirt road before him. Dye found himself delighted with the recent catch, and so had the men he often traded with. They were so impressed by the little royal he had brought, they tossed her crescent necklace in along with the gold they paid for her. Dye held the stone up, trying to eye the value of it. He knew it was unlikely the stone was worth much, but at the very least he could pass it off for a few gold pieces.

For months, he had been trailing young women away from their troubled lives with talk of adventure, escape, and freedom— but he always left them in that forest, with his pockets a little heavier.

On his walk, he did wonder, though, what exactly Alyssa had been running from. Dye had never found such a catch, a royal child running from the riches. He was curious indeed, but curiosity wouldn't feed him, unfortunately.

The street rat kept his prance up, all too happy about the deed being done until he noticed another traveler coming down the road. Guessing the royals of Valacore were still looking for Alyssa, he made a quick dash for the bushes and hid. He crouched low, watching the figure as it walked down the road, going in the opposite direction. Such a strange traveler. He had shoulder-length black hair and was as pale as a ghost. The fact he wore a black robe in the middle of the heat amazed Dye even more.

The man stopped directly in front of where Dye had taken cover. His head turned, and like magic, his eyes met Dye's. Dye swallowed hard. The man's dark eyes had him frozen solid.

"I can smell you, boy. How do you think I tracked you this far?"

The words caused a lump in Dye's throat, and without hesitation, he took off into the woods behind him. He had no clue who this man was, but those dark eyes—they were enough to run from.

Dye tripped and fell, pushed and shoved his way past every tree and log he ran into. Finally, he hit a tree and stopped. His chest pounding, he used the tree to hold himself up. Dye looked over his shoulder, looking back down the trail of broken branches he had left. He knew the man couldn't have kept up. He couldn't even see him from where he had run.

"I have little time for your idle games."

A cry escaped Dye's mouth as he turned and found a hand wrapped around his throat. The man lifted Dye off the ground, attempting to choke the life from him. Dye fought the man, scratching and kicking, but nothing seemed to work. He looked down at those eyes and knew he was going to die.

"Tell me where you took the girl," the man growled. "Save me the trouble of tracking her, and I promise to kill you quickly."

Four days the two had traveled. Gabriel was slowly adjusting to

Grant and his silence. It was evident the young knight had something personal at stake, but Gabriel hadn't dug into the matter. The two had ridden all day, and the evening sun was now high above them. Gabriel had often requested a rest but never received a reply from Grant. He was always riding a bit ahead, never looking back at Gabriel. Gabriel couldn't even recall the last time he had seen the man drink anything, and he barely slept through the nights.

"Hey, pup, you okay?" Gabriel shouted ahead, noticing Grant's steed drifting some. "Hey, pup!"

Gabriel rode closer. Without warning, Grant toppled over, hitting the ground with a thud. Gabriel jumped from his horse, rushing over. He turned Grant onto his back and looked him over.

"By the gods, pup, you look half dead!" Gabriel wrapped his arms around Grant's waist and pulled him off the road and across the small field until he reached a tree.

Grant woke to the blue sky stretching out before him, his back against a lone tree. He was exhausted and could feel his hair sticking to his forehead. He brushed his hand through his hair.

"Wet?" Grant could barely keep his eyes open.

"Aye, I splashed you to wake you up." Gabriel came up from behind the tree, offering a jug of water. "You damn near rode yourself to death. You won't be finding any lost girls if you keep running yourself ragged, little pup."

"Don't call me that." Grant snatched the jug from Gabriel, taking a large drink, far too fast. Water shot from his mouth as he choked. Once he had calmed down and caught his breath, he looked up at Gabriel, who had perched himself on a log across from Grant. Between the two, Gabriel had set up a small area for a fire.

"What is this?"

"What's it look like, ya fool? It's for a fire." Gabriel shook his head, taking his dagger from his side. He stabbed it into the log next to him, so deep it stood up once he left it.

"No, we have to keep riding." Grant tried to lift himself up, but fell back down, spilling the jug of water. He couldn't slow down, every hour left resting was putting more distance between their goal. Alyssa wasn't getting any closer, only further away.

"Damn it, pup, stay the fuck down! You need to eat and drink, we can ride once you're more able." Gabriel stood, placing a foot on Grant so he fell back against the tree. "You couldn't sword fight a kitten if it attacked you in the sorry state you're in now, so sit down and drink your goddamned water. If you haven't spilled it all."

Gabriel grabbed the jug from the ground and gave Grant a sober glare before he walked off. A small creek flowed a few feet from the tree Gabriel had pulled Grant to. It would supply the two with water.

Despite Grant's objection, the two camped near the stream. Grant spent most of the day lying against the tree, his strength slowly coming back the longer he rested. He had watched Gabriel play with his daggers, cleaning and sharpening them throughout the day as if he had nothing better to do. On occasion, Grant had noticed a small locket around Gabriel's neck.

"What is that?" Grant asked, lifting his tired arm to point at the locket.

Gabriel looked down at it, then pulled it from his neck. He flipped it open, and for the first time since they had started their travel, Grant noticed a sincere expression on the man's face. Joy, followed by sadness. Why the mixed emotions?

Gabriel looked over, handing the locket to Grant. Once he opened it, he found a small, old painting of a young Gabriel near Grant's current age of twenty-five. Beside him, a beautiful woman held a small child.

"Your family?" Grant looked up and found Gabriel nodding his head as he sharpened his dagger once again.

"Aye... My wife and daughter." The memories seemed too much for Gabriel, and so Grant didn't ask any more questions. Instead, he handed the locket back and shifted some.

"They're beautiful," he said simply, knowing full well something horrible had happened to the two. Why else would Gabriel be out drinking and roaming the lands for gold instead of being with them?

"What about you, pup? Got any family or loved ones?"

Grant looked to his father's sword, Valor. "My adopted father. He took me in when I was just a toddler. I don't even remember my birth parents."

"That sword, he give it to you?"

Grant nodded, struggling to lean up and reach Valor. He pulled the blade from its sheath, revealing its crimson-red, glass-like edge.

"I always wanted to be like him, what I knew of him, anyway. He was always a mystery... When I was young, he would disappear for weeks and come back... colder. I wanted to be a knight like him. Everyone respects him, and always has, no matter what kingdom we've been in."

Grant pushed Valor back into its sheath and sighed, leaning back. He wondered if his father was alright.

"Any ladies in your life?" Gabriel gave a huge grin, slipping the locket back around his neck. "That head of blonde hair must drive those Valacore gals wild."

Grant managed a weak snort. "No, nothing like that. I did have a friend, though... She means a lot to me. We have to find her."

Grant almost looked sympathetic. "You get rested up, pup. We'll find her."

By the time the morning sun had risen, Gabriel and Grant were up and riding. Grant insisted he felt fine, and after a quick bath in the creek, he was ready to ride. They traveled several miles before Gabriel came to a stop, looking around the roadside.

"What is it?" Grant brought his horse back around and went over to Gabriel.

The tracker's eyes jolted left and right as if he were looking for some clue that was hiding among the trees. He dismounted and stepped over to some bushes beside the road. He rubbed a few leaves, smelled his fingers, and then walked into the woods. His body turned and shifted to check each tree and branch he passed.

"What is it?" Grant asked, scrambling to follow behind. "Is it her?"

"Maybe."

Gabriel kept his eyes on the ground until he spotted a drop of blood on one of the leaves. Gabriel lifted his head to find the blood leading them further. They followed the trail for a few feet, and then Gabriel placed a hand over his mouth.

"What is it?" Grant pushed Gabriel out of the way.

The trees were painted red, a boy's body hanging from the largest trunk. His hands were impaled to keep him hanging, and the skin from his neck down to his hips had been stripped clean from his body, revealing his muscles and organs. Grant took a step closer, his eyes trying to make sense of what had happened to the boy.

"This is him, the one that was traveling with her." Gabriel seemed sure of it, continuing his search of the area for more clues to sniff out.

He looked familiar...

"I know him..." Grant said slowly, the pieces clicking into

place. "Alyssa met him in Valacore once, a street rat."

Heart pounding in fear and hope, Grant took off in a mad dash, looking around the area for Alyssa. He prayed he wouldn't find her near, not if this had been done to her companion.

After the two found nothing, they met back at the dead boy. When Gabriel began searching the boy's pockets, Grant snapped, "Have some honor, Gabriel!"

"Oh, shut it, pup! I'm looking for clues and whatnot, ya fool." Gabriel pulled the small necklace from the dead boy's pocket and looked it over until Grant stole it away.

"This is Alyssa's! I bought it for her!" His heart skipped a beat.

"Well, not sure if that's a good sign for the little lady or not." Gabriel moved over, trying his luck at the next pocket.

"Who do you think could have done this to him?" Grant held the blue stone tightly in his hand.

"If I had to guess, bandits. But I've never seen bandits do this kinda handy work... Some sick bastard did this." Gabriel pulled a sack of gold coins from the second pocket and peeked inside. "Our boy here is packing some serious coin for someone you call a street rat."

"That means it wasn't a bandit."

Gabriel did his thing for a bit longer, searching the area for a direction. He couldn't find Alyssa's trail, but he found the path of whoever had killed the boy. He was headed east, toward the mountains.

"I recall there being a cave some bandits used to call home up near the mountains between Valacore and Mirelos. Could be where they're headed."

"Then that's where we go," Grant said grimly, determined now more than ever.

CHAPTER TWENTY-FIVE

B ooks had piled up along the table Kaiser most often used. He had found several ones that spoke of the Glas, but none of them had gone into any sort of depth. What books he could find about the Glas were often missing pages or were half-destroyed from the generations of priests trying to erase the Glas from existence. It was a shame, really.

Kaiser sat at his table, his cheek resting against his fist, propping his head up as he read. On occasion, he found pictures—pictures depicting men cutting themselves. The blood swirled and twisted around the drawn men like snakes. He traced the red snake with his finger in awe.

Kaiser shook the idea off, knowing nothing so magical could be real—but as Kaiser sat looking over the artwork within the book, his arms tingled. He could feel something under the skin of his arms. Alarmed, he grabbed at his arm, feeling like a creature had burrowed under his skin. He could feel it slithering under his hand.

Kaiser panicked, slamming the book shut and pushing himself up from the table. He stared down at his skin, waiting to see something, but nothing ever came.

"Kaiser?" Seeath stood in the doorway, a troubled look on his face. He looked at the books that had fallen to the floor from Kaiser's push. Seeath kneeled, picking the books up and returning them to the table. The books were old, and being too rough with them would undoubtedly cause them to be unreadable before too long.

Seeath looked down at the page, seeing the image Kaiser had found. "Do you know what it means?" the Phantom asked. "This image?"

Kaiser shook his head, finally pulling his attention from his arm to face Seeath.

"Blood manipulation. This is what the Glas were most known for. Not all, of course, could do it. But most." Seeath traced the image with his thumb. "I've seen it myself."

Kaiser blinked in shock. "You have? T—there are more like me?"

"More Glas? Yes, two more that I know of, but not like you. The Raven and the Beast. That's what they go by." Seeath pulled the neck of his shirt down to reveal a long scar that went from his shoulder across his collarbone.

"The Raven's given name is Laderic Velstavor. He gave me this scar the first time we met." Seeath chuckled, lifting his arm to reveal the fresh scar that crossed over the old one. "Would seem I have a scar from both my encounters with the Glas."

It was the scar Kaiser had given him.

Kaiser looked down. He remembered somethings from that night, the night he tried to save Nick from Seeath on the battle-field. He recalled the mud between his fingers and toes, the smell of the dead overtaking the field. He could remember clearly, the sounds of men crying, and flesh being cut through. He couldn't remember anything after Seeath drove him through.

"You should feel proud. These are the only scars I have in all my years as general, a testament to what you're capable of. This is why I brought you here, Kaiser... So, you can hone that potential, use it for a cause rather than for only yourself, as Laderic and his brother do. I hope you understand this... What I'm trying to do."

"I understand." Kaiser whispered. He did, to some extent. Seeath wanted a weapon, Kaiser was beginning to see what sort of weapon.

Often during his training, Kaiser glanced down at his arms, fear creeping into him. Such distractions had caused Seeath to get an easy hit, slamming his practice sword into Kaiser's skull.

"Pay attention!" Seeath barked while Kaiser held his hand to the wound. He could feel the blood, and so he kept his hand tight.

"I—I'm sorry..."

Seeath grunted, shaking his head as he turned his back to Kaiser.

"Don't apologize... Unless it's to your king, apologizing shows weakness, and you aren't to show such things to your enemy or anyone else." Seeath swung his sword in the air a few times.

When Kaiser brought his hand away, he looked down at the blood. He could feel it, as if it was burning lightly against his skin.

"Show weakness to anyone, friend or ally, and they will use it to destroy you," Seeath told him grimly.

Julius, who had apparently been watching from afar, pushed off the wall and fetched one of the practice swords from the wall.

"May I?" the prince asked, waiting for Seeath's approval.

Kaiser pulled himself to his feet, rubbing the knot on his head. When he noticed his new opponent, he began to worry. Would he be punished if he landed a hit on the young prince?

Julius stepped forward, his stance more suitable for fencing than the longsword practice Kaiser had been learning. The tip of Julius' sword hit Kaiser in the chest, causing him to take a step back. Before Kaiser could regain his focus, Julius started circling.

Kaiser tried his best to parry any small attacks Julius came at him with, but before too long, his back hit the castle wall behind him, and Julius' wooden blade came in with a quick thrust.

Kaiser quickly jumped to the side, his whole body struggling to avoid the attack. The sword hit the castle wall hard, and Kaiser instinctively rolled forward, swinging his sword straight into Julius' gut. Julius fell back, his hands on his midsection.

In seconds, Kaiser and Seeath both rushed to the young prince. Two of the guards nearby also came to investigate, one even grabbed Kaiser by the shoulder and held him back.

To everyone's surprise, the young prince began laughing between coughs. With Seeath's assistance, the prince returned to his feet and smiled, patting Kaiser on the shoulder. "Those reflexes of yours, incredible! To dodge my attack and immediately counter. Seeath is correct in the potential he sees in you."

Kaiser all but blushed at the prince's compliment, relieved when the guard stepped away. The young prince was nothing like Devon Sull, who would have had him killed on the spot.

After the prince had calmed down and dusted himself off, Seeath gestured toward Kaiser. "Perhaps you two should spar more often. Julius is more within your skill range. It could be good for you both."

"I was going to suggest the same," the prince agreed. "Father would like that. If Kaiser does not mind, that is."

"I—I don't mind at all!" Kaiser said, finally beginning to feel more comfortable with Ragnovok.

After his training, Kaiser left the castle, returning to the field he had stumbled upon previously. He found a large rock, big enough for him to sit on and read. It was a calming place with a beautiful view of Castle Novok. The castle rested high above the kingdom, built into the side of the mountain.

Kaiser sat with his legs crossed, wondering how many people had fallen from the castle's high wall. Even from the courtyard where he trained every day, a person could see the kingdom from one side and the ocean over the cliff on the other side. It was more than Kaiser had ever seen in Sullvain.

Kaiser sighed, holding the book in his lap. Solitude had been something he had been given much of the last several months, like it or not. His time in the cell left him starving and nearly mad before Rageal helped him escape. Despite that forced lonesome- ness, he found peace in the fields, alone. He thought about his sis- ters—not their deaths, but before that. Alice, how he missed her. The only real family he had were those two. Despite having differ- ent mothers, their love never faltered.

Another topic Kaiser found himself thinking of in the field was his mother. He had never met her, but it was clear now she had been a Glas. Kaiser questioned why she had left, or if she had been killed.

One of the books he'd been reading told of the Glas extinction by unknown means. Years after the extinction, when the Glas be- gan to rise again, the Given Church formed parties of Hunters to seek out the remaining few. Maybe she had been fleeing from such hunters, leaving him with his father out of safety. Kaiser could ask himself a thousand questions, but none of the books he had access to could tell him what fate his mother had met.

As his mind wandered on about his past, Kaiser noticed some- thing from the corner of his eye. Half a mile or so from his rock perch was the forest edge, the vast woodland that divided Ragno- vok and Dreava, straddling the two kingdoms.

A figure with red hair stood near the trees, but the distance kept him from making out any details.

The sounds of horses pulled Kaiser's attention, and by the time he looked back, the figure had disappeared. It took him a moment to brush the person's appearance out of his thoughts, but he left his rock and went to investigate the sounds back in town.

Three knights rode through the center of town, and behind them, Magus was mounting his horse. Kaiser had only met him in passing, but Seeath had spoken highly of the man.

"Well, if it isn't the Glas, come to see me off?" Magus led his horse closer.

"You're leaving?"

"Yes, it would seem my words of wisdom are needed among one of the smaller villages, what with deserters running about... Nothing uncommon." Magus looked to his companions, who had already ridden ahead, then turned back to Kaiser.

"With any luck, you will have run off by the time I return... This kingdom is mine to look after, and I see no place for a creature such as you." Magus turned his back to Kaiser.

"Seeath doesn't think so..."

Magus twisted around, grabbing at Kaiser's neck and pushing him back until he hit the side of one of the village houses.

"Seeath is clouded by the power he has seen in others of your kind! You are a creature, a wild dog he hopes to train, but I would put you down and save everyone the trouble!"

Kaiser sank down. He hadn't been prepared for his words to cause such an outburst from Magus, who had always seemed calm and collected.

Magus brushed his hand through his hair, returning a strip of white hair to its original position among his head of brown. He took a deep breath and smiled as if he were sorry for the action.

"Run, little Glas, while you still have the chance." Magus

pulled himself up onto his horse and looked down.

In Ragnovok, Kaiser wasn't safe.

CHAPTER TWENTY-SIX

I t had been so long since Foster had taken the time to truly see the things around him. He had settled for growing old in his little house near the kingdom. He had even forgotten how heavy his sword was. Painting had always helped him to forget the hardship. How many times had he drawn that image? How many pictures littered his wall, all that same sun drawn on a different day?

It was moments like this, sitting outside the walls of Dreava, that Foster realized the sun he had drawn so many times looked just as beautiful here, peering out over the ocean. Foster sat atop some rocks, his view overlooking the cliffs along the coast. For miles out over the water, he could see icebergs as they flowed with the current. The bitter wind bit at the exposed skin on his face.

"Sir Foster, I've been looking for you all morning."

Oran stood behind the rocks, his eyes on the sunrise. As Oran silently peeked in at the art, Foster went on, his hands making small, precise strokes across the paper. Oran stepped back and took the moment of silence to explain his orders.

"How did the meeting with the court go?" Oran waited for a reply.

"There wasn't a meeting. The court, all three grounds, refused to see me." Foster said, shaking his head. He hadn't expected a meeting with the king, though that would have been ideal, but he expected more than he had been given.

"What? But Prince Harrion and Princess Dawn know you!"

Foster sighed. "It's probably for the best. The Dreava family has ties to Ragnovok. No matter how loose those ties may be, it's best we keep our full intentions hidden from those who may side with Ragnovok." Foster painted while he spoke.

Oran joined him near the cliffs. "What will we do then? How will we kill the Glas?"

"Before we left Sullvain, I received an unmarked letter, someone in Ragnovok claims they can help, someone I believe. Talking to the king has failed, now we see what this stranger knows." Foster put a few more touches on his picture, fixing the clouds.

"You're loyal to your king, Oran, a trait not found in many." Foster raised his hand, using his thumb to determine the best way to paint the large icebergs miles out at sea. "Loyalty is good. We need it to protect those we trust, but we must offer it only to those who deserve it. When I was young, I worked for the Given Church... The Glas were few, and the Church recruited mercenaries to hunt what remained of them. I was skilled, hotheaded, and ready to do anything for a few coins."

Oran smiled. "For some reason, I can't imagine you ever being hotheaded as a youth."

"Believe it or not." Foster paused and then told him, "The Given Church knew a single Glas was too much for a normal man so they would pair the hunters in twos. I remember the first day I met her, she was beautiful and by the gods, did she know how to fight! Better with a sword then I ever was."

Foster sighed, not used to sharing such happy memories. His eyes fixed on the ocean, but his mind wandered to images of her. He could recall her walking along the golden steps of Valacore, that mischievous grin.

"She's the one you spoke of back in Sullvain," Oran murmured. "The one you had to kill."

Foster looked away. "Yes, and the Church made damn sure I did it... All those years, I stayed loyal to them, as did she. It's impossible to spot a Glas from a normal man. It isn't until after they experience death that they show their true form. The Given Church call it Rebirth when a Glas dies and gains its full power. She was a hunter, my partner. We were after the Raven, long before he ever bore that name. He proved fiercer than we had expected and she was cut down, only to awaken as a Glas. Their bloodline lies dormant within them until they have their rebirth. She had no idea she was one of them."

It hurt Foster to think about her, brought up feelings he hadn't felt in years. She deserved a better fate than what she had been dealt.

It had become cramped and dull inside the tavern rooms, so Servis had taken to walking the kingdom. He had never been to any of the other kingdoms, and the beautiful white snow piled atop the black bricks of Castle Dreava did much to get his mind off the events unfolding in Sullvain. Their stay was friendly so far, but he was too wary to take his armor off.

During his walks, he often got strange looks, the people in Dreava not used to such a heavily armored man.

Oran had gone off to find Foster, and Servis had left the tavern to walk closer to the castle than usual. He had always heard rumors of the dragon bones inside, but knew he couldn't just step within the castle doors and look around. Servis stood in front of the magnificent castle, one of the largest in the lands, until he was spotted by a girl, one he assumed was the princess. She had a servant at her side.

"You must be one of Sir Foster's men," Princess Dawn Dreava said, giving a sweet smile as she approached.

"I travel with Foster, yes. I don't serve him." Servis crossed his arms, keeping a fair distance from the princess.

Dawn giggled, shaking her head. "I did not mean to imply anything... You seem like a strong-willed man. I doubt you kneel to anyone."

Her words were right to a point—Servis had served the Sull family, but very poorly. He could see she meant no harm and let his guard down.

"Your kingdom is beautiful," Servis said, lightening his tone, not wanting to be rude with her.

"Thank you, Sir...?"

"You may call me Servis... I prefer it over any title." Titles had never suited him.

Dawn gifted him with another one of her easy smiles. "Well, thank you, Servis. It is always an honor to hear outsiders speak highly of our kingdom. It seems too long ago we were credited with killing off the ever-majestic dragons."

Dawn's servant leaned in and whispered something in her ear.

Dawn looked at Servis. "If you are interested, I will show you around the castle some time. Most outsiders enjoy seeing the skulls, as depressing as they seem."

"I'd like that." Servis took Dawn's hand, giving her a kiss on the back. His polite kiss brought chaos, however, as Dawn's body jolted and seized before falling back into the snow.

"Go! Get help!" Servis shouted at the servant, who rushed off.

Dawn's eyes rolled back and turned utterly black before her body went limp. Shit.

The visions were becoming more of a curse than a blessing.

Dawn had never had one during the day, only in dreams—but she was now sure the visions meant something.

She woke up in her chamber, tucked in and safe. A small throb in the back of her head immediately made itself known. Likely from falling backward, she assumed.

Dawn brushed her brown hair from her face and yawned, looking to the window to see if it was dark yet. Instead, she found her brother, Harrion, fast asleep in a chair near the window. She smiled, knowing full well he must have been worried sick.

She pulled the blankets off, but before she could get out of the bed, Harrion stirred from his chair and took a knee next to the bed.

His hands grasped hers, and he shook his head, his eyes grave. "You nearly put me in an early grave."

Harrion had always been such a brave and able young man, hunting and serving in the kingdom's guard when able, but she saw the softer side he kept hidden.

"I'm fine."

"Was it another vision? I thought you only had them at night. Do you remember it?"

Dawn nodded, thinking back to Servis and the kiss he gave her on the hand. His touch must have triggered the vision.

"I saw our castle, the halls drenched in blood." Dawn rested her chin on the top of Harrion's head. "Outside our walls was an army led by a man in armor. The one-eyed lion stood in our halls, its mane covered in blood."

Servis' armor. She had seen him wearing it and knew it was the one from the vision. The one-eyed lion she had seen before in several dreams.

"What did they want? Why were they at our walls?" Justice, or maybe revenge?"

She wasn't sure all of them wanted revenge, but she felt the hatred and sorrow, just like her last vision.

"I came to see the young princess."

The two siblings turned to find Foster at the door. "Should I come back later?"

Harrion stood, shaking his head. "No, if she is ready for visitors, I will allow it."

Harrion leaned down, giving her a kiss on the head before exiting the room.

Once Harrion had left, Foster approached her. "Servis told me what happened. I trust you are all right? He was scared half to death."

"Tell him he need not worry, I am fine." Dawn looked up at Foster as he shuffled through his notebook, pulling out the sunrise he had painted earlier in the day. The art made her blush, and she sat it across her lap.

"How long have you had visions?"

The question caught Dawn off guard. Not many knew she had the visions. Dawn folded her hands in her lap and returned to the formal lady Foster had met the day he arrived.

"I do not believe that is any of your concern, Sir Foster." She whispered the warning, but Foster didn't leave.

"I know you don't completely trust me, Princess. A wise choice, as it seems most everyone is too trusting nowadays. But trust me or not, you will continue having the visions, I suspect. They'll get clearer with time, but will always remain a puzzle. I know a woman who stays within the Coast of Scales. If you wish to control your visions, seek her out."

"Wait... How do you know about the visions and the woman?" Dawn had planned to ignore him and handle the visions herself, but Foster seemed to know more than her.

"When I worked for the Given Church, we used many means to hunt down the Glas. A person who is born with visions—and is able to control them—can pinpoint a single person anywhere in the realm. When you need help, go see her."

With that, Foster bowed respectfully and left her alone. Dawn sighed, falling back into her bed.

Foster made it sound like the dreams could be solved, but she had no idea where to begin. The one-eyed lion had appeared the most, but its attention had never been on her, only elsewhere. She had no idea what to make of Servis, the man in his armor, at her castle gates with an army. If she were to put meaning to her visions, she feared his appearance meant he was a threat.

The glass man was the only one who approached her within the vision. She could still feel his cold touch on her hips even covered in her blankets. She took a deep breath, shaking off those thoughts.

Dawn sat back up in her bed and looked to her right, where a stack of books sat. Elder Hollen must have had them sent to her chamber. She gathered herself, determined to get the glass man out of her mind, and picked up one of the books. A small note attached from Hollen suggested the book she held was the best bet she had of finding answers on the glass man, despite its abundance of missing pages.

Dawn opened the book and whispered the first sentence out loud.

"Here follows the known history of the Glas."

CHAPTER TWENTY-SEVEN

Tracking the young street rat's killer had turned out easier than Grant and Gabriel could have imagined. Once they were within view of the mountains, Gabriel could almost smell the stench the bandits left behind, but something was amiss.

The two had left their horses behind, approaching the mountainside caves on foot so they could keep the element of surprise. Grant could barely see his hands in front of his face. All he could do was keep close to Gabriel, who seemed able to find his way in the dark.

Gabriel followed the small rocky trail up the side of the mountain, discovering a few entrances he passed. His senses lead them further and further.

The two finally ventured into the cave, Grant trying his best to stay close. Once the two were deep enough, Gabriel stopped, sniffing the air like a dog.

"What is it?" Grant asked.

"Blood... Lots of blood." Gabriel led Grant further into the darkness.

Aside from the sounds of their steps, Grant found the sounds of dripping water the eeriest of all. Puddles splashed around their feet, and with each step forward, the water rose until Grant found himself knee-deep in water.

After a few more steps, Grant's boot became wedged between

two rocks, bringing Grant to a stop. He reached into the water and struggled with the stones until his foot was free. When he stood back up, he could no longer hear the sounds of Gabriel's footsteps ahead of him.

"Gab? Gabriel!" Grant's voice echoed through the darkness. His eyes narrowed, trying to see through the black and determine which direction he had been traveling to begin with. Confident in his decision, he pushed on, his hands waving blindly in front of him to keep from colliding with the cave walls.

For what seemed like hours, he sloshed around in the water, becoming desperate to find an exit or Gabriel.

Then, like a blessing, Grant found the end of the water, finally pulling himself onto some dry patch of dirt. He sat for a moment, resting against the wall while he gathered himself. *If only I had some sort of light*, he thought.

While taking his breather, he heard a sound bounce about the cave walls up ahead. Assuming it was Gabriel, Grant picked himself up and moved on, finally seeing a light flicker in the distance of the narrow cave walls.

Grant came to a small opening. The path had taken him to a large, well-lit room. His eyes struggled to adjust to the light, but when he could finally see, he laid eyes upon a massacre. A dozen or more bodies were scattered about the room's interior, and the pleas of a single survivor came from the far corner.

Grant jumped from the small hole and entered the room, creeping his way toward the pleas. He found a large man in a black robe cornering the last bandit.

"Please! Please! I've told you all I know!" the rough-looking bandit cried out, his hands together in a praying position, but the man seemed to be unaffected by the gesture. "Mirelos, go to Mirelos!"

Suddenly, the man turned his head, two glowing eyes peering at Grant. Now that he had been found, Grant stepped out of the shadows.

"Did you do this?" Grant demanded, his right hand gripping Valor's hilt. "Did you kill all of these men?"

The robed man turned to face Grant, his focus now completely off the bandit. With each step the man took toward Grant, he shifted, finally pulling his robe from his shoulders. The man's hair was as black as night and his eyes glowed with a dark swirl of purple.

This was no ordinary man.

He tried to move, but before Grant could get Valor from its sheath, the man had his hand wrapped around Grant's throat. As his feet left the ground, all the air rushed from his lungs. He let go of the sword handle and used both hands to try to pry the attacker's fingers off his throat.

"A feisty one, you are..." The man's grip tightened, and Grant struggled for air.

Then a loud thud came from behind the man, and he released Grant, moving toward the entrance of the room.

After Grant took in a few deep breaths, struggling for air, he looked up and found a dagger in the man's back, right above his shoulder blade. Gabriel stood near the entrance, another dagger ready to be thrown.

"You okay, pup?"

Grant tried to reply, but his voice was hoarse and broken from the recent struggle. The man disappeared in a dark cloud of smoke and quickly reappeared behind Gabriel. His senses kicked in, and Gabriel rolled forward, barely avoiding the man's large hands. Gabriel and Grant now stood side by side, Valor drawn and ready. The bandit took his chance, dashing out the door.

"Gabriel, stop him! He may know where Alyssa is!"

"You sure you can handle this... thing? By yourself?" Gabriel looked over, clearly worried.

"I'm fine, go! Now!"

Gabriel dashed forward, exiting out of the room after the bandit. Now only Grant and the strange man remained.

"What are you?" Grant held his sword ready, the two beginning a small circle around the room. He had never seen anyone capable of the speed and movement this man showed.

A sinister smile formed under his black bangs. "I am the Beast."

"Wait, you're a Glas?" Grant hadn't expected that. "Where is Alyssa?"

The Beast rushed forward, disappearing right before Grant's eyes. For a solid minute, Grant was alone, his eyes darting around the room, waiting for an attack. Though his heart pounded against his chest, his hand was steady and sure.

Without a sound, Draston appeared behind him, lunging forward. Grant spun to the side just in time, swinging Valor with such precision that the blade ran directly into Draston's arm, leaving a gash running up his forearm. The Beast let out a roar, his massive build fumbling away toward the wall, where he stopped to rest.

"How?" Draston growled, slamming his fist into the wall. When he finally turned back to Grant, he stepped to the side, picking up a massive battle-ax that had fallen from one of the dead bandits.

"Where is Alyssa? Tell me!" Grant's bark was just as loud as the beast's roar had been, his body shifting to regain its stance after his counter.

"The marked one? The bandit told me where, but you'll not live long enough to worry about such things. Wait, you must be the little knight the Church sent for... and that sword." Draston's face lit up with surprise at the sight of Valor. "You're far too young to be the Dark Stalker, boy. Who are you?"

"Grant Dalfair... Dark Stalker?" Grant had heard the name before somewhere, but it was long ago. He looked down at the red blade his father had given him. "Father?"

It all fell into place. It was Foster that Grant had heard someone call the Dark Stalker years ago, but it had been so long ago, and Grant had been so young, he had never stopped to ask about it.

"Ah, then the Dark Stalker had a son... What a pleasure it will be to take you away from him."

The Beast began a quick step toward Grant, raising the battle-ax so high above his head, the blade screeched across the cave roof. When the blade came down, it carried such force that, even blocked, Grant was sent tumbling back, slamming against the rocky wall.

Draston didn't hesitate as he pulled back, swinging from the side. Grant quickly dropped down, the blade barely grazing the ends of his hair.

A knee came flying in, landing hard against Grant's cheek, bouncing his head off the cave wall in an explosion of pain. He fell to the side, trying to pull himself away from the Beast, but his eyes were blurred and a loud buzzing in his ears made even crawling difficult.

Draston laughed, watching Grant struggle to get away. "The legendary Dark Stalker's son... Who'd have thought he would die so easily?"

Draston reached down, his large hand grasping Grant's shoulder. With a hard jerk, Grant narrowly avoided being lifted, but Draston's second attempt couldn't be avoided, and Grant was pulled up to his knees. Draston slammed Grant's head against the cave wall again, and his body fell to the floor.

Nearly unconscious, Grant was lifted to his knees once more. Blood ran down his head from the cuts and scrapes, and a portion of the left side of his face was badly bruised. Valor remained in his grasp but only barely, its red glass blade out in front of him, its hilt swaying in his weak hands.

"A beautiful trinket for my queen," the Beast said. He pulled the ax back and, with a loud grunt, brought the blade full force at Grant's neck.

Grant pushed himself forward and twisted, letting the ax blade swing past him as he landed on his back. He brought Valor up with all the strength he could muster and cut through Draston's right hand, sending the ax flying to the side, his right hand still latched onto it.

"Ahh!" Draston took a step back, blood spraying about the ceiling and walls until he forced his hand over the wound. "You son of a bitch!"

With a snarl, Draston lurched toward Grant, but before he could reach him, a dagger punched through his chest. He let out a bear-like growl, ripped the dagger from his chest, and glared at Gabriel, who had reentered the room.

"I'll kill you, you bastard!" His purple eyes targeted Grant with a murderous stare, but he quickly retreated a few steps and disappeared into smoke.

"Gods be damned, pup, you nearly got yourself killed!" Gabriel pulled Grant up, resting him in his lap. He pushed Grant's hair from his face, trying to get a clear look of the bruising along the side of his face.

"Did you catch him? The bandit?" Grant wrenched in pain, his eyes remaining shut. "Alyssa?"

Gabriel looked down at Grant in shock. "Yeah, I caught him, made him spill the goods. She's in Mirelos, just a day's ride south..."

Gabriel wrestled to get Grant on his feet, wrapping his arm around his shoulder so he could help him walk. Grant's legs felt like they were on fire but he pushed forward, ready to reach Alyssa.

"Let's get you patched up first, pup. You're no good to the girl if you show up half-dead."

How foolish she had been, running around acting as if she could live freely outside of the castle walls. Her curiosity of the world had gotten her here, to a dark cellar room.

Alyssa tried to focus on the water droplets as they hit the stone floor—it was the only thing she could do to bear the cries around her.

The men Dye turned her over to had taken her to Mirelos, or so she guessed. She had seen a glimpse of the mountains as they rode in, and based on the tip she had gotten from the old man before, she was in the South. She had been sold into slavery—the Princess of Valacore, turned into a slave. She wanted to cry, but she didn't, holding her tears in.

Half a dozen young girls were scattered in the dark room, some younger than Alyssa, some older. Their cries and whimpers were enough to break Alyssa's heart.

The small girl next to her looked to be no older than ten.

"What is your name?" Alyssa whispered, looking over at the girl. At first, the girl didn't respond, her eyes red from crying and her knees pulled tightly to her chest.

"Helen, w—where are we?"

"I...do not know." Alyssa sighed, looking up at the ceiling. In some spots, the light from above could be seen, but no sounds came down to them, just shadows moving above.

Alyssa felt a touch at her side and looked. Helen held her hand out, and Alyssa took it, holding it gently.

"It will be okay, I promise."

The girls near the door began scratching and pulling, trying their best to break it open, but the iron bolts holding the wooden door in place proved to be stronger than any of the children. The sounds of their struggle were loud enough to drown out the sound of the approaching footsteps.

When the door swung open, the girls scattered, each rushing to different corners of the room like wild animals hiding from a predator.

Two men entered the room, followed by an older lady. Her sunken eyes and wrinkled face gave Alyssa chills. She had the look of a cruel and unforgiving mother.

"All of you against the wall," one of the men commanded, gesturing.

No one moved.

"Now!" the old lady shouted, and like magic, all the girls

whimpered and fled to the wall, lining against it.

Alyssa and Helen stood side by side as the old lady started at the right of the room. Her crooked fingers touched the first girl's cheeks and chin. She was examining each of them, and when she found a flaw or imperfection, she shook her head and moved to the next.

Alyssa wasn't sure if being found unwanted by the lady was good or bad, but the closer she got, the harder Alyssa's heart pounded.

Helen let out a small cry when the lady touched her, those fingers holding the poor child's chin hard so she didn't squirm. The old lady took her time, but finally shook her head, shifting over to Alyssa. Once more, the lady used her fingers to poke and check. Alyssa closed her eyes tight, feeling the old finger run over her nose. Her eyes remained closed even after the finger left, and then she felt the old lady lift her sleeves. The old lady revealed the markings along Alyssa's arm and pulled at the sleeve to look further.

"What are these? Speak, girl!"

Despite the old lady's commands, Alyssa remained silent and scared. The lady pulled at Alyssa's shirt once more, peeking down her neck at the markings. She nodded her head and left Alyssa alone, moving on to the next girl.

After the lady had looked over each of the girls, she stepped back as the two men grabbed Alyssa and three other girls the lady had chosen. As the men pulled the girls to the door, Alyssa twisted in a desperate attempt to look back at Helen.

"It's okay!" Alyssa could see Helen crying as the door shut. And then she was pulled up the stairs and sat at a table.

"Clean these four up and keep them upstairs until we can sell them... Take the others across town and sell them for whatever you can get for them."

She was to be sold alongside the other three, but Helen would be taken elsewhere. She had lied. Alyssa told the girl she would be okay, but Alyssa realized she couldn't protect anyone.

She was a victim herself.

CHAPTER TWENTY-EIGHT

K aiser watched as a small trail of red ran down his palm, its direction shifting and flowing down the easiest path. He had read so much about his kind, yet he had no idea how to control the power he knew he had inside him. His eyes focused on the blood, trying to alter its path, but once it reached the edge of his hand, it ran off.

He had spent the better half of the day sitting in the field atop his rock. His training with Seeath had bruised his body, but each morning, his training wounds were gone entirely—another Glas trait. Unlike his bruises, the small cuts he had poked into his index finger would often heal within the hour.

He had learned this throughout the day, poking and trying his best to change the course of blood against its will, always resulting in failure.

Kaiser sighed, tossing himself back, so he laid out on the rock. He knew he could go no further than the fields, that he was still a prisoner, just of a different king—but with the wind blowing through his hair and his eyes closed, he finally felt free. Kaiser let out a quiet sigh and looked up at the clouds. As he reached out his hand toward them, a small drop of his blood slipped from his palm and landed on his cheek. He wondered if he could have saved his sisters somehow if he were stronger.

He sighed and mumbled, "And when the dragon woke, he

asked them to be fed; but when no one would feed him, he fed on them instead."

"What are you daydreaming about?" Seeath's voice came from behind Kaiser, snapping him out of his thoughts.

Kaiser closed his eyes, his hand no longer reaching for the clouds, just reaching. "The past."

"You should never dream of the past. Nothing to be gained from it but regret." Seeath had gotten closer, and Kaiser rolled to his side and sat up, looking at Seeath. He had brought two horses with him.

"Do you know how to ride?" Seeath asked.

"No."

"Let's go." Seeath jerked his head toward the horses.

After Kaiser had finally gotten onto his horse, Seeath led him out of the fields, toward the forest. Kaiser had only seen it from his rock but had painted a visual image of what he believed it looked like inside. His struggle to stay on his steed took away some of his excitement, though. When the two reached the forest, Kaiser finally got settled.

"Why are we here?"

"Deserters... When the king declared war against Sullvain, we had many men flee. The cowards hid in the forest between Ragno-vok and Dreava." Kaiser could tell by Seeath's tone that he was sickened by men who ran from war. Kaiser didn't blame them, though—if he thought he could have made it, he would have taken his sisters and fled.

"Normally, we have a few patrols scout the forest edge, but I thought maybe you could use the air." Seeath looked back at Kaiser, who had slid sideways on his horse, fighting to get back on his saddle. "It wouldn't hurt you to get some practice riding in either. Come on!"

Seeath kicked at his steed and took off through the woods, leaving Kaiser behind.

"Sir Reinhart! W—wait!" Kaiser's horse tried to follow, its sudden jolt of speed sending Kaiser falling to the ground. He lay flat on his back for a moment, the pain from the fall subsiding. When he had made it to his feet, Kaiser looked around, his horse now out of sight through the trees.

Kaiser sighed, having no idea which way he had come from. He began walking, hopeful he would run into Seeath or the tree line one. As he pushed through the brush, he heard something from afar.

"Sir Reinhart?" Kaiser whispered, worried he would run up on deserters. Before he could ask once more, something tackled him from behind. Kaiser tumbled through the dirt until he hit a tree. Once he had regained his sight, he looked around for whoever had attacked him.

A few feet away, a girl was crouched low to the ground like some sort of wild cat, a jagged rock in hand.

"C—calm down." Kaiser raised his hands, trying to show her he was no threat, but the girl just hissed at him. Her hair was fire-red, and she had yellow eyes. Kaiser noticed the twigs and branches scattered in her hair, the rough scratches and dirt on her cheeks. She was no deserter—she was a wild beast, and her eyes were unyielding.

She inched back, waiting for an attack, but when she realized Kaiser was no threat, she rushed away into the trees. Kaiser reached out his hand to stop her but gave up, just relieved she hadn't killed him.

"Well, this isn't the wild one we were after, but he does look like a royal."

Kaiser looked toward the voice. Three men stepped from deeper in the forest. He shook his head, wondering where all his luck had gone.

"I'm not a royal, I came from Ragno—"

One of the men pulled Kaiser from the ground and punched him hard. "Shut your mouth. Royal or not, you have a family. You're worth a ransom to someone."

The men nodded in agreement.

Kaiser smiled, finding it near hilarious how wrong they were. As if anyone aside from his captors cared about him.

"What are you smiling about, boy? Think this is a joke?" The man pushed him against a tree. Kaiser could smell his breath as he got in his face. "Well, boy, gonna tell us what's so funny?"

"I'm not worth much." Kaiser laughed, shaking his head. He wasn't sure if it was his lost hope from earlier in the day or just a mental break, but he just laughed.

When the man turned to give his friends a puzzled look,

Kaiser struck, headbutting the man in the jaw. The strike gave him a second to move, and Kaiser slipped out of the man's grasp, making a dash to escape. Despite his head start, Kaiser tripped, slamming face-first into the ground.

He covered the back of his head with his hands, ready to be beaten for his attempt. He heard the men behind him, but nothing came. Once the sounds of ruffling and grunts stopped, Kaiser opened his eyes, afraid to turn around. He jumped when he felt something touch his leg, but calmed when it wasn't a strike or kick, just a touch.

Kaiser built up his courage and flipped over onto his back. A set of bright yellow eyes hovered right above him. The wild girl had climbed on top of him, and now that Kaiser was flipped, the two lay face to face. Kaiser, finally pulling his focus from her eyes, noticed she had blood around her mouth, trailing down her neck and the rags that covered her breasts.

She moved closer, her whole body pressed down on Kaiser's as she sniffed the small wound on Kaiser's forehead from his failed escape attempt. Like an animal trying to heal its wounds, the girl licked Kaiser's forehead, then pulled back as if surprised by the taste. Once the shock wore off her face, she leaned in again. Her cheek touched his, and when she pulled away, she left blood on Kaiser's cheek. She slowly backed away from him, giving him room to sit up.

"W—what's your name? Mine's Kaiser," Kaiser tried, but the girl just tilted her head. Before Kaiser could get to his feet, the girl leaped into the woods. Again, she was gone.

Kaiser looked toward the three men who had attacked him, his eyes wide. Each of them was dead now, their throats bitten into and ripped apart. Kaiser looked back at the girl, but she had disappeared. He was thankful she hadn't done the same to him.

Gathering himself for the trip back to Ragnovok proved harder than expected. With his horse missing and Seeath nowhere to be found, Kaiser was unsure if he was even walking in the right direction. The forest was thick with trees, and he imagined Seeath was looking for him at that very moment, somewhere across the trees. Kaiser trudged on.

For the first time in his life, he was happy to finally see a castle in the distance. He had finally made it back to the tree line, cleaning the branches off his shoulders and from his hair.

Once he was back at the castle, he learned that Seeath was still out in the forest. Kaiser wondered if maybe Seeath would be upset with him for getting separated, but after finally sitting down, he realized he was too tired to care. The halls of the castle were cluttered with guards and maids running their errands, and Kaiser slipped out into the courtyard to avoid crashing into anyone.

The sun was beating down hard, and Kaiser was exhausted, so he walked across the courtyard. During training, he had often noticed the small, tower-like room attached to the castle wall. It sat across from the courtyard, away from the castle, and he couldn't think of a time he had ever seen anyone enter it, so he decided to explore. The room was refreshing in comparison to outside, and Kaiser found himself fighting through cobwebs and dust when he opened the doorway.

Every room in the castle had candles and every hour of every day they were lit, but Kaiser found no light inside the room, only rays coming from the single window. The view was a beautiful one, looking over half of the town down the hill and then the cliffs and ocean.

Kaiser raised his hand, drawing the G shape he had seen in more than one of the books Seeath had given him access to. Once the G was poorly drawn into the dust against the window, he looked to his right, lifting his shirt. He shared the same G shape, branded on his skin almost directly over his rib cage. His mind had wandered from Seeath and the red-haired girl in the forest to all he had learned about his people. Or what little he had heard.

Kaiser dropped his shirt when he heard the door creep open.

"Kaiser?" Prince Julius entered, having an equally hard time getting through the mess. He seemed just as amused by the secret room as Kaiser.

"I have not been in this room for some years now. It used to belong to Sir Reinhart when he was just a knight serving under General Croft."

The two looked around the room until Kaiser heard Julius give a small gasp. He was holding a short sword, its hilt littered with gems.

"General Croft gave this sword to Sir Reinhart when he be-came a knight... I'm surprised he left it here." Julius lifted the blade up to the light and its hilt shined a hundred different brilliant colors.

Kaiser glanced at the sword, then continued to scan the room. "Sir Reinhart has he always been so... cold?"

Kaiser kept looking about the room, leaving Julius to fiddle with the sword.

"Mostly. He was low-born, a blacksmith's son actually. I was not around to see him before he became a knight, but I often hear stories from Father and Magus."

"He was... low-born?" The idea of such a noble and legendary knight starting as nothing but a smith's son pique interest in Kaiser.

"Yes, Magus said Seeath would show up at the gates and watch the knights train. One day, Magus offered to let him come inside the gates and join in. Father says the two were like brothers, Magus and Seeath, always together. Magus is one of the most intelligent scholars in the realm, and Seeath one of the best warriors. I guess the two helped to complete what the other lacked. One acting as the book, the other the sword. They had balance."

Julius's story caused Kaiser to stop in his tracks. He touched his side, where the brand was.

"C—can I see it?" Julius asked, approaching with a shy blush on his face.

It took Kaiser a moment to decide if the young prince could be trusted or not, but he finally lifted the shirt up enough to reveal the brand. Kaiser felt strange, being looked over like some sort of object the prince found fascinating. Without commenting on the brand, the prince stood up straight and looked Kaiser in the eyes.

"Seeath is training you in the way of the sword. You have been training less than a month, and you have already proven yourself to me." Julius's chest rose; the prince was clearly serious about what he was saying. "I am no warrior, not like Seeath. I share more alike with Magus but you, you show promise with a sword. If you keep training, you could be a valuable swordsman."

Kaiser wasn't sure how to react as the prince held his hand out.

"I know you have been through a lot and have no reason to trust a royal, but you can trust me, Kaiser. I can help you become more than a victim. I can help you stand up."

Kaiser eyed him skeptically. "And what do you want in return?"

Because nothing was ever free.

Julius' stare was intense. "I want you to be my sword, like Seeath is to Magus."

CHAPTER TWENTY-NINE

The slumbering king remained in his bed, his chest slowly heaving. With each breath, it seemed he was losing ground. Harrion had stayed at his bedside through most of the ordeal, but his father was showing no signs of recovery, and so Harrion would go above the court's head. He would ride to the port of Isbal, a small village near Sullvain's coast, and there, he would purchase an herb he had been told of. The chances were low, but Harrion would ride across the realm if it held any possibilities of bringing his father's health back.

As Harrion sat at his father's side, Dawn joined him. The two exchanged a small smile as she approached, sitting on her heels and laying her head on Harrion's knee. The two siblings watched their father take his slow and raspy breaths.

"Will he get better?" Dawn asked, small tears forming in her icy-blue eyes. Harrion's hand began softly petting her head.

"I do not know." He sighed, knowing full well his father would die if he did nothing.

Harrion gently lifted his sister up so she was looking at him. "I need your help, sister."

Dawn's face twisted in concern. "Is something wrong?"

Harrion shook his head, comforting her with a smile. "I will be riding west tonight after the sun falls. I've asked the court for their help, but they denied me. I believe an herb from across the ocean can help our father, but... I have to ride to Isbal to obtain it."

Her eyes widened. "But if something happens to Father while you are gone... You should be here to take his place!"

"I am trying to make sure that doesn't happen."

Harrion had always been stubborn. Even when he came of age and the king had urged him to act kinglier, he rebelled. He wasn't a bad child, but a wild one, often running off during lectures to hunt or explore, leaving Dawn to listen to those long and boring lectures by herself.

"If you must go... Be careful, please?"

"Mine is but a few days ride west. It is you that must be careful. In my absence, the court may struggle for power over some decisions." Harrion looked to the door, uneasy that it was cracked and anyone passing by might hear his next words. "Dawn... I need you to keep an eye on Vale. I love him as my brother, but he has been acting strange lately. I caught him watching Father in his sleep, not with sadness or love... but anger. I cannot bring myself to believe he is capable of hurting our father, but be cautious."

Dawn looked shocked to hear such words.

Vale was their brother, even if they only shared one parent. Even if something were to happen to their father, the court would gain power if the next in line were unable to take the throne. From there, the court would decide between Dawn and Vale.

The two siblings continued watching their father, but outside the chamber door, a figure lurked just out of sight. Vale had heard

Harrion's words, heard them all. And now he would act accordingly.

Across the kingdom, Servis and Oran walked the walls of Dreava. Oran playfully kicked at the shards of ice, sending them bouncing along the black wall and into the ocean below. Dreava was an impressive kingdom, its castle and walls made of black bricks. Foster had mentioned a tale of how one of the kings had crafted the black bricks from the bones of dragons, but of all the tales, Oran didn't believe this one.

After walking the length of the wall, Servis stopped at the edge, his body leaning over to look down, almost as if he planned on jumping.

"Oran..."

"Brother?"

When Servis closed his eyes, Oran gently put his hand on his brother's shoulder, sensing his inner turmoil. When Servis opened his eyes, a sense of sadness had crept over Servis's features, one Oran had never seen before.

"What's wrong?" Oran asked, worried for his brother.

"After we help Foster find the Glas, I won't be going back to Sullvain. I can't serve that family, not anymore," Servis said bluntly. "I'll stay here in Dreava for a while, then maybe I will go somewhere north."

The news came as little shock to Oran, as he had often woken up expecting his brother to have run off.

He shook his head and joined Servis at the edge. "I don't blame you, but I'm not sure I can do the same."

The two shared a moment of silence and took in the realization that after this little quest, they might never see each other again. The wind rushed over the top of the wall, causing both brothers to shift away from the edge and move closer to the small fire that had been made for the wall's guards to get warm.

The wind came in with him, its frigid sharpness chasing Foster into the tavern. His men from Sullvain were still sitting around. The ones not drinking were playing betting games, trying to kill their idle time as best they could. Foster took a moment, watching the men. They were children, just like Oran and Servis, though Foster sensed more capability within Servis. None of the men before him fully grasped what was at stake, but he couldn't blame them. Not even the royals of Dreava could see it. The royals, all of them, had become soft in their years.

The war between Sullvain and Mirelos was the only chaos they had known, but Foster knew of the threat before that, one greater than war.

He brushed the snow from his shoulders and passed his men, taking his thoughts to his room. He recounted all the Glas he had killed over the years, and how they all seemed hell-bent on following in their ancestor's footsteps. This was the reason he couldn't bring himself to allow this one, Kaiser Noire, to live... All Glas had that hunger, that desire to dominate those weaker than them.

Even if the child didn't have that hunger now, in time, he would.

Foster stopped just short of opening the door to his room, sensing something amiss. As he reached for his sword, a voice spoke from within his room.

"Calm yourself."

Foster kept his grip wrapped firmly around his sword's hilt as he entered. As predicted, Foster found the man he had been waiting on, the one he had told Oran about. A noble from Ragnovok.

The stranger had made himself at home, sitting comfortably in the chair next to Foster's bed, idly playing with one of Foster's paintbrushes.

"I have been to Dreava many times, but I do not think I will ever get used to this cold." He spun the brush around with his index finger, his eyes watching it with intent. "How do you fair within it? I imagine a man who settled in Valacore would be more accustomed to the warmth."

The questions went ignored as Foster stepped over to take the brush and return it to its rightful place among the others.

"Did you travel from Ragnovok just to ask about the weather in Valacore? Or would you rather explain why you contacted me?"

Foster had received the letter just days after Prince Devon's death, a letter offering aid to the Dark Stalker. Foster felt as though he had seen this man somewhere, maybe during his hunts in the years passed.

"Well, my dear Dark Stalker. It would seem we have a mutual enemy."

"Kaiser Noire?"

The stranger nodded, gesturing for Foster to close the door behind him, which he did. "General Reinhart brought the Glas home with him. He believes he can turn him into a loyal little soldier, but we both know that won't happen."

Foster crossed his arms. He was becoming interested in what the stranger had to say.

"I was young then, but I remember you. I remember the Dark Stalker. You and that girl, what was her name?"

"Why do you want him dead?" Foster was uninterested in hearing stories of the past.

"Despite what you may think of my being here, I am loyal to my king and to Seeath. This boy will bring about their downfall. I've seen what the Raven has done. I've read libraries full of stories and know how dangerous they are. I also know we have no recorded way of killing one... It has all been guesswork up till now. I hear the Dark Stalker may know how."

In his prime, Foster had slain more Glas than any other, but he'd had the Church's support and far more manpower. The men he had now were children, unprepared to face a Glas, even a recently emerged one.

Foster cocked an eyebrow. "You want me to kill the Glas for you, so you can keep your hands clean?"

The man shrugged. "If I killed him myself, then I would lose my place within Ragnovok."

Foster shook his head, giving a comical laugh. "You are a strange man."

The two looked at each other, both agreeing on one thing. Foster looked down at the painting he had finished, the sunset over the icy ocean of Dreava.

"I won't risk the lives of these men. They are just tools King Sull would use to get his revenge... I will kill the Glas myself." He looked at the stranger, who had an uncontrollable grin on his face. "Can you get the Glas out of the kingdom and into the open?"

The strange nodded once, as if sealing the deal. "I can do that."

CHAPTER THIRTY

Despite his wounds, Grant and Gabriel had made it to the outskirts of Mirelos in good time. The beaten and sore Grant rode at a steady pace, unable to ride as hard as he would have liked. His swollen face had healed some, leaving just a black eye and a few cuts at the corner of his brow.

"Look at it this way, pup. Girls love a man with scars," Gabriel joked, trying to lighten the mood as they finally glimpsed Mirelos in the distance.

The kingdom was a poorly placed one, its castle and surrounding kingdom all sitting in the middle of swampland. Multiple stone bridges led into Mirelos from all directions.

Grant had heard stories about the old war between Mirelos and Sullvain. Thousands of Sullvain men died from simply being unprepared for the swamp's harsh terrain. In the end, both kingdoms backed down, Sullvain realizing it would never be able to wage war on Mirelos land, and Mirelos simply had no reason to take the fight to Sullvain.

"What caused the war between Mirelos and Sullvain?" Grant rubbed his eye some and winced as pain ran up his side.

"Resources, like most wars, I suppose. We used to call it the Coin War... Mirelos doesn't give much thought to how dirty it is, with all the whores and mercenary work going on inside the kingdom. Hell, you can hardly call it a kingdom! The king doesn't even show his face no more."

Gabriel and Grant came to a long river and began riding downstream alongside it.

"Mirelos never had a big ol' army, but they had tons of gold, and so Sullvain thought it a good idea to branch out. Thought taking Mirelos would help them keep Ragnovok and Dreava down South."

As he went on, Gabriel pulled a small flask from his side and took a swig. Afterward, he reached it over to Grant, who shook his head. "It'll help with the pain, pup."

Grant finally took the flask. Its contents sent shivers up his spine and left a hot taste in his mouth.

"Did you fight in any of the wars?" Grant asked, handing the flask back.

"Gods, no! I'm a lover, not a fighter. I saw plenty of the troops, though. During the war, I was a young man, had me a small farm between the two kingdoms, so I'd see Sullvain men marching to and fro."

Grant thought of Gabriel as a young man and wondered exactly how old the man was. His graying hair gave off the impression he was aged, but he seemed as agile and capable as any young man.

"So... you were a farmer?" Grant chuckled, pressing his hand to his side when the laugh caused a bit of pain, but still, the smile remained.

"Oh, you find that funny, do ya? Not all of us are born with shiny golden hair and live in fancy houses in Valacore." Gabriel stuck his tongue out, taking another long drink of his flask. His words were true in a sense, and Grant realized how lucky he had been.

"Speaking of the past," Gabriel said, "you said you didn't know your parents... Do you think they're still out there?" The question was an odd one, one Grant didn't expect.

"No, I was young, but I remember them." Grant looked to the side, at the slow stream of clear water running next to them. "I cannot make out their faces. They're blurred. I do remember Foster on horseback, though. He took me because I was in some sort of danger. I've never asked him about what happened... I'm just grateful he took me in."

The two rode on, both in silence now. They had started with jokes and history, but now both of them thought of the past, the darker side of it. Gabriel took hold of the locket he had around his neck. He held it tightly and sighed.

"During the war, my farm was taken from me... Sullvain soldiers used it as a checkpoint on their travels to Mirelos." Gabriel let the locket go and instead acted as if he were adjusting his red scarf. "Wasn't long before the men started making themselves at home, so we had to flee... I was afraid of what they might try doin' to my wife or, gods forbid, my infant daughter. We found refuge at a small camp outside of a temple of the Given, north of Sullvain. I started hunting, learned a lot from some of the refugees, but while I was out on a hunt... the camp was burned to the ground, and everyone in it was killed."

Gabriel took a deep breath, his hand still holding onto his scarf. "I searched through what was left of our tent and found my wife's body... This scarf, her scarf, was the only thing of hers that survived the flames."

Gabriel reached his hand up and wiped the tears from his cheeks. When he opened his eyes, he found Grant's hand out-reached. Gabriel gave him a half-smile and handed him the flask.

Deep within Mirelos, the streets were alive with people from all over the realm. Men and women shouted and tossed coins at each other for various products.

Alyssa and the other girls who had been taken from the cellar were being led through the crowd, their hands tied tightly to-gether. Each girl was tied to the next by a rope that gave them just a foot or two of space to move. They stopped on the busy street as the two men leading them came to a halt.

Alyssa looked over all the objects for sale on the stall next to where they had stopped. Stone figures decorated the wooden stand, and next to that were hundreds of foreign coins, currencies from across the ocean that had little value on this side of the sea, more for decoration or collection.

Alyssa leaned in, her small hands struggling to pick one of the coins up while tied. The currency had the image of a serpent on it, its body wrapped around a mountain as its head opened as if to take in the shining sun above it. On the back side were two men who kneeled to a standing man in the center of the coin. The two kneeling men had their arms outstretched, but someone had carved into the coin, leaving cuts on their wrists.

"You don't look like someone who plans on buying my wares, girl," a dark-skinned woman said. Most of her figure remained hidden in the shade of the canopy, but Alyssa could see a set of beautiful eyes from under the cloth wrapped around her face. She had clothes unlike anything she had ever seen.

"I—I did not mean to—"

"Hush, girl, you're in no trouble." The woman reached her hand toward the coin, taking it from Alyssa so she could look over it. "Do you know where this coin comes from?"

Alyssa shook her head. She had read many books but never had she seen an image like the one on either side of the coin.

"Back before the Given God and his ways, there were many gods. This god is Malkar, the god of blood and eternity. His worshipers would give their lifeblood to him, and he would allow them to live forever. His Goddess, Kessa, would also drink the blood of her worshipers."

The woman grinned and offered the coin back to Alyssa. "Keep it. Across the sea, it's worth a trunk full of coins, but here it's just a trinket. No one in these kingdoms worships the old gods."

"Thank you." Alyssa tried to give the strange woman a smile but was quickly jerked forward, her body stumbling and knocking into the girl ahead of her. The two men had started moving again, dragging the girls with them.

Further down the street, they were led onto a small wooden stage. Alyssa looked down at the crowd, and her heart raced. Men and women shouted and roared, tossing hands up and pointing at the girls. Alyssa had feared this was her fate, to be sold off. Stories of Mirelos and its seedy happenings had reached Valacore, but she never thought to see them firsthand.

They were quickly joined by the old lady from the cellar. The woman grabbed Alyssa, pushing her forward so she stood out among the other girls.

"Clean and pure, this one is the steal of the batch!"

The crowd eyed Alyssa, and she grew sick as the old men in the back grinned and nodded while others began tossing their hands up and shouting offers.

"Two hundred and fifty silver!"

"Three hundred!"

The two men who cried out locked eyes, and without warning, they threw punches at each other like wild dogs fighting over the meat on a bone. While the two tried to kill each other, a third offer sounded.

"Six hundred!"

Alyssa and the entire crowd looked to the voice and found a woman. It was the exotic woman who had given Alyssa the coin.

"Sold for six hundred coins!"

The old woman had Alyssa removed from the stage, the two

men dragging her around to the back. They found the strange woman waiting with the bag of money.

"Your name, girl?" the woman asked, leading Alyssa into the back of a small wagon. The woman must have lived inside it—all her artifacts and coins were laid out inside. She offered her food and drink, and Alyssa took it in handfuls, completely forgetting the polite way to present herself while eating.

"Alyssa," she said, food still crammed in her mouth. She had barely eaten since Dye had left her, and her slender figure showed such.

While Alyssa continued, the woman reached out, lifting Alyssa's sleeve. She seemed amazed by the markings. It wasn't long before Alyssa pulled her arm away some.

"You are a rare find indeed, girl... Where do you come from?"

"Valacore."

The woman pondered what she had seen. The markings seemed to amaze her, but she also seemed quite familiar with them.

She shifted, getting closer to Alyssa. "I will take you home, to Valacore."

The offer stunned Alyssa, leaving her with her mouth wide open.

"B—but why? Why would you do that for me?"

"Because there are powers beyond us at work here, girl, and I can see them." The woman pointed to her right eye and smiled. "You are more than a princess, and you are certainly no slave."

"H—how did you know I am a princess?"

The woman touched Alyssa's wrist, and Alyssa allowed her, realizing this woman knew something about her markings.

The sun had set, making their search for Alyssa that much harder. Grant and Gabriel had made it to Mirelos, but the city had died down, and barely anyone walked the streets. The heavy rain had caused the shops and traders to close up early, and only the two men stood among the muddy streets.

"I say we wait and ask around in the morning." Gabriel tied their horses next to one of many taverns in Mirelos.

"No, you go ask around inside, and I'll look around out here." Grant gestured toward the door, and Gabriel had no objections. "And, Gabriel... try not to get drunk."

"If they got cold ale and half-naked women in there, no promises, pup." Gabriel gave a playful wink and disappeared into the tavern.

The rain was beginning to pick up, and so Grant moved quickly, his hood fashioned tightly around his face. He was a stranger in Mirelos, but he ran about the streets as if he knew where he was going. His opinion of Mirelos grew darker and darker with each house. Homeless beggars and whores hung around each corner.

Grant shook his head, gently pushing past one of the beggars before he found the wooden stage in the center of the market area. He had no real way of knowing, but something in his gut told him she had been here, and so he stopped, turning and spinning, trying to look for any sign of where she might be. He was desperate and afraid she had come and gone from here.

Finally, he stopped. Across the street from him, he saw a wagon. The owners were loading their stocks, and sitting under the wagon's canopy was a small girl.

"Alyssa...?" Grant took a step closer, and with each new step, the weight of the world lifted. He knew it was her. "Alyssa!"

She heard her name and looked forward, shocked and confused, but soon she recognized the voice and stood from the crate she sat on.

"Grant?"

She saw him, rushing toward her in the rain, and she ran to meet him.

Without words, the two collided and Alyssa wrapped her arms around him. Tears poured down her face, hidden by the rain. Grant clutched onto her, a profound sense of relief coursing through him. Part of him had feared he'd never see her again...

"I am so sorry, I never should have left!" Alyssa cried, her voice barely audible and muffled by Grant's chest.

He shook his head and pulled her in tighter. "All that matters is that you're all right."

Grant pulled away, his hands grabbing her shoulders to hold her still, allowing him to look her over. "Are you okay?"

Alyssa nodded, unable to stop her smile.

The two headed back down the street, leaving the wagon. The odd woman didn't stop the two. She just shook her head, and pointed to her eye again, aware of the path Alyssa had taken.

Alyssa went on about her journey, talking about Dye and the bandits, how they took her and brought her to Mirelos.

She licked her lips. "Father Adan... he told my father that I needed to be killed, that's why I ran."

Grant stopped dead in his tracks, looking down at Alyssa. "What? Why would he say such a thing?"

Grant looked up and found Gabriel standing in front of the tavern. He looked from him to Alyssa, a smile on his face.

"I found her, Gabriel."

"Aye... that you did."

Gabriel seemed off—the upbeat drunk Grant had come to admire was gone and the man standing before him in the rain was someone else.

"What's wrong?"

Gabriel shook his head, his right hand pulling one of his many daggers from his belt.

"Gabriel...?" Grant lifted his arm, pushing Alyssa behind him. "What are you doing?"

Lightning lit the sky above them, and Grant got a clear view of Gabriel's face, sadness and pain etched on his features.

"The Church played you, pup. They knew you wanted to be the hero, just like your father. They used you. They had you be my muscle while I tracked her... and now I'm going to do what they

paid me to do." He stepped forward, and Grant instantly unsheathed his sword.

"Don't do this, Gabriel... She's just a child. Why would you kill
a child for the Church?"

The sky lit up again, giving Gabriel the opening he needed.
Grant had no chance to stop him.

The nimble tracker closed the gap between them within seconds, and sharp pain ripped into Grant's side. Once Grant had
processed what had happened, Gabriel stood next to him.

"Don't fight me, pup. Please," Gabriel whispered in Grant's ear
before he removed the dagger from Grant's side. A direct kick to
Grant's chest sent him falling to his back.

Alyssa screamed. Even with the pain shooting through his
ribs, he could tell Gabriel had purposely missed any vital organs.
He didn't want to kill Grant.

Now that Grant was out of the way, Gabriel set his eyes on
Alyssa. The young girl backed up slowly, eventually hitting the
side of a building. She was cornered, her only hope lying on the
ground. Grant struggled to get up.

"I'm truly sorry for this... If there was another way."

"Gabriel!" Grant rose to his knees. Using Valor, he pulled himself up. "Leave her alone!"

Gabriel shook his head, stepping over to deliver a powerful
kick to Grant's chest, which sent him back into the mud.

"Godsdamn it! I don't want to hurt you, pup!" Gabriel cried
out.

Alyssa gasped as he approached her slowly, his fingers pulling his last dagger from his belt. His hand grabbed hold of her shoulder to keep her still. She grabbed onto his scarf, trying to push him back.

Grant managed to get to his feet, gripping Valor tightly.

"Forgive me, Tes—" As Valor ripped through Gabriel's guts, his eyes widened, and his words were silenced. With a sudden cough, blood shot out and across Alyssa's face.

Grant pulled the blade out and caught the man when his body fell limp.

Both men hit the mud. Alyssa stood a distance from the two, Gabriel's scarf still clenched tightly in her fist.

"Why?" Grant asked, his body adjusting to rest Gabriel in his lap. Gabriel had little time to live, blood trailing from the corners of his lips.

"The Church... They have something of mine... S— something I thought was gone."

Grant gritted his teeth. "We could have gotten it back together. I would have helped you!"

Grant began to cry, but he opened his eyes when he felt Gabriel's hand. Gabriel grabbed hold of Grant's head, pulling him down some. He coughed, trying to catch his breath to speak.

"K—keep being the knight, pup. Even the knight can take the king and end the game." Gabriel used the last of his strength to rip his locket from around his neck, pushing it hard into Grant's chest.

Grant closed his eyes as Gabriel took his last breath, his body finally giving in. Grant rested his head against his friend, his cries hidden in the sound of the falling rain.

On the outskirts of Mirelos, Grant said his goodbye to Gabriel. Although Alyssa didn't know the man, she could see how much he had meant to Grant. She placed her hand on Grant's shoulder. The two stood around a small pile of rocks, unmarked and forever forgotten by all but Grant and Alyssa. Grant's sadness was soon replaced by anger as he lifted up the locket.

"The Church and all its temples, even the Given God himself... I'll kill the—"

"Grant." Alyssa took his hand, pulling him back from the dark place his thoughts were heading.

The two couldn't return to Valacore, not knowing how the Given Church wanted Alyssa killed, so they went south.

There was only one man Grant could trust now, and last Grant had heard, he was in Dreava.

CHAPTER THIRTY-ONE

The sun had yet to glimpse over the mountains, and every-one in the kingdom slept. Foster was the only one astir, his arms crossed as he gazed out to the west. Somewhere beyond that horizon awaited his destiny, be it victory or death. He took a sharp breath, puffs of air forming from his mouth. He was old now, not like before, and he wondered if he could bring himself to kill another Glas. At his side, he had only two things—his long sword and a large flask of oils. If he could bring himself to do it, he would only have one chance.

Foster broke his stare from the horizon and turned to his steed, giving it a few pats along its side. His old bones were begin-ning to give him small aches from the cold in Dreava, a problem that would bother him no more.

"Are you leaving?" Oran asked, standing near the stable wall. "Alone?"

"I am." Foster pulled himself up onto his horse.

"You talk about how dangerous the Glas are... I can tell you don't want to do this."

"No, but I have little choice." Foster reached into his satchel and carefully removed his notebook. Flipping through the pages brought a warm smile. Dozens of sketches and drawings filled the book, it had been filled with good memories. Like all good things, he reached the end of the notebook and closed it again. "If I don't return within three days, you and your brother are to go back to Sullvain and report my failure."

He looked down at Oran and tossed him the notebook. "If you could find a way, get it to my son back in Valacore."

Oran returned to the tavern, where he found Servis sitting at a table alone. He had been drinking, something Oran had never known him to do. The two brothers didn't say anything as Oran took a seat across from him. Servis was hunched over, his head resting on his forearm as he looked sideways into the fireplace a few feet away. He seemed worn out. Lack of sleep, Oran thought.

"Did he leave by himself?" Servis didn't raise his head, just tilted it a bit so he could look over to his brother.

Oran nodded.

"Good," Servis mumbled, directing his eyes back to the fire. "I had no intention of dying for the Sull family."

"I'm used to you hating the Sull family, but what has Foster done to you? Why do you hate him so much?"

Oran respected Foster, even if he hadn't fully trusted him at first.

Instead of an answer, Servis shrugged, the glow of the fire highlighting his face.

"Foster isn't like the other royals..." Oran insisted. "He's not going after that Glas for King Sull, he's doing it because he realizes how many people could die if he just stands by and does nothing." Oran pushed his chair back, his emotions rattled. "You could learn something from him. You talk about how cruel the royals are, why don't you try doing something and helping someone instead of whining about how much you hate it!"

Oran turned, storming up the stairs to his room.

"Oran..." Servis buried his face into his arm, rubbing the drunkenness from his eyes. He wanted to go after his brother, but he couldn't bring himself to do it. He knew Oran was right.

Foster wasn't the only one to ride out of Dreava before the sun rose. Dawn had seen her brother off just hours before. She stood near her window, dried tears on her cheeks. She felt childish—crying was unlike her.

A cold breeze rushed into her room, causing her to tighten the fur collar of her robe. It didn't take long for her to realize where the wind had come from and she turned. Vale stood near the door, his hands still holding to the doorknob.

"What is wrong, dear sister?" Vale tilted his head as if he was worried, but Dawn could hear the mockery in his voice.

"Nothing," Dawn said in a cold tone, her glowing blue eyes looking to his hands, tucked behind his back. "What is it? Why have you come to my chamber?"

"It's Father."

A jolt of alarm shooting through her, Dawn gasped, quickly running for the door to check on her father, but Vale stood firmly in place. His hands finally revealed themselves, a pillow gripped within his fingers.

"He passed just minutes ago."

Dawn's legs abandoned her, and she fell, her palms hitting the stone floor. As she wept, Vale pushed the chamber doors shut and moved closer. Dawn's cries became growls as her teeth clenched, and her head jerked up. He had killed their father, she was certain.

"You killed him!" She stood, running at him. Vale's hands were quick enough to grab both of her wrists and hold her still in her rage. "You're a monster! A bastard!"

"There we go, tell me how you truly feel about me."

His mockery enraged her more. Yet despite her struggle, she soon found herself pushed back, her head smashing against the window. She let out a small whimper as the glass behind her cracked and blood ran down the back of her head.

"He was our father!"

"He was your father, not mine! I was a bastard he had too much heart to cast into the streets!" Vale wrapped his fingers around her small neck, squeezing hard enough to cause her to lift up onto her toes.

"L—let... go..." Dawn's fingers fought at his hand, desperately trying to free herself so she could breathe.

Vale finally let go, allowing her to slide down the wall, onto the floor. "Harrion isn't around to protect you anymore, and soon, I'll be sitting on the throne."

"You think the court will just let you sit on the throne?" Dawn's words were hoarse between her gasps.

"I'll take care of the court. I've called for a meeting to discuss Harrion and his disappearance. My only problem now is you, and I would rather keep you around, dear sister." The doors to Dawn's chambers opened and two guards entered.

"Take her to the dungeon. Make sure none of the Elders know where she is until after the meeting."

Dawn struggled against the men, her legs kicking at them, but she was no match for them, and as commanded, the two guards rushed Dawn out of her chamber. The men seemed in a daze, carrying out Vale's will.

Under the keep, Dawn was thrown into a cell, her hands the only thing that stopped her from running into the wall.

When she turned, the guards marched off like mindless drones. They wouldn't willingly listen. She stepped over to the bars of the dungeon cell, looking around but finding herself alone.

She wanted to cry but fought it back. She wouldn't be weak, not in Harrion's absence. She had spent her life picking up the slack for Harrion—their lessons and teachings always fell on her, while Harrion ran off to play.

Now she would borrow that willpower her brother often had. She would stay strong and fight back.

After Vale was left alone, he raised his hand to the broken window, his finger running through the fresh blood. He pushed his fingers into his mouth and closed his eyes, sighing deeply as the bitter taste filled his mouth. His pleasure was interrupted when he felt eyes on him.

"You should have her killed," a voice from behind Vale commented. The man's face was hidden under a dark cloak lined with black feathers.

Vale smiled, welcoming the man. "She's my sister. I'll need her to keep the common folk's trust. I can kill the court and all its Elders, but I can't kill the entire kingdom."

"You could," the man replied, serious with his suggestion.

"Oh, Laderic, that's not how you rule a kingdom." Vale stopped, looking around curiously. "Where is your brother?"

"He was wounded by the Dark Stalker's son," Laderic said, showing a glimpse of a white mask hidden under his hood.

Vale was surprised. Since he had come into contact with the two Glas brothers, he had thought it impossible to harm them. It was just weeks ago that Laderic and Draston showed up in Dreava, feeding Vale promises of power. And more. He wasn't so naive as to accept such promises without knowing full well they would ask for something in return, and he had the feeling that was why Laderic stood before him.

"My queen sent Draston to find a girl, and he failed."

"But you thought ahead... Didn't you?" Vale was no fool—he knew how methodical Laderic was, even if they had only met a handful of times.

"The Dark Stalker's son is making his way here with the girl as we speak. He believes his father to be here. When they get here, you'll secure the girl for us. In return, my queen has promised to eradicate the Elders of the court for you."

"What about the Dark Stalker? He's riding west to kill the Kaiser boy; will you stop him?"

Laderic pulled the hood back, revealing his coal-black waves resting over the white mask with a single eye hole on the right.

"If Kaiser wants to be a predator like the Glas before him, he must prove himself able to survive. Only then will my queen take him in."

CHAPTER THIRTY-TWO

A lyssa's skin had grown numb. She wasn't used to the harsh winds of the South. She had never felt anything like it. Back home, in Valacore, she often read about the South more than any other place—its extinct dragons and ancient temples made it sound like a fanciful place full of imagination. She remembered reading about snow and dreaming to see it, but now that she had, she sure hadn't missed much.

She shivered, and Grant tightened his already tight hold on her hand. It was thrilling and concerning at the same time. He seemed so desperate to keep her close. He had given her most of his heavier clothing, including the red scarf her would-be killer had been wearing back in Mirelos.

She wanted badly to ask him who the man was; she knew little about the Church except it bore the actual blame for the man's death. All this seemed to change Grant. She could imagine what he was feeling. He had trusted them and been betrayed. She remembered the feeling well. Her own father had ordered her murder.

Right now, she missed the younger Grant. He was playful and kind, always protecting her—but now she found a serious man in his stead. Just his expression was proof enough, his chapped and freezing face unwavering, determined to make it to Dreava through the mountain of snow.

The two finally came to a stop, Alyssa's small frame bumping into Grant's backside when he broke his stride.

"W—what is it?" Alyssa asked, peeking around him.

They stood in front of a massive crevasse in the land, its depths traveling too far down to fathom. The Scar, a bottomless cliff that separated the North from the South. Only two bridges crossed the span. The first was north of Ragnovok, connecting and entering Sullvain territory, while the second joined Dreava and Mirelos.

"There." Grant pointed further up the cliffs at a wooden bridge. They pushed forward, quickly reaching it. At certain parts of the Scar, the gap could be up to a mile apart, but thankfully, Grant and Alyssa had found a relatively small fracture.

Grant moved ahead, his hands grabbing tightly onto the ropes as he placed a single foot on the wooden bridge. The sudden jar sent snow falling from the bridge, quickly disappearing into the darkness of the Scar.

"Traders who want to skip the trip to the major bridges and avoid the tolls build these makeshift crossings."

"Is it safe?" Alyssa rubbed her hands together over her mouth, trying to stay warm while Grant investigated.

"I believe so... We have little choice. We won't make it another night going east to the main bridge. If we cross here, we should make it to Dreava by sundown, which beats freezing to death."

"That it does."

She watched Grant venture forward. Once both feet had left

the snowy ground, he inched ever slowly toward the other side. Each step caused the planks to crack and scream as if in pain. The wind hit the bridge, causing it to drift dangerously to the right. Alyssa held her breath.

Once he had made it halfway across the bridge, he removed Valor from his side and tossed it ahead, onto the ground.

Alyssa watched on from behind, her hands firmly against her lips for warmth, and to hide her fear. She let out a thankful sigh when he placed his foot on the other cliff. She could barely see him through the snow, but she heard his voice shout for her and the figure of his arm waving.

She wasn't as fast to trust the bridge, her legs shaking beneath her. Her first step was quick, but the ones to follow were slow. She could feel the bridge swinging. Her weight wasn't enough to keep it as still as Grant had.

Alyssa closed her eyes in the hope that not seeing the drop below her would keep her moving, but even then, the wind and sounds of whining lumber under her feet reminded her.

When she opened her eyes, she could make out Grant, his hand gesturing for her to continue. After two more steps, she felt the wind hit the bridge, jerking it hard. Alyssa dropped to her knees and let out a whimper.

"Grant!" she cried in panic as she wrapped her arms around the rope next to her and tightly closed her eyes.

"Alyssa, you have to keep going. The wind is picking up!" Grant shouted, unable to help her from the side.

She nodded, pulling herself to her feet and taking another step, but the wind hit again, sending her falling flat. Her arms hit the wooden planks hard, and she felt her whole body shift and begin sliding.

One of the ropes had snapped further back, and now the bridge was hanging to one side. Alyssa grabbed hold of the ropes, using all her strength to hang on.

Grant reacted within seconds. He snatched Valor from the ground and shoved the crimson blade deep into the ground at the cliff's edge. He held onto its hilt with his left hand and reached his right out to Alyssa.

"Jump!"

Grant's fingers dangled just inches from Alyssa, and with a leap of faith, she released the ropes and reached for him. Her small body hit against the cliffs and went limp from the impact.

When Alyssa came to, she found herself gently swaying left and right. She could see small specks of blood hitting the snow right behind a set of boots. With every step the boots took, another few drops of blood followed as if chasing them. She shifted, looking about. She was hung over Grant's shoulders. His chest heaved as the snow fell around them.

"Grant."

When he heard her speak, he stopped, bending to allow her to get off his shoulders.

"Are you okay?" Grant reached his hand up, his fingers examining the small cut on Alyssa's head, hidden under her bangs.

"I'm fine. You're going to wear yourself out. You shouldn't have carried me."

"We need to keep moving, we won't last much longer out here."

Alyssa nodded, taking Grant's hand as he stood. The two went on, fighting through the winds.

The ground rode along the Scar, to the west. Harrion, with three of his men, had left Dreava in secret and would soon be in sight of the West Bridge. They were accustomed to the cold, and the Dreava steeds were the fastest in the South. Harrion and his men had stayed tucked close to the Scar, riding along the ledges.

On their right was the endless plummet into the Scar; on their left were jagged cliffs that dropped off into the forest that grew between Ragnovok and Dreava. They took the high path in hopes of avoiding any other travelers, a plan that had worked thus far.

As the West Bridge came into sight, Harrion heard one of the men cry out. The man had fallen from his horse and lay on the ground holding his arm. Harrion dismounted, rushing over to check on the man.

"Are you okay? Can you still ride?" As Harrion placed his hand on the man's shoulder, he suddenly felt a sharp pain in his side. He staggered back and grabbed his side where the pain had hit him.

Looking down, Harrion found his hands covered in blood and the glint of a silver dagger lodged into his side. The three men he had been riding with surrounded him, drawing their swords.

He had been betrayed by his own countrymen.

"Why are you doing this?" Harrion held his side, backing away from the three men until he felt the cliff edge crumble at his heel. The fall to the forest would be deadly, but the men approaching him were more so.

"Our king is dyin' and you royals would rather hide the fact from us than do something about it. The people are starving, we need a leader, not a dyin' old man. Vale promises us he'll help Dreava," one of the men said, looking shamed but determined in his actions.

"Aye, and the coin doesn't hurt." The man stepped closer, pulling his sword from his sheath. Before the blade was unsheathed entirely, Harrion leaped forward, painfully pulling the dagger from his side. He plunged it deep into the man's chest and grabbed his blade's hilt. With a kick, the man's body fell back, and his sword remained firmly in Harrion's grasp.

"Godsdamn it! Just kill him!"

The second man came at Harrion quick, his sword bringing more force than he could handle. The first two blocks sent him stumbling about until he was once again on the cliff's edge, but this time, his legs gave out, and he was sent tumbling off the jagged rocks, falling into the trees below in a wild whirl of colors and wind.

At the bottom, he hit the ground hard, all the air rushing from him. His body screamed in protest.

Harrion lay limp for a minute before he allowed his eyes to flicker open. The sounds of the wildlife around him stirred him, and he lifted himself up. He found a small fox several feet away, his nose sniffing the air. Harrion looked over his wounds, and finding no broken bones, he thanked the gods and pulled his beaten body to the nearest tree to rest.

The winter winds were gone due to the trees, but he would still have to worry about freezing to death come night.

For his first course of action, he ripped the sleeve from his coat and wrapped it tightly around his waist. The wound wasn't as deep as it could have been—another reason to thank the gods. He had gotten lucky more than once and didn't plan on pushing such luck. His thoughts fell on Dreava and what could be stirring there. Vale had betrayed him, something he had never considered. Harrion feared for his father and sister.

Once he had himself wrapped up, he stood, working the pain out of his legs. He would need to find shelter for the night. Even as warm as the forest was, the cold of night would take its toll.

CHAPTER THIRTY-THREE

K aiser yawned. The half-finished book sat before him, but he was far from interested in it. The last three books he had read about the Glas had turned up recycled folklore. He had learned nothing new. Every time he thought he was reading something new, he would find pages missing or images scribbled on.

The Glas had many enemies, that much Kaiser had learned, but he was beginning to realize one of those enemies went out of their way to try and erase the Glas from history. Kaiser had written all of the unanswered questions down as if someday he would meet the one person who could answer them.

He rubbed his eyes and looked over his list, generally asked questions any child would ask after hearing the bedtime stories.

One question stood out more than most, though—the kingdom... The Glas once had a kingdom. It was there they branched out and began conquering other kingdoms, but in all the books Kaiser had read, he couldn't find a location, not even a name.

Kaiser had less than three books left, and he had low expectations of finding anything of value in them. He had drained the Novok's library of any and all Glas knowledge and had learned very little. Who or what had killed the Glas remained a mystery, as did the whereabouts of the kingdom. Kaiser flipped the next page, knowing full well that reading on was a waste of time.

"The Raven," Kaiser whispered to himself.

He had heard Seeath and Magus speak of the Raven on numerous occasions, but had only learned the Raven was an enemy of every kingdom. The idea seemed fitting—the Glas had no allies, and now the last remaining Glas, the Raven, had no allies.

How Kaiser wished he could speak with the Raven. The information he must know. Kaiser knew little of his race, but the people he lived among knew even less now. The Raven was the only one who could teach him more, and Kaiser doubted he would ever get a chance to speak with him.

"You must be tired." Julius stood in the library doorway, sweaty and heaving.

Kaiser had taken the day off training due to Seeath preparing for Magus' return home. Kaiser had taken the free day as a chance to read the last of his books.

Kaiser smiled, nodding his head some before Julius joined him at the table.

"You have been training and reading every day, you must be worn out."

Following behind Julius was one of the castle servants, a tray of food in hand.

"You should eat." Julius pushed the tray to the center of the table, and Kaiser took a piece of bread from it.

When Kaiser had arrived in Ragnovok, he had devoured a tray of food like a wild animal, but now he was comfortable, taking his time. He had picked up on the habits when eating alongside

Seeath.

As Kaiser ate, he looked across the table at Julius, who was flipping aimlessly through the books.

"Have you learned anything new?" Julius said, looking up at Kaiser, who shook his head. "Seeath travels sometimes. If he ever goes to one of the other kingdoms, I will ask him to gather more books."

The two had only spoken a few times since Julius offered to help Kaiser, and although Kaiser was willing to agree to the partnership, he wanted to make sure he knew what he was getting into.

"We should go into the forest later today; we can look for that girl you saw." Julius was trying too hard.

Kaiser hesitated, remembering how she tore out the throats of those men. "I'm not sure she's the type of girl you want to find. She was so... feral."

"Nonsense, we will at least look for her."

The two turned, hearing a commotion coming from the main hall. They left the library and found a crowd of people gathering at the castle entrance. Kaiser and Julius pushed through the gathering, and upon reaching the front of the crowd, they found Magus and his small escort trailing up the steps.

As elegant as ever, Magus tossed his cape to the side and dismounted his horse. Kaiser watched as Julius stepped forward, approaching Magus. He knew the prince looked up to Magus, but Kaiser didn't follow. He remained in place and slowly stepped back, disappearing into the crowd.

"Magus! Did you find any deserters?"

"Not this time, my prince. Even if I had, Seeath would be the one to dispatch them, or at the very least, give the order." Magus gave Prince Julius a smile. "What are you up to?"

"Kaiser and I were about to go to the forest and..." Julius stopped, looked around.

"Are you sure spending time with Seeath's Glas is such a good idea?" Magus asked, worried for the young prince.

"Do you not trust him, Magus?"

He shook his head, gesturing toward the castle doors. Once the two had broken through the spectators, Magus and Julius found Seeath standing in the throne room. He approached Magus, and the two men gripped the other's hands. Seeath was obviously relieved to see his comrade return. The three of them walked further into the throne room.

"Any news?"

"No, the deserters remain hidden inside the forest, and there were no signs of Sullvain men near the West Bridge." Magus noticed the thoughtful look across Seeath's face.

"Does that worry you?" Magus asked, gently taking a glass of wine from the maiden who had been summoned over.

"It does. Kaiser killed the Prince of Sullvain... I find their lack of retaliation strange."

Both men agreed, but Magus already knew his secret trip to Dreava had something to do with it. Magus knew full well Seeath would piece things together if he were given the time, so he finished his glass and gestured for Prince Julius.

"Would you like to help me get my things back to my chambers?"

"I would, but Kaiser and I are going out later."

"Nonsense, he can wait."

In his escape from Magus' presence, Kaiser found himself standing along one of the main halls. He recognized the rooms he had passed; his own room was just around the corner. Along the way, he passed the royal family's chambers. He had never seen inside and never would.

He walked the hall, his hand sliding up and down the walls as he went. He looked over more of the paintings he had seen his first day in the castle, just as eerie as ever.

Kaiser had rarely ever considered the history of Ragnovok, though Seeath mentioned it daily. The kingdom was more attuned to the old gods and their ways, while Sullvain and Valacore claimed only one god, the Given God. During his time in the library, Kaiser had regularly looked up information on the Given God. He doubted the two had any connection, but he had found the first churches dedicated to the Given God had sprung up just years after the Glas disappeared. That was over four hundred years ago, however—and thanks to missing pages in all his books, Kaiser would never truly be able to connect the two events.

"K—Kaiser?" A shy voice spoke from down the hall, and Kaiser found Princess Fiona.

"Princess?" Kaiser took a bow, showing his respect, something Seeath had taught him. He didn't show the same formality to Julius due to the time the two had spent together. Julius was more a friend than a royal, and Kaiser believed the prince preferred it that way.

Fiona shined a weak smile and approached, her hands holding each other near her waist. "My brother said you two were going to meet at the forest later? I was wondering if you would like to play with me sometime, too?"

The question had caught Kaiser off guard, and the look of shock was apparent on his face, causing the princess to blush.

"I'm sorry, I should not be bothering my brother and you." Fiona looked down.

She seemed shier than any royal Kaiser had ever met.

"No, It's okay." Kaiser rubbed the back of his neck, embarrassed by the fact she was embarrassed. "I would love to."

Fiona was younger than Julius and had a childlike attitude, even asking to play like Lilly used to. Julius was already a young adult at seventeen, and Kaiser was just a year older than him.

The words brought a shy smile to Fiona's face, and her cheeks reddened to the point she had to look away.

"T—thank you, Kaiser," Fiona whispered as she turned to walk down the hallway. Before turning the corner, she looked back at him. "Oh, one of my brother's men sent word. He will be waiting for you in the forest."

The forest was empty, just the rush of wind and dust dancing about. Kaiser had found the edge of the forest, but didn't see Julius, so he entered to look for him. The last time he ventured into the woods, he'd nearly lost his life, but despite his apprehension, he felt welcomed, as if the trees beckoned him to enter.

Knowing the prince intended on looking for the red-haired girl, Kaiser had brought his sword along. He stopped somewhere in the woods, a ray of light breaking through the trees and hitting his face. The warmth was welcomed, and he closed his eyes to embrace it. Such a dangerous place with deserters, wild animals, and a feral, murderous child—yet there he stood, more relaxed and freer than he had ever felt in his life.

The feeling stirred up the past—how he would stand in the middle of the crops and soak up the sun before Guile scolded him back to work.

One thought led to another, and he wondered how the old man fared, if he was still alive. Kaiser hoped the old farmer didn't get himself hurt when Devon's men took Alice and Lilly.

Kaiser's thoughts had gone from relaxed to worried, and he opened his eyes. Across the small opening, he saw a figure staring back. Kaiser's hand grabbed hold of his sword's hilt, and he readied himself.

"Who are you?" Kaiser shouted across the opening.

The figure stepped out of the tree's shadow and revealed himself to be an old man in full armor, his graying hair barely visible under his helmet.

"Foster Dalfair of Valacore."

The man removed his helmet and brought his sword up, its shining steel tip pointed at Kaiser. The armor alone was intimidating, but he had read the name in one of the library books. Foster Dalfair was also known as the Dark Stalker.

The Glas had vanished over four hundred years ago, but every time their race began to sprout up again, a Stalker would appear and slay them. None of the books knew who ordered them to keep the Glas race from regaining a foothold, but he played the role well.

"You're the Dark Stalker?" Kaiser drew his sword, trying to hide his fear.

"I am. We met once, in Sullvain... I'm truly sorry for what they did to you." Foster stepped forward and poured something from a flask onto the old knight's blade, and once the blade was fully coated, Foster struck it with a rock. The blade caught fire, its flame swirling around the sword's steel. "I'm also sorry for what I'm about to do. Gods forgive me."

Foster rushed at Kaiser, his flaming blade coming down from overhead. The force caused Kaiser to stumble back, but he regained his stance and tried to counter. Foster was experienced in the way of the sword—far beyond Kaiser—and he dodged Kaiser's attack with ease.

Foster's blade swung so close, Kaiser could feel the heat of the flame against his cheek. He was distracted by the dancing fire, and Foster landed a kick into his gut, sending Kaiser rolling back.

Once Kaiser had gathered himself, he lifted his hand up and stopped Foster's follow-up attack. Foster stood above him, pushing down with all his might as Kaiser held his own blade up, trying to keep Foster's from coming down. Kaiser's right hand gripped the end of his blade, allowing him to hold his enemy's attack. Blood ran down Kaiser's arm, his own blade cutting into his palm.

"You don't belong in this world, not anymore." Kaiser felt the man push down with all he had, and his flaming sword shattered Kaiser's blade in half. When Foster's blade finally hit the ground, it had made its way down Kaiser's chest, leaving a deep, bloody gash on its way.

Kaiser fell back against the tree behind him. He touched his wound and lifted his hand. His fingers were covered in sizzling blood.

Foster stood, giving the boy a moment before he finished the kill. He wanted to give Kaiser a quick death. He didn't want him to suffer.

"You remind me so much of her, you don't deserve this... Forgive me for making the same mistake." Foster lifted his blade, preparing to deliver mercy to the dying Glas. As his blade fell, Foster was tackled, sent rolling across the forest opening. He struggled to his feet, his armor making the ordeal all that harder.

When he finally rose, a wild girl stood between him and his target. She growled, baring fangs like a wolf. She crouched down on all fours and scratched at the dirt in front of her, daring Foster to approach.

Foster dusted himself off, ready to accept her dare, when a wolf emerged from between the trees, joining the red-haired girl.

He was taken aback, but his blade was ready in an instant.

"Are you protecting him?" Foster shook his head, confused by the redhead's actions. He pushed the attack, nevertheless.

The wolf leaped at him, clamping onto his sword arm, its teeth biting into his iron brace. He threw his arm back, trying to swing the beast loose, but before he could, the wild girl jumped on his back, her nails clawing at his armor.

By the time he managed to get the wolf from his bracer, the girl had bitten down into the side of Foster's neck, trying her best to rip what she could from his skin. Foster lifted his left arm, taking hold of the girl's fiery hair.

When he saw the wolf coming back in for another attack, he raised his sword, driving it through. He quickly dropped his weapon, using both hands to fight the girl off his back. A strong throw sent the girl hurtling through the air and slamming against a tree. She let out a loud cry and fell to the ground.

The chaos settled, and Foster touched at the wound on his neck, trying to decide how serious it was.

When Foster turned back to the Glas, he was standing again, his wound still bleeding—but Kaiser seemed unaffected. The whites of his eyes were now black. As he took a weak step forward, Foster looked to his sword, still lodged into the dead wolf. Even if he could fetch it, the flame that allowed him to harm Kaiser was now extinguished, making the blade useless.

"I didn't ask for this!" Kaiser's scream echoed through the woods, and the earth responded with a gust of wind that sent the leaves around them into a frenzy. "Why do you all hate me?"

As Kaiser got closer, Foster stepped back. The Glas wasn't of his own mind. The young man Foster had sought to put down had been replaced by a creature, baring the most primal instincts of a Glas.

The blood on Kaiser's palm began swirling around his arm with a life of its own. Foster made a dash for his sword, quickly ripping it from the wolf and swinging it toward Kaiser. The steel blade was stopped—Kaiser's grip held onto it firmly.

Foster tried to pull the blade back but couldn't. With ease, the Glas twisted his wrist, breaking the sword. Foster jumped back, holding half a blade.

The sorrow Foster had going into the fight was gone. Now he worried the threat was greater than he had expected. Kaiser's corrupted eyes looked at the broken steel in his hand, then finally they looked to Foster. He took one step toward Foster, and Foster jumped toward Kaiser. The two collided, what was left of Foster's sword stabbed deep into Kaiser's chest. The other half found its way into the opening of Foster's chest plate.

Foster looked into Kaiser's black eyes and tried to find humanity. As the two stayed locked together, Kaiser's eyes began to gray, returning to normal. His frenzy had died down, and his body fell back, landing hard on the ground. The life-like blood returned to normal, and only a defeated man remained.

Foster grabbed hold of his fresh wound, trying to breathe through the pain. He was unsure if the Glas was finished, and looked around for his blade.

Before he could find it, he screamed as pain rushed through his leg. The wild girl had awoken, her teeth and nails now digging into the flesh of Foster's leg.

With the likeness of an animal, the girl jerked her head to the side, ripping a large chunk of meat from Foster's calf. He smashed the backside of his gauntlet against the girl's cheek, knocking her across the ground. Blood spurted from the missing flesh, and he fell against a nearby tree. He wouldn't last long.

Once the girl regained herself, she would surely finish him in this state.

"Dammit!" Foster looked to Kaiser, lying limp and lifeless.

Making a quick decision, Foster turned from the scene, disappearing into the forest as quickly as his wounds allowed.

CHAPTER THIRTY-FOUR

Two nights had gone by, and the small cramped cell was growing colder each night.

Dawn sat with her back against the wall, her hair a mess and only her fur robe to keep her warm. She wondered if anyone outside the dungeon had begun to question where she was, if Vale hadn't already killed them all.

She gritted her teeth and cursed his name. If only Harrion were still around, he would have quickly dispatched the snake she had mistaken for a brother.

Her body shivered as she pulled her legs closer together. The dreams she had been having since arriving in the cell had caused her a lack of sleep, and she was beginning to feel it.

Her recent dreams were free of the glass man, the armor, and the one-eyed lion. Her newest visions, however, had caused her to be sick. She found herself in the throne room, a pool of blood flowing over the marble floor, pouring down the steps like small red waterfalls.

She walked barefoot through the red mess, up the stairs, and to the throne. A body sat on the throne, but it wasn't anyone she recognized. The young man was blonde, his limp hands hanging off each side of the throne.

Each time she had the dream, she was able to walk closer to the body, and she had begun having the dream even during small moments of rest, with her eyes closed tight. After several attempts, she finally walked the whole of the throne room, standing directly in front of the young man. Her hands covered her scream as she found a long dagger piercing his left eye, its silver blade sticking through the back of the blonde man's skull, turning red with blood.

After the image of the dead man had become too much, she let out a muffled scream and woke from her vision. She knew it had been nothing but a dream, but they were becoming more real than the cell she sat in.

It took her a moment to regain her breath, and once she finally had, the dungeon doors swung open. Vale was alone, one of Harrion's heavy coats wrapped around him, the fur of a wolf lining the neck. He seemed pleased by the disgust on Dawn's face.

"Does it offend you? That I wear our brother's coat?" Vale's lips pierced into a thin smile, and he pulled the coat on tighter. "It seems fitting for a king, and Harrion won't be needing it anymore."

Dawn was catapulted into a rage as she leaped forward, her chest and face pressing against the cell bars, allowing her small arms the reach they needed to grab hold of the fur around Vale's neck. Dawn's grip was that of a beast, and she threw herself back, pulling Vale against the bars. In the chaos, she couldn't see his face, but him gasping for air brought her pleasure.

"If you harmed him, I'll kill you! You bastard!" Dawn screamed, tears in her eyes as she tried to choke the life out of

Vale.

The struggle echoed through the hall of the dungeon, and a guard quickly ran to Vale's aid, his sword hilt smashing hard against Dawn's wrist until she released the fur.

She fell back, holding her throbbing wrist, more harmed by the fact she hadn't finished Vale, who had dropped to his knees. His hands held his neck, trying to ease his breathing.

"You bitch!" His voice went in and out, red marks decorating his neck. Once back on his feet, he returned to his royal posture, fixing his stolen coat.

"You said you would kill me, you missed your chance... Harrion's body is lying at the bottom of the Scar as we speak." Vale gestured for the guard to return to his post and looked down at his sister.

Dawn buried her face into her knees, muffling her whimpers. She didn't want to hear this, not about her brother.

"Tomorrow, I will gather the court to discuss my place on the throne. I will leave you here, give you time to think over your options. You need not remain in a cell forever... I would love to have my dear sister at my side, someday soon."

Dawn looked up from her knees, glaring at the man in front of her with pure hatred.

"Wipe that look off your face," Vale said. "I'll be back after I tend to my visitor."

At the gates of the kingdom, two figures entered, their bodies shivering and covered in the soft snow. Grant had all but carried Alyssa the rest of the way, her small legs trying to give out under her. Grant wanted to push on to the castle, to ask for Foster, but Alyssa needed the warmth of a fire, and Grant quickly rushed her to an inn near the kingdom's entrance.

The tavern was empty save for a few soldiers in the corner, and he led Alyssa to the fireplace. As the snow melted away, Alyssa looked up to Grant, giving him a weak smile.

"We made it," she boasted, causing him to smile. "We did."

He took a seat next to her, his hands reaching out to warm them over the flame. He could hear one of the soldiers across the tavern whisper, causing Grant to look toward them.

"Sullvain men?" He had seen the emblem before while traveling with Foster—a snake wrapped around a sword. "Stay here, get dry."

Grant left Alyssa's side and walked toward the soldiers. Halfway there, he was stopped by a tall man with dark brown hair.

"Can I help you?" the man asked.

"Those men, do you belong to them?"

The man raised an eyebrow, but he nodded. "Yes, these are my men. My name is Servis Belouve, and you?"

"Grant Dalfair of Valacore."

Servis stepped back, looking Grant over.

"Dalfair? You're Foster's son?" another man asked from behind the two, having stepped into the tavern from outside.

Grant explained what had happened, leaving out certain information about the Church he felt no one should know but himself. He told them of his search for Alyssa and how circumstances had caused them to go south in search of his father.

"He left for Ragnovok two days ago and hasn't returned." Oran stood in Foster's room as Grant looked through his father's things.

Grant flipped through the papers on the desk and sighed. He had missed his father, and now worry was beginning to fill him.

"Your father asked me to hold this for him... I was to help it find its way to you if he didn't return." Oran held out an old notebook, offering it to Grant. Its contents were mostly sunrises and sunsets, but between them, he found portraits of random folk doing their everyday chores.

"Thank you, Oran." Grant held the book tightly to his chest and stepped away from the desk, giving up on his search.

"What will you do now? The prince, Harrion—he seems to respect your father. If you request his aid, he could help you with supplies and such, for whatever location you choose to travel."

"I've met Prince Harrion, though that was many years ago. Nevertheless, the ear of someone my father trusted would be a godsend right now. I'll try and speak with him at once."

Oran nodded. "I'll take you there."

The two returned downstairs to find Alyssa still huddled close to the flames. When she spotted him, she smiled at him, clearly trying to cheer him up.

"With any luck, Prince Harrion will see us this late," Grant muttered, hoping the prince was in a good mood.

Grant and Alyssa waited at the door for Oran, who had been stopped at the stairs by his brother.

"I'll return shortly," Oran was saying. "The least I can do for Foster is make sure his son's safe within the castle."

"You care for others too much…" Servis shook his head, smiling, and Oran smiled back.

Oran pulled his hood over his shoulders, tightening it around his neck. Before Oran left, he looked back at his brother. "When I return, we should talk about where we go from here."

"Y—you'll come with me?" Servis stumbled on his words.

"We will discuss it tonight."

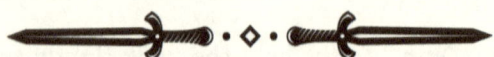

The three found no guards at the castle gates and the halls were silent. Grant reminisced in the memories of this place. He had run these halls as a child with Harrion. He couldn't picture the young prince or princess in his mind, but he remembered the times they had during Foster's visits.

Alyssa moved closer to Grant, grabbing hold of his arm when the walls became littered with dragon bones. The further down the hall they went, the larger the bones became until finally, they entered the main hall. They found it empty, but a voice was heard up the stairs, within the throne room. Grant approached the great doors, not wanting to disturb whoever was inside. He only wanted to know if it was the prince.

"You fools... Laderic and Draston will..."

He could barely hear the exchange of words, as the men were whispering, but one name stood out.

He stepped back, his hand reaching for Alyssa's. "It's not safe here."

As Grant spoke, three Dreava men approached from down the hall, and the throne room doors were pulled open. Inside were six guards and the bastard prince, Vale Dreava. All six of the guards drew their swords.

"The Dark Stalker's son," Vale said, overjoyed by their arrival. "We heard you might show up."

Grant didn't answer. Instead, he counted his enemies, realizing he had fallen into a trap. He quickly looked behind him and found Oran with his sword drawn, Alyssa standing between the two men.

"Where is Prince Harrion?" Oran looked to Vale, inching closer to Grant to keep Alyssa safe.

"Harrion?" Vale laughed as three more guards entered the room behind Oran. "Harrion is no longer heir to the throne... Wait."

Vale spotted Alyssa and smiled, his teeth showing. "Drop your weapons now and I won't have you killed on the spot."

Grant growled, his grip tightening around Valor. There was no way Grant was letting this man get his hands on Alyssa. He would die first.

"Unless you think yourself capable of fighting off my men, good luck protecting the child as well."

After a moment of hesitation, Oran dropped his sword.

Alyssa grabbed hold of his waist. "Grant... Please, I don't want to lose you."

Alyssa's plea hit their mark, and Grant sighed. He sat Valor on the ground, and the guards swarmed them. Grant and Oran had their hands quickly bound.

"Oh, you poor, foolish boy." Vale stepped over to the two men and took a knee, picking Grant's blade up. The prince struggled to hold it up correctly as he admired the crimson blade. "The Dark Stalker's blade."

Vale quickly swung the blade, its edge cutting the flesh across Oran's neck. Alyssa cried out in horror, and Grant struggled against the guards, but they were too strong.

Oran was released, only to fall to his knees, desperately trying to hold the gash in his neck where blood gushed. Within seconds, his face turned snow-white, and the young man fell to the floor, lifeless.

"I'll kill you!" Grant kicked and punched, trying to free himself, but he was only restrained by more guards.

Vale wiped the blood from Valor. "Take the Dark Stalker's son to the dungeon. Fetch the other Sullvain soldiers from the tavern and have them join him. We can plan a splendid execution! Lock the girl in my sister's chamber. Maybe having an innocent to tend to will straighten her out."

The guards separated Grant and Alyssa, breaking what little hope the two had managed.

CHAPTER THIRTY-FIVE

"You are to pursue the Dark Stalker?" Julius lengthened his stride to keep up with Seeath. The Phantom had armed himself and rushed out of the castle, storming down the steps toward the stables, Julius on his heel. "Should you not stay and tend to Kaiser?"

"Kaiser has proven resilient in the past. I have no doubt he'll heal overnight as before. The Dark Stalker made an attempt at Kaiser's life, on Ragnovok land... I would see that he regrets ever setting foot here." Seeath motioned, and three other soldiers mounted their steeds.

Before he approached his own horse, he turned to Julius, placing both hands on his shoulders. He gave Julius a confident look and then looked past him, toward the castle.

"Keep a watch over the castle for me. The enemy is wounded and shouldn't be far. I'll return shortly." He gently ruffled Julius' hair and turned, leaving the castle grounds with his men.

Although he felt powerless, Julius would do what he could and remain at the castle. Giving a quick prayer to the old gods on Seeath's behalf, Julius turned, only to find Kaiser standing near the castle gates. Julius rushed over.

"Kaiser! Should you be out of bed?" Julius asked, his eyes looking

Kaiser over.

The wound down Kaiser's chest hadn't fully healed, and its pain remained while the other injuries had vanished overnight. Kaiser had slipped from his room unseen, afraid he would be ordered back to bed—and from the look he gained from Julius, he was correct.

"The worst of your wounds may have healed, but you risk opening the remaining one."

The young prince nudged Kaiser back into the castle gates and back to his room. Every objection Kaiser voiced was shut down, and before he knew it, Julius had him back to his room. As the prince went to close the door, Kaiser grabbed it.

"Wait, I'll rest," Kaiser promised, "but first I have a question... Why did you not show up at the forest edge?"

Julius tilted his head, looking puzzled as he knitted his brow. "I sent one of my servants to tell you I could not come. Magus requested I help him report his trip to father. Did they not tell you?"

"I must have left before they could reach me, no worries." Kaiser gave a smile, but the look remained on Julius' face until the door closed.

His wound sent a sting of pain through his chest, and he hurried to sit on the bed. Small traces of blood seeped through the bandage. Kaiser pulled the white fabric away to reveal the wound. Another keepsake from his enemies, sure to leave a long scar down his chest. He drifted to the mirror, his eyes looking at the fresh wound.

The man Seeath called Dark Stalker, he'd used a flaming sword to inflict a wound Kaiser wouldn't heal from—just the sort of tactic Kaiser had read about in his books. Although scared beyond belief, Kaiser found himself curious about the words the man had uttered. The Dark Stalker had mentioned Kaiser looked like someone.

Another wave of pain broke his concentration, and he held his hand tightly against his wound.

He pulled the bandages back over his wound and turned his attention to a small dagger on the table next to his bed. Kaiser had been in bed most of the day, but while resting, one thing stood out above everything else.

How had the Dark Stalker found Kaiser so easily in the woods?

Were it not for Julius' servant sending Kaiser off to the forest, he would never have run into the legend. Of course, Kaiser trusted the prince, so he didn't think him capable. Which left only one man—Magus.

Kaiser lifted the dagger, holding its sharp edge against his palm. He was tired of running, sick of being hunted.

He would make the next move.

"I will have his head!" Roaring, the king chucked a wine glass, and it shattered against the stone wall.

Julius watched the argument between his father and Magus

with more than a little shock.

"My king, Sir Reinhart and his best men ride after the Dark Stalker," Magus said. "It is only a matter of time before we—"

The king rounded on Magus, his eyes flashing. "How did you miss such a person in our land!"

"My king?"

The room was heated. Julius remained silent as the two quarreled, though it was more of a parent scolding a child.

"You went out to the villages with the sole purpose of gathering information on the deserters. Did the presence of the Dark Stalker never pass your fucking ear?" he demanded.

Magus diverted his eyes to the floor. As mighty and noble as the snake was, he knew his place. "Forgive me, but I feel none of this would have come to pass if the Glas boy had been dealt with sooner, not trained as a pet. His presence within our walls, Prince Devon's killer, is the reason for the Stalker's arrival."

Magus looked to put the blame elsewhere. That wasn't going to happen. Julius stepped in, defending his new-found friend and ally. "Kaiser had nothing to do with this. Sullvain has been an enemy of Ragnovok and remains so, no matter the company we keep. The fact King Sull sends someone as revered as the Dark Stalker just furthers Sir Reinhart's claim. Kaiser is of value, and King Sull would see us rid of him before we make him an ally."

Magus glared across the room in Julius' direction, something Julius had never received. The debate had come to a close, King Novok circling his study chair as he weighed both his adviser and son's statements. His rage subsiding, he returned to his chair to ease his bones.

"You let my son outmatch you in words," King Novok mocked Magus, slipping back into his chair.

"The outcome of this is not Magus' fault," Julius said. "I have learned many skills from him. Kaiser is to be trusted, and if it were my decision, I would allow Seeath to continue his training. I believe he will serve us loyally one day."

The sun had fallen, allowing the wounded Harrion to move without the worry of being found. He'd stopped the bleeding on his side by using the sleeve of his coat as a makeshift tourniquet, but the fall had left a branch stabbed into his right shoulder.

He remembered all the times his father had taken him hunting, and he prayed the tips and tricks he had picked up would see him alive to return home.

He stumbled through the woods, a straight branch tightened to his leg. He didn't think it was broken, but walking had been a problem.

For two days, he had been out in the woods, and being no stranger to the wild, he had tended to his body, removing the branch and patching all his wounds. He tried to make his way back east, to Dreava. He'd been on guard in case his brother's men came looking for him—but after the first day, he allowed himself some rest.

Sitting on a small stump in the woods, Harrion began skinning the meat from a little squirrel, the only thing he had been able to catch since his fall.

Once skinned, he steadied the fresh meat over the small fire he'd made. As his food cooked, Harrion leaned back, resting his sore body against a tree. The snow in Ragnovok territory was light and nowhere near as bad as in Dreava, which Harrion was thankful for.

His thoughts were interrupted when he heard rustling in the distance. Armed with his small knife, Harrion stood, wobbling toward the sounds. He held the dagger up as he rounded a large tree to find a man lying face down in the snow.

Approaching with caution, Harrion gently turned the man over. "Foster?"

Harrion gasped and quickly pulled the defeated knight up, dragging him back toward his fire. Once he had Foster next to the flames, he addressed his wounds, pulling his broken and shattered armor free. His injuries were severe, much worse than Harrion's had been, and the large gash in his calf needed treatment or he would lose most of his leg.

Harrion was amazed at how far north the old man had crawled. Harrion's stomach twisted at the sight of white bone peeking through all the ripped flesh. Knowing he needed to get him out of the weather, he pulled the old knight up and slowly took him to a small cave he'd found after his fall. It was deep into the mountain ridge, safe from the snow.

K. Vider

After making a new fire for Foster, Harrion quickly returned with the cooked meat and sat down next to him. Harrion worried for him. The leg wound needed tending, and so Harrion ripped what little remained of his coat sleeve and tightened it around Foster's leg. Once he had it in a place, he tried his best with the smaller wounds.

A few hours went by, Foster's wounds had been tended to the best of his ability, and he was now resting next to the fire.

With Foster resting, Harrion wondered what was happening back at home. Had Vale planned this betrayal all along? A spike of fear ran through him as he wondered if his father and Dawn were okay.

"Prince Dreava?" a familiar voice whispered into the cave. A voice Harrion would normally be joyful to hear, but with Foster next to him, his heart raced. The Phantom had always been an ally to Dreava, but with Foster having set his sights on the Glas, Harrion began to worry.

"Seeath Reinhart." Harrion stood, stepping over so he was in front of the wounded Foster.

"What happened?" Seeath asked, then caught sight of the wounded Dark Stalker, his hand going for his sword.

"Sir Reinhart, wait." Harrion quickly put himself between Seeath and Foster.

"He came into our country and tried to kill one of my men. I'll have his life!"

Seeath tried to push his way past Harrion, but Harrion

331

wouldn't budge, placing his hands firmly on Seeath's chest.

"No! This man is near death as it is. You will not kill him in his sleep!" His protest was short-lived as Seeath grabbed hold of Harrion's wrist and twisted, causing him to fall.

With Harrion out of the way, Seeath stepped over to the slumbering Foster and put his sword to his neck. "Reinhart, put that sword away! As Prince of Dreava, if you kill that man, I will take it as an act of war!"

His blade still firmly against Foster's neck, Seeath looked over his shoulder at Harrion. "You would spare his life and risk war against Ragnovok?"

"I would beg for his life, beg mercy from a friend."

Seeath let out a silent huff and put his blade away. He turned his attention away from Foster and helped Harrion up, a stern look on his face.

Once Harrion was back on his feet, he smiled and patted Seeath on the shoulder. "Thank you, Reinhart."

"Thank your father... if not for all that he's done for Ragnovok, I would've already taken that man's head back to my king. I owe your father much from the past. Consider the debt paid," Seeath said, looking over Harrion's wounds.

At the snap of his fingers, a soldier entered the cave and reported to Seeath. He rummaged through the soldier's sack of supplies and removed some bandages and food.

"Here... Why you are out here in this condition is your own business, but I'll not have you die in the woods like an animal."

His eyes shot over to Foster. "I would offer you haven back in Rag-novok, but the Dark Stalker would be killed on sight. If you insist on helping him, I suggest you head for Sullvain. He won't make the trip back to Dreava."

Once Seeath had finished unpacking the supplies, he turned, him and his soldier heading back out.

"Seeath!" Harrion stopped him just short of his exit. "I'm truly thankful... I will not forget your kindness."

"I'd rather you did, Prince Harrion. If I set eyes on that man again, I'll have his head." Seeath turned his back on the cave and gestured for his men to follow. "If he wakes, be sure and tell him as much."

As Seeath left, Harrion blew out a breath and went back to the fire. He had saved Foster from Seeath but he wasn't sure he could do the same when it came to his wounds. Harrion sighed, stoking the fire some before glancing over at Foster. He hoped the old man would live to hear the warning.

Magus had spent the day trying to calm his rage. The prince had always looked up to him like a hero, but then he so quickly made a fool of him in front of the king.

Holding no grudge against Prince Julius, Magus remained in his chamber, his desk littered with his work. The repercussions of Devon's death would come knocking, and Magus found it odd Sul-lvain hadn't already made a move. When the time came, he would show his loyalty to the Ragnovok throne.

Magus' slammed his fist down upon his desk and forcefully pushed the books and papers off it, taking deep breaths. No matter the degree of loyalty he had, being belittled in the eyes of the king was too much. Kaiser's presence and the Dark Stalker's attack were causing more chaos than Magus would have thought, yet he could do little. Staring out his window, he sighed, finally gathering himself.

He would wait for Seeath's return. The capture of the Dark Stalker would complicate things, though Magus believed the Dark Stalker was experienced enough to keep his mouth shut about their unlikely alliance. Still, Magus would have to find a new way to rid the kingdom of the Glas boy.

Magus poured himself a small cup of wine, his mind easing and returning to ways to fix what problems had risen. He stood at the window, sipping his wine as he looked through his reflection to survey the rest of the kingdom below.

As he thought and plotted his next move, pain echoed through his back and gut. His eyes barely glimpsed the shine of the blade in the reflection. His hand touched at the spot, and when he lifted it, blood covered his palm.

The blade retracted, leaving a gaping wound in his gut, piercing him from the back. He quickly turned, dropping his wine to the floor.

"My... What do we have here?" Magus fell back, smiling at the sight of Kaiser, the last person he expected.

The boy stood a few feet back, the bloody dagger clutched in his hand. He seemed as frightened as ever as Magus took two steps forward. In fear, Kaiser stabbed the stumbling Magus three more times. Magus fell against the wall and slumped onto the floor.

"Gods be damned!" Magus pulled himself over, trying desperately to get himself up and into his chair. "Who would have thought... a child would be my undoing?"

He finally got himself onto his seat and laid his head back, his hands pressed tightly against the four bleeding wounds Kaiser had inflicted. He could taste the blood pooling in his mouth but couldn't help but smile. He had been put down by a whelp, a young boy who didn't know anything at all.

"W—why did you send that man to kill me? Who ordered you to do it?"

Magus laughed before a sharp shoot of pain cut it short. "Ever the fool. I did what was needed for the kingdom, for Seeath. You're a monster, even if those around us cannot see it. I would kill you and your whole gods- damned family if it meant protecting the Novok family."

Magus sat up, looking at Kaiser as he trembled. He could see the boy's hands were shaking.

"Not that any of this is needed... You allowed the Sullvain to kill your family, do you know why?" Magus tried to raise his arm, pointing at Kaiser. "You are a weakling, you cannot protect anyone. You go from one prison to the next... you have no control over your fate, you are nothing."

His words hit their target. As tears ran down his face, the boy's arm rose to wipe them away.

"You're a monster and everyone, even your loved ones, will die in your wake... As your sisters did, because of you."

"SHUT UP!"

Kaiser lunged forward, stabbing his dagger deep into Magus' chest. His onslaught didn't end as he latched on and thrust over and over.

Blood pooled around the two, and by the time Kaiser's rage had calmed, he was drenched in blood, his pale skin now crimson. He swallowed hard, the sight of Magus' butchered and bloody corpse causing his stomach to turn.

He stumbled back and vomited, the silver dagger clanging as it dropped to the ground.

"J—just... shut up, please." Kaiser remained on all fours, his head pressed against the floor as he cried. He could feel the blood under his fingernails, over his skin. He hadn't wanted to do this, but it was the only way. Magus would have kept trying to have him removed from Ragnovok, one of them had to die.

He closed his eyes tightly and repeated the dragon's rhyme to himself. In the middle of his regret, he heard the chamber door shift and quickly looked toward it. A set of blue eyes peeked in, and when they met Kaiser's, they widened and darted off.

Knowing he would be put to death for his actions, Kaiser rushed after her. He threw himself toward the door and fell into the hall. The witness cut the corner, but Kaiser fought to his feet and took chase.

The halls were empty, and by the time Kaiser had caught up, the chase had led to Princess Fiona's chamber. Slowly pushing the door open, Kaiser found the princess hiding in the corner, her eyes full of fear for what she had seen. He had full intent on killing the witness, but the idea of it sickened him when he saw her look at him the way she did.

Kaiser took a step back, ready to leave her be and accept his fate when the door busted open behind him, sending him to the floor. Princess Fiona screamed.

When he turned over, two men in black were entering the room. Their faces were covered with masks, and their swords were long and foreign.

One of the men drew his blade up, ready to cut down the princess, but Kaiser jumped up and grabbed a vase from the princess's vanity. He smashed it against the attacker, sending the man to the floor. Kaiser fumbled with the man's sword, finally picking it up off the ground in time to face the second man.

"Get under your bed, stay there!" Kaiser shouted before he lunged at the second man, sending them both tumbling into the hall.

The princess did as she was told and hid, her hands covering her mouth. She could hear the chaos out in the hall and let out a small gasp when she heard two more men come. She jumped at the sounds of steel colliding.

After a while, the sounds all stopped. Fiona opened her eyes and crawled to the edge of the bed. She mustered the courage to approach the doorway and bravely looked outside of her chamber. The walls were red with blood, and four corpses were scattered on the floor. The victor stood in the middle of the carnage, slowly removing his blade from his last victim.

Kaiser turned to her, and she shuddered. She couldn't control herself as she began to shake. She had heard Magus refer to Kaiser as a monster, and a weapon by Seeath, but she saw neither.

She was, without a doubt, looking upon a god.

CHAPTER THIRTY-SIX

"**H**ow I miss the chill from the castle. I remember my mother chasing me through the halls late at night. I was never one to sleep when commanded. I was no more than ten, waking everyone while I laughed, running ass-naked at that!"

Harrion's memories kept him going. The rocky mountain was behind him, and now he was on flat land. His feet ached under him. Harrion had carried Foster throughout the night, heading north as Seeath had suggested. They had passed the Scar, and now the snow and cold weather were gone.

Harrion had never experienced the warmth he found this far north. He hardly recognized the sun above him, shining without the snow. He had taken to talking to Foster, but sadly, the man was still out cold, and so he spoke mostly to himself.

He had yet to pass anyone on the road, and even if he had, it would be best to keep Foster from sight to avoid raising suspicion. It had been a day's trip since he had spoken to Seeath, and if it hadn't been for Foster's condition, Harrion would be heading the opposite direction, storming back into Dreava to deliver justice to Vale.

He wondered how the kingdom was. His father's wellbeing worried him beyond words—yet even as he worried, his feet carried him ever farther away from his family.

Harrion sighed, stopping at a small log next to the dirt path.

His feet throbbed, and his wounds pained him even more now. He had hardly rested since the sun came up, and the long walk had left his own scars little time to heal. He stood up, stretching his arms out, trying to prepare himself for the rest of the trip.

"Do you need some help, son?" An old man on a wagon approached from behind, an equally aged woman sitting next to him.

Harrion struggled to turn, his legs almost giving out from his burden of carrying Foster the distance. He considered his options, not wanting to bring anyone else into the matter.

"Drink up, rest your legs." A warm, welcoming smile split the old woman's wrinkled face. She reached a small cup of tea out to Harrion as he sat in a chair near Foster's bedside. He had taken them up on their offer—he knew his limits and didn't expect to make it to Sullvain, no matter how close it was from their current location.

"His wounds are severe," the old man said. "He won't walk the same, if at all."

Foster's wounds had been re-wrapped by the old man, his touch showing a hint of experience in the matter.

"It ain't none of mine, but what happened to him?"

The couple joined Harrion, all sitting at the table near Foster.

"His honor got the best of him." Harrion looked over to Foster and the peaceful look on his face as he slept. Harrion was set on leaving him here. The couple seemed kind enough, and in all hon-esty, Foster was with an ally. He had even arrived in Dreava with Sullvain men.

"I would have you send word to Sullvain. Tell them Sir Foster is here and needs help."

The old man shook his head. "I doubt the king will send men this close to the Scar with the attack on Ragnovok and all."

Harrion looked at the couple, puzzled. "Attack?"

"Aye, the word is King Sull sent some foreigners from across the sea to kill the Novok family."

"What of the family? Do they live?" he asked sharply.

The old man's head bobbed. "They do, thanks to the Glas they've been housing. Heard he killed them all by himself, then devoured their bodies. Could just be rumors, though. Ragnovok gets darker and darker as the days go by. My old lady hates that I go down that way for selling my crops and such."

Harrion all but ignored the man as he went on. An attack on Ragnovok, in their own home? Another war was around the cor-ner, and one had just ended. Harrion understood to some degree —the Glas had killed Sullvain's prince. Even Harrion would seek vengeance on such a thing, and it was such thoughts that brought Harrion back to his worries of his home.

"I need you to watch over this man. He is a dear friend of mine, and I will see you rewarded for the effort." Harrion stood, grabbing anything he might need. He was of impressive build, but even he had his limits, and before he even made it to the door, his legs threatened to give out. The long journey carrying Foster had proven too much for him.

The old woman came to his aid, her frail but strong arms helping him stand. "Oh, dear, you won't make it a day's trip in any direction before you pass out!"

"At least stay the night," the old man insisted. "You can get some rest and head out in the morning. We'll watch over your friend until we can arrange to get him to Sullvain."

Harrion nodded, knowing they were right. He would die of exhaustion on the way back to Dreava. He would head out bright and early after some rest.

The night had grown considerably colder than Harrion expected, but he was used to the chill. He lay out on a small place on the floor he had made, and the wooden floor under him was welcomed compared to the last few nights out in the wild. He was glad to have Foster inside and warm, allowing him some rest.

Harrion stood, pulling a chair over to Foster. After taking a seat next to the sleeping man, he pulled the blanket up over him more.

"I could use your advice right about now." Harrion sighed, looking over Foster's graying hair and the healing wound across his neck. Foster had always been a wise man, offering counsel to many kings, Harrion's father included. He sighed again, thinking about his home.

"I cannot leave my father and sister to be used, or worse, by Vale... I have to go back." He stood to leave but felt a sturdy grip latch onto his wrist.

His head whirled around to see the old knight's eyes open. "Foster!"

"W—where am I?" The old knight pulled himself up as best as he could and looked about, seeming comforted by the sight of Harrion. "Dreava?"

Harrion shook his head. "I found you wounded in the woods."

Harrion explained the series of events leading them to Sullvain—how Harrion had been betrayed by Vale; how he had found Foster lying injured in the forest; how Seeath spared his life and advised he be taken north. Harrion spared no detail in explaining why they sat so far from home.

"You say Vale means to take Dreava?" Foster asked, his voice rough. "Oran and Servis. I hope they heeded my command and returned to Sullvain."

Harrion watched as Foster struggled to sit up, his eyes assessing his leg wound. "Harrion, I need your help. I know you wish to return to Dreava, but far greater threats lurk in the cold lands, south of the Scar."

Harrion frowned. "The Glas? He must have been far stronger than expected to have defeated the Dark Stalker."

Foster nodded, covering his leg back up with the blanket. "I cannot travel by myself, and I fear the only means to ending the Glas may be hidden within one of the Church archives. Most tales of the Glas are fabricated, but their books hold the true outcome of what happened to the race four hundred years ago. If we can find out how they were exterminated back then, we can—"

Harrion interrupted him. "They would freely give us this information?"

Harrion could see in Foster's eyes that the old knight had little hope—but whatever Foster had seen when facing the demon, it had shown him how dire the situation had become. No one had listened to Foster, and he knew now they would all regret that fact.

"On the west coast, there is a church. The Raven killed everyone in it... I have hope we can learn something from what is left there."

Harrion knew what Foster was asking him to do was important, not just to Dreava but the realm, but he would have to leave Vale in control of Dreava. He would be condemning his home.

"Do this for me, with me, and when it is finished, I will personally assist you in retaking Dreava. I need you, Harrion." Harrion look away, unsure he could say yes to such a thing. He knew Dawn was strong and she had the counsel with her. Even if Vale declared his desire for the throne, many things stood between him and it. Harrion looked back to Foster and sighed, he couldn't leave this broken man to die trying to travel alone.

CHAPTER THIRTY-SEVEN

Rattling chains and the sounds of empty threats ran down the dungeon halls. Grant hung tightly against the cell bars. He had failed again, this time by walking Alyssa right into their hands. For a moment, he gave up, laying his head against his prison and sliding down to the floor. Across from him, in another cell, sat Servis. He stared blankly at the ground, a broken man.

"We have to get out of here," Grant suggested, shifting closer to the silent man. "Servis, was it? We have to find a way out."

His words fell on deaf ears. Nothing Grant said impacted the Sullvain knight.

"They left him there..." Servis mumbled. "My brother. His body was still lying on the floor when they brought us here... He meant nothing to them."

Grant could see him holding back the tears, his head hanging low. He couldn't begin to understand how Servis felt, but he would gladly take Vale's life for what he did to Oran.

"Servis... You have to live for him. He wouldn't want you to die here." Plus, if he didn't focus and help Grant come up with a plan, neither of them was getting out of here alive. Grant had counted the guards; he knew the exit and how far from their cells it was but he couldn't find an opening. Without a weapon, he was unlikely to escape.

Grant watched as Servis perked up, something finally getting through to him. As Servis began to show himself, three men approached the cells.

"Hey, pretty boy, King Vale said to get you ready." The cell doors swung open, and the three men overpowered Grant before he could even attempt to fight back, slapping chains around both his wrists.

"Don't you dare give up, Servis!" Grant shouted, being pulled down the hall.

The castle had been locked down since Dawn had finally been released from her cell, but it was only to find another prison. She was locked away inside her chamber, two guards at the doors. She was still allowed outside of her chamber, but only with one of the guards with her.

At first, she was unsure why Vale would allow such a thing—but then she was brought a girl, Alyssa. The girl was frightened beyond words, but throughout the night, Dawn had calmed and tended to her. She somewhat fit into Dawn's clothes, and so she allowed Alyssa to get out of the rags.

They lay on Dawn's bed, Alyssa's head in Dawn's lap. Dawn felt for the child.

"I watched him kill that man... without a thought." Alyssa didn't speak his name, but Dawn knew precisely who she spoke of.

"He is a monster, hidden in the flesh of a man." She softly brushed Alyssa's hair.

"Is he... your brother?"

Dawn's jaw ticked as she clenched her teeth. "I only have one brother, and that monster took him from me, along with my father."

Alyssa pulled herself up, looking to Dawn. Dawn turned her head some, wondering what Alyssa was thinking.

"Sir Grant will save us. I know he will," Alyssa said, confidence saturating her tone.

"Grant? Is he a knight?" Dawn was unsure if the girl was fully aware that the man could already be dead.

"Not anymore, but he saved me back in Mirelos. They took him to the dungeon with the other Sullvain knights."

Dawn's eyes widened as she looked to Alyssa with hope. "The Sullvain men, they are here? In the castle?"

Alyssa nodded. Dawn shifted, a plan coming together in her mind. She quickly rushed over to her dresser and pulled a pair of silver shears from the drawer.

"Listen, Alyssa, I need you to stay here and hide... I'm going to try and free the Sullvain men, give them a chance to take the castle back from Vale."

Alyssa nodded and watched as Dawn made her way to the door. She slipped the silver shears up her sleeve and gently knocked on the door. Once the two men opened the door, she stepped forward.

"I would like to retrieve some things from one of my maid's room..."

The two men looked at each other, and finally, one nodded. He let Dawn pass and quickly started walking behind her. Acting as a shadow, every step she took, the man mimicked. Dawn led him through the castle, finally reaching the main hall. On her way across the floor, she stopped, glancing toward the throne room. She could see men in white robes gathering—the Elders. Vale would be making his move soon and had called them to the throne room.

"Keep moving, Princess."

She nodded and started walking again. It wouldn't be long before the man realized she was going in the opposite direction. She was leading him toward the dungeon.

When they arrived at the stairs, he asked, "Where do you think you're going?"

Dawn looked around as if confused, already a few steps down the stairs. She finally faked a smile and started to turn around, brushing by him at the top of the stairs.

"I have not been out of my chamber in some time, I must have taken a wrong turn." Once she was passed the guard, she quickly turned and threw herself at him, knocking him down the stairway. She caught herself on the wall and made sure she didn't go with him.

Dawn rushed down the stairs and found him laid out on the stone floor, alive but unconscious.

She couldn't believe that worked. A sense of satisfaction flowed through her. Now, she was free to look for the men if she didn't run into more guards.

Blood dripped from his chin. His arms hung above his head, the position excruciating for having been like that so long. His feet swung inches from the ground, his weight only worsening the pain in his wrist and shoulders.

The three had taken turns beating him, explaining the new king wanted the son of the Dark Stalker prepared. The beating Grant could bear—the scars along his back from his past punishments were proof of such, but he needed to get himself free.

"Where's my sword?" Grant asked, spitting blood out to the side.

One of the men laughed, looking to the others. "That fancy red sword? King Vale kept it, said it was elegant enough to be a king's sword. Why?"

Grant met them directly in the eye, wanting to make sure they understood his next words. "I'm going to kill you three with it."

The tone and promise in Grant's voice silenced the three men, and to regain their courage, one of them delivered a solid punch to Grant's stomach, sending him swinging from his chains.

As they beat him, one stopped to look in the direction of a sound coming from the hallway, then stepped away to investigate. After several minutes, the two became a bit worried, turning to Grant.

"Now don't go anywhere, we'll be right back for you."

As the two went to leave, Grant heard them cry out. His back was turned to the entrance, so he was unsure what was happening. He swung back and forth until finally, a hand grabbed hold of him and turned him. Servis and his men stood before him.

"Are you okay?" Servis asked, grabbing Grant and lifting him from the hook that held his chains.

When he lowered Grant, Grant's arms protested, having been held in the same awkward position too long. Grimacing, he rotated his shoulders.

"Are you Grant?" A young woman stepped forward.

"I am, and you are?"

"Dawn Dreava, Princess of Dreava. Alyssa told me you—"

Grant stood up, pushing Servis aside so he could get to Dawn. "Is she okay? Where is she?"

Eyes widening, Dawn backed up some, putting some distance between them. "She is in my chamber. She is in good health."

Grant let out a sigh of relief and stepped back, looking to Servis. He didn't want to see more brave men die. If he could get his men out without more bloodshed than need be, he should.

"Servis, take your men and get away from Dreava," he commanded, his tone leaving no room for argument.

"What of you? Are you coming?"

Grant shook his head, pulling at the chains around his wrist. "No, I have to get Alyssa... and make sure Vale pays for what he's done."

Servis nodded, placing a firm grip on Grant's shoulder before he turned back to his men and led them away.

Dawn remained. Grant noticed her staring at him, like she was trying to figure out if she knew him.

"Grant, if you go to the throne room... you will die. I have visions, vague as they may be. I knew I had seen you somewhere."

"Visions?" Grant smiled, wiping the blood from his chin.

"I'm serious! I saw you sitting on the throne, a dagger through your left eye and skull."

Her words didn't stop him from walking past her and down the hall. Dawn ran after him, grabbing hold of his arm to stop him. The two locked eyes, his intent to kill Vale stopping her from protesting more.

"If you won't listen to reason..." Dawn conceded. "He's in the throne room. I think he plans on assassinating the Elders."

Grant nodded and continued toward the throne room. Time to pay his respects to the new king.

The Elders of Dreava gathered together. An important meeting had been called within the throne room, but once they arrived, no one was present. As they grew impatient and were about to leave, the doors to the throne room opened. Vale entered with his men, young Alyssa in tow. The Elders seemed confused, watching as he brought her up the stairs and to the throne.

"I have gathered you all here for a significant announcement.

As you all know, my father has passed, and with my brother's untimely disappearance, I am the last male Dreava."

"A bastard, not fit to rule," one of the elders said, and more agreed. "When no one can take the throne, the court Elders will decide the kingdom's fate until an heir from Princess Dawn is capable of rule."

The dozen or so elders all spoke up, each agreeing on the subject. Despite their protest toward Vale's claim, he smiled and stepped over to the throne. The Elders watched in disgust as he sat on the throne, a sinister grin on his lips.

"This matter is no longer up for debate." Vale snapped his fingers, and two men came from the shadows. Laderic and Draston. The Elders all gasped, unsure of what was happening. Along with the two Glas brothers, a dozen masked men appeared, each wielding swords.

"As promised, the girl is yours. In exchange, your queen will command these Elders to obey me like she does her puppets." Vale looked on at the masked men, a deep fear for the power the queen had over the weak-minded.

Alyssa struggled as Draston picked her up, the stump of his right hand still wrapped in bandages. Laderic removed his hood and shifted to the throne, laying his hands gently on Vale's shoulder. Even as allies, the movement and aura of Laderic caused Vale to shudder.

"Yes, as promised. Before you now, the one and only King of Dreava." Laderic lifted his hand, and the men stepped forward, drawing their blades. As they did, Laderic dropped a small dagger into Vale's lap. "Long live the king."

The men moved on the Elders and even Vale. Their intent—to kill everyone. Realizing the betrayal at last, Vale struggled from his throne, barely escaping the attack.

"What are you doing? We had a deal!" Vale crawled along the floor on all fours, trying to follow Laderic as he rejoined Draston behind the throne.

"The Glas need no one, especially a prince as weak as you. If you want to rule this kingdom, take what is left of your throne."

The escape had been easy. Most of the guards had been heading in the direction of the throne room, allowing Servis and his men to slip out of the castle unseen. They found the gates unguarded, and after exiting, Servis closed the large wooden doors behind him. Men and women had gathered, all watching in confusion as the group of Sullvain men rushed through the streets.

It grieved him to leave Oran. His little brother deserved a knight's burial, but if he turned back now, his men would never make it home, so he pushed on.

The group of men made it through the gates, and once they had reached the snowy fields outside the kingdom walls, Servis knew of only one place they could make sure they weren't fol-lowed—the forest.

During the trip south, Foster had mentioned how deserters

and outlaws had used the vast woodlands to escape from Ragno-vok and Dreava. Servis knew his men could at least rest safely within it.

Most of the Sullvain men had been beaten while imprisoned. Servis had no plans on returning to Sullvain, but he would do what he could for his fellow knights.

He was about to lead his men into the forest when he heard a commotion. It was the sound of people gasping and crying out.

"Go on ahead," Servis told his men. "Get to the trees and take over as deep as you can. I'll catch up."

His men trusted his orders and went on.

Servis knew something was going on, something he could feel in his gut. He wondered what would become of Grant, the stranger who had talked hope back into him.

He ran back, unable to leave Grant to the wolves.

As the slaughter raged on, Grant broke through the door. His eyes looked past the bloodshed to find Vale and the Glas on the further side of the room. He watched as the two Glas disappeared, Alyssa with them.

"Dammit!" Grant growled and instead turned his rage on Vale. His hatred boiled.

As Grant made his way toward the throne, he was met with a sword swing that he dodged with ease and then wrapped his chains around it, flipping the masked man around and impaling him with his own sword. He ripped the blade from the man and gripped it tightly.

"Vale!" Grant's body shook as his scream echoed through the high walls.

As Grant marched closer, he dispatched the incoming threats, slashing and hacking his way through everyone who stood between him and his target. Vale whimpered, grabbing the dagger he had been left with, hiding behind the throne.

Grant rounded the throne, and Vale leaped out at him. Narrowly avoiding the attack, Grant slid across the floor and crashed hard into the wall, his sword tumbling down the steps, leaving Vale with the upper hand. Blood dripped from his head, and by the time his eyes focused, he saw Vale coming at him with the dagger, throwing himself on top of Grant.

"You think you're better than me? Because of your honor?"

As Vale put all his weight into the dagger, Grant's chained hands tried their best to hold him back, but the blade inched further down. Further and further and further...

The tip of the knife pressed against Grant's eye, and with ease, the tip pierced Grant's left eye socket. Blood gushed out and poured over Grant's face. A sick laugh escaped Vale as he watched the scene beneath him, but Grant barely heard him through the horror and pain of having his eye stabbed.

Still struggling against Vale with all his might, Grant tried to stop the blade from plunging into his skull. He bucked against the man atop him, giving him a moment to flip Vale over him. With a quick roll, the tables turned.

He smashed Vale's hand against the floor and took control of the dagger, thrusting the blade toward Vale, into his mouth, and with a quick jerk to the left, Vale's cheek ripped apart.

Grant stood, leaving the bastard to bleed to death. Stumbling toward the throne, he lifted his hands to cover his eye.

The Elders were all dead, and the surviving masked men had disappeared. The screams coming from Vale in the back of the room reached a peak as he gurgled on his own.

Grant found Valor lying on the arm of the throne and grabbed it on his way past the bloodshed.

Outside of the castle, people had gathered. His good eye looked out over the people, and he took one more look back at the slaughter he had left behind.

He had survived, not for the Church or for his kingdom, but for Alyssa. The Church had lied to him—they had led him along, everyone had.

Grant was finished being a pawn.

He would find Alyssa, even if it meant going against the entire realm.

Grant stepped forward, his legs shaking under him. He did all he could to push forward, using his sword to keep his balance. The people gathering began to whisper and point as they tried to make sense of the scene.

Grant took one final step forward and collapsed, the crowd backing away from him in fear.

CHAPTER THIRTY-EIGHT

K aiser had seen the inside of a cell enough for one lifetime. His hands were bound before him in the Ragnovok dungeon. He sat in silence. The two other prisoners sat whimpering, pressed against the other side of the cell.

At first, he had been confused by their fear, but then he recalled the blood. As soon as the chaos has settled, and the intruders who attacked the princess had been dealt with, Kaiser was taken to the cell.

The blood still covered most of his torso, drying and flaking off like a second skin. Words of him betraying the kingdom had echoed from the stairs leading out of the dungeon, but the words meant little to him. He had no tears to shed or fears to hide from. He was no stranger to imprisonment.

He wondered if they had cleaned up the mess since last night. He had no idea who the men were, but they had come for the princess, that much he was sure of. As Kaiser replayed the night in his head, he couldn't shake the image of Magus from his thoughts. His face and chest mutilated by the blade. He wondered if he were truly capable of such an act, or if he had dreamed it all up.

Then he returned to his senses, noticing the brown-colored blood still stuck under his fingernails.

"Stand up, Glas."

Four guards had come to escort Kaiser. He had thought the number a bit high, but considering what he had done to the intruders the night before, it seemed prudent. The two men in the cell with Kaiser gave two long sighs of relief as he was taken from their sight and up the stairs.

Things had spiraled out of control. His life was so simple once, a farm boy caring for his sisters. Kaiser remembered the most he had ever worried about was waking up in the morning to help Guile tend to the crops. Simple things he gradually realized he had taken for granted. He missed that person, that child he was and how all he needed was his sisters and their love.

Now, he had become something else—a Glas.

They had taken him from the dungeon and bathed him, dressed him, and now he was being presented in front of all. Kaiser stood in front of the king. His crown rested atop his head as he pulled a beautiful sword from its sheath. A crowd of people gathered in the throne room, their eyes on Kaiser as he took center stage, his own eyes on the blade the king held.

The moment reminded Kaiser of Sullvain when he was chained to the floor, all the royals watching with such hatred, their laughter accompanying each abuse. This time was different —he wasn't chained down or laughed at. He was being respected. He knelt before the king as the royal blade came down and firmly rested upon his shoulder.

Kaiser had saved the princess from the assassins, the same assassins who had supposedly taken Magus' life the same night. Kaiser took the honor, his eyes peeking up only to see Fiona and Julius watching him. She had watched Kaiser kill Magus, yet she kept the fact a secret. The two of them seemed happy enough, given the recent attack on their lives.

"Kaiser Noire," King Novok declared, "the last of the Glas, you came here in chains as a victim of war. You were not trusted or welcomed among us, your presence an insult to some. On this day, you shed that past. You are no longer of Sullvain, but a welcomed citizen of Ragnovok. We have lost valued members of our kingdom, but thanks to you, my daughter remains safe."

The king lifted his blade from Kaiser's shoulder and placed it on the opposite. "I hereby recognize you as a knight of Ragnovok under Seeath Reinhart's command."

After the honor had been served, the royals swarmed up to him, patting Kaiser on the back and thanking him for his bravery. Honor swelled inside of him as they congratulated him. Kaiser wished for a moment Seeath had been there to see him—the smirk he would have on his face, his pet taking bloom. The royals drank and celebrated; none of them knew Kaiser, but they all used his knighthood to indulge themselves, not that Kaiser cared.

He found his way out of the throne room, away from the gathering. He ended up on the balcony at the end of the castle hall. At this view, he could see the courtyard and out over the kingdom below. He had so much on his mind.

After killing Magus, he'd expected death to follow—but instead, without the truth, he was being celebrated. So long as Fiona kept his secret, Kaiser would never be punished for his crime, only praised. Kaiser wondered if this was how it worked, how you rose among the royals. Waiting for what he deserved was pointless. Kaiser was beginning to find taking what you wanted was how things worked.

"They honor you, yet you stand alone out here?" came a male voice.

Kaiser turned, finding the prince and princess standing in the hall. This was the first time he had seen Fiona since the bloodshed.

Julius looked at him seriously. "I wanted to thank you for what you did for Fiona."

Kaiser shook his head. He could hear the honesty in Julius' voice—he truly loved his sister.

"A gift from my sister and me. She was the only witness to your battle against the assassins. She said you used one of these to fight them?" Julius held out the foreign blade.

Kaiser recalled its light weight as the prince placed it in his hands.

"My father said they call the blade a katana. Men skilled with it can wield it one-handed or two. My sister said you were very proficient with it?" Julius looked over to Fiona, who was now blushing. Before Julius continued, his name was called from down the hall, three men waving for him. "If you will excuse me, Kaiser,

I must attend the party. Come along, Fiona."

The two left down the hall, Fiona turning once she had gotten a few feet away. Kaiser was relieved to see she was unscathed by what she had seen. He wondered what she would eventually demand as payment for her favor, but for now, his secrets would remain in silence.

Exhausted from the last forty-eight hours, the only thing Kaiser could think about was heading to his comfortable bed. As he headed to his room, he heard a commotion and stopped to look over the balcony. Seeath was returning, but he didn't want to talk to anyone, so he continued to his room.

"In the dead of night, those bastards!" Seeath muttered, slamming his fist down.

"Yes, Sullvain's doing, it would seem." The king and Seeath had retired to the king's meeting room, leaving them alone to discuss what had happened in Seeath's absence.

"If not for Kaiser, I would have lost my only daughter." The king gestured for the servants to fetch some wine and looked at Seeath. "Because of this, I thought it just to knight him."

"Kaiser is to be knighted?" Seeath looked up at the end in surprise.

"It has already been done, you missed it by mere hours."

Seeath was shocked at first. Even with the rise in status, he believed Kaiser capable.

"What of Magus? Surely he didn't approve of such a thing. He loathes the young man." Seeath held his drink to his lips but stopped just short of taking the drink. The king's expression told him everything.

"Magus was found dead in his chambers. One of many targets the assassins were hired for, no doubt."

They had fought more than their share of wars together. The two had grown up together, rose among the castle ranks. Magus was the closest thing to a brother Seeath had ever had. He held his emotions in, not allowing the king to see them.

"Sullvain will pay for their actions, in time." The king reached across the table, his hand resting firmly on Seeath's shoulder.

The ceremony had ended, and now the halls were empty and silent, as they were most nights.

Seeath had stood in the hall, staring at the door leading into Magus' chamber. He had fought the urge to go in, knowing full well the memories that would flood him. His hand rose, resting softly against the wooden door until he finally pushed it open and entered.

As he feared, the room was still stained with the actions of the night before. Bloodstains still remained, littering the stone floor and along the walls. Seeath wondered if his friend had suffered much as he stepped across the room and sat down at Magus' desk. He sat in silence, staring at the contents of the room, trying his best not to stare at the blood at his feet.

When he turned, he found a half-finished painting, a hobby of Magus'. It was of Seeath, out in the courtyard training with a soldier. Seeath couldn't recall the moment Magus must have started it, but he imagined there were many times he hadn't noticed his friend.

Since the day he was knighted, the two had slowly grown apart. Seeath took the piece of paper and folded it as he stood. He wanted badly to take one last look about the room, but couldn't bring himself to do it, and instead, he quietly left.

The wind sent chills across Kaiser's skin as he walked the courtyard. He had never experienced such a cold night back in Sullvain. He didn't mind it. He actually enjoyed the breeze.

He'd retired to his bed, but the events of the day had his mind racing, and he couldn't sleep. Instead, he walked the halls, his new status dismissing any guards from stopping him. He had rested along the wall, peering out over the sleeping kingdom.

So many thoughts flooded his head—thoughts of Magus, and what Seeath would do if he knew the truth; thoughts of Fiona, the attack, and the intruders he had killed. He looked at his hands, the blood long since cleaned, but still, he now knew what they were capable of, and it scared him. Not because he thought himself a monster, but because he had never tasted power like he had now. He had been cast into a cell, branded a threat to the realm, and forever titled a Glas.

All he had learned of the Glas was that they held immense power and wielded it without thought—why they were wiped from the realm. He had never considered himself one of them. How could such a weak boy have that sort of power inside of him? These were the things he had told himself during his training with Seeath, but now?

Now, he was beginning to see it, feel it, believe it.

"What do you become when you've lost everything?" Kaiser whispered to himself.

He slipped a blade from his belt and held it tight against his forearm. His heart raced as he pressed it down hard, until the skin broke and blood emerged. He pulled the blade away and watched the red begin to run down, but the harder he focused on it, the slower it became until it stopped.

Soon it shifted, the blood running the opposite direction, up his arm. On command, the red swirled around his forearm like a snake until it stopped at his fingers and hardened into red glass.

This was Kaiser's heritage, not a farm boy from Sullvain, but the last of his race. Not a prisoner or weakling, but a survivor.

SPECIAL THANKS

To my daughter, the reason I strive to better myself.

Thanks to Karine Green and Keith Gordon for going above and beyond in reading and editing. Without them, no one would be able to decipher my gibberish.

Andrew, Sabrina, and Micheal for helping me bounce ideas and listen to my rants. And of course, Jessica for helping better flesh out my creation.

Keep up to date with announcements involving the series and other books by following K. Vider on Twitter: @authorKVider.

Please consider leaving a review for this book on the site you purchased it, or on Goodreads. Reviews help others discover new books.

Art and cover design by Sam Mayle Arts.
Interior formatting by Edward Van Winkle.

www.ingramcontent.com/pod-product-compliance
Lightning Source LLC
Chambersburg PA
CBHW051943240626
47153CB00005B/1603